A is for Apocalypse

All copyrights remain with original authors
Published by Poise and Pen Publishing
2014

ISBN-13: 978-0993699016
ISBN-10: 0993699014

http://www.poiseandpen.com

Cover art: Ig0rZh - Fotolia.com
Cover design: Jonathan Parrish
Story title art by Jonathan Parrish using stock art by okalinichenko

CONTENTS

RHONDA PARRISH ANTHOLOGIES

Available Now

A IS FOR APOCALYPSE
B IS FOR BROKEN
C IS FOR CHIMERA
D IS FOR DINOSAUR
E IS FOR EVIL
F IS FOR FAIRY

FAE
CORVIDAE
SCARECROW
SIRENS
EQUUS

MRS. CLAUS: NOT THE FAIRY TALE THEY SAY
TESSERACTS TWENTY-ONE: NEVERTHELESS
METASTASIS
NITEBLADE MAGAZINE

FIRE: DEMONS, DRAGONS AND DJINNS
EARTH: GIANTS, GOLEMS AND GARGOYLES

GRIMM, GRIT AND GASOLINE

Coming Soon

HEAR ME ROAR
SWASHBUCKLING CATS: NINE LIVES ON THE SEVEN SEAS

A IS FOR APOCALYPSE

Book 1 of the Alphabet Anthologies

Edited by Rhonda Parrish

Poise and Pen Publishing

EDMONTON, ALBERTA

Brenda Stokes Barron

When I was selected, my mother held me close for a
moment then pushed me away as though she needed
that extra force to let go. I was taken straight away to the
cabin where the doomsayers reside before their journey. I laid
awake in the bed where so many people slept their last
comfortable yet fitful night's sleep and wondered what the end
of the world would look like.

I wondered if I'd be the one to set it in motion.

The tower sits at the edge of the wilderness beyond the
boundaries of Culridge. The older, jaded few of our community
who hadn't been selected to walk to the tower in all their years
called the whole thing the Culling of Culridge. I wasn't old but
I understood their cynicism—it would seem a convenient way
to keep our numbers under control.

Still, many believed in the tower and what it was promised
to hold—the end of our world and the hope of our future. Every
year one of us failed to grasp the unknown from the sacred
hands, and our people lived another day. Success wasn't the
goal but the attempt had to be stalwart. Only the most valiant

failure would qualify to appease the tower, or so the stories went. Failure to go when called meant our certain death. At least when summoned, there was the chance of failure. And a chance of failure meant a chance at living.

His arms were around me as his name was called. I was standing there with my family, waiting to hear the announcement and barely registered the sound of his name, my father's name, before the world around me was blotted out and my face was buried in his chest.

"Be brave," he said, whiskers scratching the side of my face. He pulled away slightly and examined me. "Be brave," he said again and took my hand in his and kissed the back of it. The cold metal of his turquoise ring pressed against my palm. I knew I'd never see him again, that he'd go to the tower and never come back, but I didn't cry. I held the tears until his back was turned from me forever.

That night, I sat in my room and listened to the sound of my mother sobbing. I prayed for the world to end then. But the destruction didn't come.

I walked for days. Or maybe it was only hours. It's hard to say when you're outside of Culridge. Time goes funny. The world bends and buckles. The shapes of things distort. I walked through tall grass and dense forest. I walked across a desert made of pebbles. I cut my way through brambles with a pocket knife.

And I stood at the base of the tower watching its shape emerge from the ground and disappear into the sky as though it always was and always will be.

It wasn't as I'd pictured. In the stories my father told, the tower was made of black stone, obsidian and slick like glass. It was angular and sharp, perfect in its construction.

But this tower was rough and rounded. It seemed thrown together in a heap with large turrets sticking out at right angles made from knotted tree branches or clay. I pushed through the gate and walked closer, still out of breath but anxious to get started.

Once I was about ten feet away from the tower, I noticed it. It wasn't hastily affixed branches making the tower's irregular form. The rounded protrusions were knees and feet and hands and ankles. The knotted twists, faces.

The tower was made of bodies, bent and screwed together and I understood then that my quest was already over. The only ending in this story would be mine. I knew I was going to die. Might as well get it over with.

I closed the gap to the tower in seconds and leapt onto its structure. There was no stench, no hint of rotting meat. All the bodies were smooth as stone, hard and set. They were frozen in time and in thought. I didn't feel the softness of flesh beneath my fingertips which made it a little easier to step on faces and grab onto hips and collarbones.

I hoisted myself upward, ever upward. The air grew thinner. My breaths turned shallow. Gripping onto the smooth stone became more difficult. Then, I saw it. A hand jutting out from the mass of bodies. A once-turquoise ring on one of its fingers.

And I cried then. My body shook with the force of it and I leaned down to take that hand in mine. I pressed my lips to it.

My eyes fluttered. The world flashed gray for an instant. For half a breath, I was made of stone. I felt the tower encase me, beg that I become it. Plead that I join its misshapen ranks.

But then I heard my father's voice in my head. The world beamed bright in color.

Then the stony hand in mine turned warm. My fingers indented the flesh. His ring slipped off into my hand as his hand fell away. I saw his face, mouth agape, like waking suddenly from a horrible dream.

We were falling. All of us. The tower crumbled as all the bodies, all the people, were made of skin and bones again.

Lightning flashed above. I looked up and saw the sky splitting open. The clouds had cleared and I could see where the tower had held it in place. It was a horrible dream and real all at once. It was a moment's realization, that our little part of the world was no longer supported on our backs. We fell.

And we fall and fall and fall and my father's shouting, "Be brave."

"Be brave."

A is for Ascension

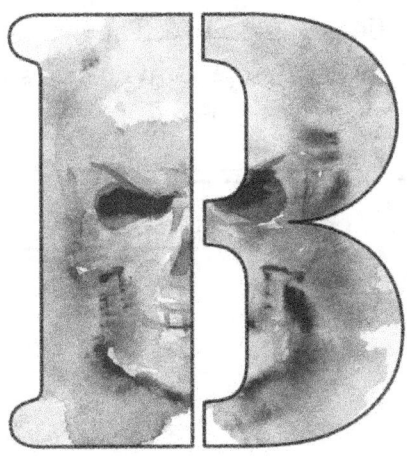

Marge Simon and Michael Fosburg

We wade through the tide, regroup on the shore. The last enemy was vaporized in that blind frenzy that held no allegiance. With none left in command, we march as one, our weapons meaningless. Stick men, grown thin as nails.

More and more of us pour in to join our straggling company, we walk through a dream. We stand surveying sea and sand, wiping our eyes, waiting for a sign, a spark to wake us up.

Just ahead, the shores give way to green. Someone has brought a cello to the beach. She spreads her skirts and smiles. There are yellow flowers in her hair. She has an air of long forgotten grace. Perhaps she is what we were fighting to preserve, perhaps not. Why should that matter now?

She draws the bow across the strings, a common language, easy to identify. Debussy's Sonata leaves us in tears. But the sad timbre of each note is too near the pitch of falling mortars, the moans of gut-shot friends.

Her bow is a rifle poised to fire. The grassy knoll, a new delta to breach. There is a ringing in our ears that will not stop. Weapons drawn, we advance...

B is for Beachhead

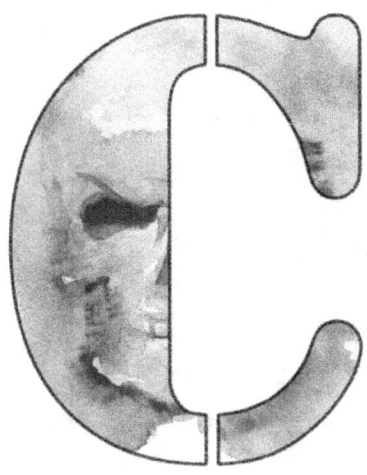

Milo James Fowler

They all said he was crazy. Dangerous. Maybe they were right. But I had to find out for myself.

Nine months had come and gone since Mama passed, and the ache inside me hadn't dulled at all. I still woke up every morning expecting to find her on the cot beside mine. Had been a long while since it smelled anything like her. More often than not, her pillow lay wet with my tears.

"Where you think you're going, girl? Past curfew." Hartley blocked my path with a sawed-off shotgun at rest against one shoulder. "You know better."

"Going for a ride."

"Under moonshine?"

"Bring you back a coyote." I tapped the crossbow slung over my shoulder. "Grill it for you myself."

Hartley licked his lips. Some who knew him from way back said he once weighed a hundred pounds heavier. Hard to believe. As it was, he outweighed everybody else in the compound. Stood taller, too. I might've been intimidated if I didn't know he squealed like a piglet when you tickled him behind the ears.

"I don't know, Madeline. You going out alone..." He frowned. "We all get to feeling cooped up from time to time and with you being the only female and all, I'm sure you could use some space away from us oafs. But I really don't think—"

"You're welcome to tag along."

He cursed under his breath and hefted the shotgun in explanation. He had to stand watch.

"Draw the short straw again?" I winked up at him as I leaned against the concrete stairwell. I was in no hurry—or so I hoped it would seem.

"Starting to think all there is are short straws." He glanced past me up the stairs as if he might've been overheard. Complaining never went over well with Boss Man Carson. "How long you gonna be?"

"Long as it takes." I shrugged. "Carson would've sent Judah or one of the others, but they just got back from scouting the east ridge—"

"Beauty sleep," Hartley grumbled with obvious envy.

"They've earned it." Braving miles of open terrain in sunshine was enough to garner anybody's respect, even mine. A bunch of misogynistic ego-trippers, they never looked at me above the neck. "Heard tell they sighted some marauders. Had to cover their tracks."

"Long as they don't lead 'em back here." Hartley shuffled to one side, allowing just enough space for me to squeeze by. "Reckon we've gotta eat. But why so late, Maddie?"

"Coyotes don't wear watches."

He snorted at that and almost smiled. "Be back before sunup. Otherwise, I might have to start worrying."

"Won't be that long." I patted his belly as I passed, dropping down the steps two at a time. "Breakfast is on me."

I eased my bike from its stall and walked it out of the
garage. Ginger, I called her. Ridiculous, I know, but all the
horses had been butchered long ago for the meat, and she was
the closest thing to that roan mare I'd always wanted as a kid.
Just a whole lot uglier. Lowering the door manually, I reset the
alarm and glanced over my shoulder to be sure I was alone.
With the moonshine to guide me, I pushed the bike hard to get
it rolling across the dusty hardpan, leaning into it with both
hands on the steering grips. I usually had to give her a running
start before I revved up the engine, but tonight I planned on
waiting until I was over the rise and coasting half a mile away
before I kick-started the thing. One backfire in the front yard
and Boss Man Carson would have me scrubbing latrines for a
month.

I deactivated the gate alarm and rolled through. Carson
liked to change the code every now and then, just to keep us on
our toes, but Hartley was good about keeping me updated.
With Mama gone, he was just about the only friend I had left.
Doc was nice, but always busy and Carson held the indifferent
air of a leader. As for Judah and the others—they gave me the
creeps. Like stray dogs they were, always circling. I could feel
their eyes on me when I passed them by. So far, they hadn't
tried anything. Knew better. Boss Man would've cast them out
if they did. I was under his protection.

But I didn't feel safe anymore. Not inside the compound.
Not outside either, but I had Ginger, and we could keep ahead
of marauders well enough. Strike out on our own, take my
chances? Or stay? Mama would've known what to do. Hated to
admit, but I was lost without her.

I gazed out toward the city ruins in the distance, what
remained of the "urban cityscape" down in the valley that the
desert hadn't reclaimed. Carson always referred to the city in

eloquent terms that no longer held any meaning for the rest of us. The gate squealed as it closed, and I cringed, quickly reactivating the alarm. I shoved my bike onward, and as it picked up momentum down the steep grade, I threw one leg over the seat and squinted against the cold rush of air.

We hadn't suffered many run-ins with marauders lately. They were keeping their distance. Ever since Judah and his bunch stumbled across that cache of RPGs and blasted the hell out of a couple convoys headed into the city, the marauders hadn't ventured out of their territory. If they had, it was doubtful I would've attempted a trip alone in the middle of the night—and even more doubtful that I would've gotten as far as I had already. Only Hartley standing watch? A sure sign the Boss Man had grown lax.

I glanced back and saw our compound perched on a hillside half a mile behind me. Time to let her rip.

I stood up as the bike continued to roll forward. Squeezing the clutch, I kick-started Ginger, and she growled and revved as I twisted the throttle, spitting gravel from her chunky tires. Shifting into gear, I leaned to the right and steered us toward the southwestern ridge. Unguarded, a run-down shack sat five miles away. I'd seen it once before but never got close.

Some said the man who lived there never slept. That he didn't need to, because he wasn't exactly human. Others said marauders knew better than to mess with him, and that was reason enough to leave him alone. A man who frightened off cannibals? I'd heard the guy was clean out of his mind, that when the plagues came, he'd tried to kill himself but couldn't do it. Managed to off his wife and three kids but was too much of a coward to do himself in. Living with that had driven him over the edge.

Maybe all of it was true. Or none. Only one thing I'd heard mattered to me: that he could speak to the dead.

☠

Wasn't long before I caught sight of the shack—only structure in sight, lit up inside with warm light. Smoke spewed up from the stovepipe in the lopsided roof. Clearly, the man did not fear marauders. Or he was just too loco to care. Sure the nights were cold, but who in his right mind would strike a fire way out here, unprotected? Sending up smoke sign to be seen for miles around?

A man cleared his throat behind me.

I whirled around, reaching for my crossbow. He clubbed me hard across the face. I went sprawling to the ground but managed to get off an arrow before darkness swallowed my senses—and me right along with them. Just as my vision clouded around the edges, a tall, grizzled man with my arrow in his chest leaned over and scowled at me.

"You really shouldn't be here," he said.

☠

When I came to, I was lying on the floor—rough-hewn planks and dust. The smell of smoke filled my nostrils. I sat up with a start, facing a shadowy figure.

"What's your name, girl?" a deep voice came from the faceless man. He sat backlit by a glowing wood stove. Flickering light played across the arrow that pierced his chest.

"Where's my bow?"

"You want to shoot me again?"

"Once is usually enough."

"Not with me, I'm afraid. You got a name or don't you?"

"Maddie—not that it's your business."

"No, probably not," he allowed. "But whose business would it be then? Carson's? He got you with child yet?"

Heat spread across my cheeks. I clenched fists and tried to get to my feet, but the stove's light went off-kilter as I did.

"Take it easy now, Maddie. I hit you with a Louisville Slugger. You know what that is?"

"A club." I sank onto one knee and stayed there. The room hadn't stopped moving.

"Baseball." He chuckled quietly. "The plagues took so much life from this earth. No way to reclaim it all, I suppose. But it was a game. With a bat." He thumped his weapon against the floorboards. "A bat and a ball and a couple hours to kill. Wasn't that the life?"

What the hell was this? A conversation?

"You live here." I squinted into the gloom, but I still couldn't see his face.

"That I do. And you're from that compound the other side of the hill. Know who used to live there, back in the day?" He paused. "*Movie* stars. That's right. Can't remember their names, but they were real A-listers, let me tell you. Didn't leave much behind, but the same can be said for all those so-called *important* people in politics and sports back then, soaking up the limelight like sunshine, no idea the sky would fall on them someday."

Couldn't understand half the stuff that came out of him. "Tell me your name," I said.

"Which one?" He fingered the arrow's shaft. "You can call me Mercer. Most people did, right up to the very end."

"I've heard of you—"

"Truth mixed with lies."

"That you can speak to the dead. Is that much true?"

The crackle of the wood stove held the moment.

"In a manner of speaking, yes. But it's been a long time since anybody could afford my services."

I'd come prepared to barter if necessary. It was the way of things, after all. "Name your price."

"Eurasian whiskey."

"I don't—"

He chuckled. "Don't suppose you'd ever heard of it. I'm sure it's the first thing the hospitals turned to once they ran out of proper supplies—alcohol in any form."

"Alcohol." I nodded. "Yes, I can get you alcohol." Doc had plenty.

"Didn't use it all up on your mother? Assuming it's her you want to see on the other side."

My mouth opened and closed without sound.

"First the mother, then the daughter," Mercer said. "Carson hasn't tried to impregnate you yet? Only female in that compound, aren't you? Just a matter of time."

"You don't know a thing about my mother."

"Easy now, I meant no disrespect. With those flesh-eaters roaming about, you and your mom couldn't be too picky. Carson offered you his protection. And in return, he gets to play Adam to his choice of Eves—"

I stood then, dizziness be damned, and cursed him out. "You want the alcohol or not?"

"How long till he comes looking for you?"

"He won't." Not if Hartley kept quiet.

"You leave whenever the mood suits you, is that it? He lets you go off solo?"

"I'm a hunter." One of the best. Only Judah could out-shoot me. Boss Man hadn't tried.

"Right." Again, he fingered the arrow in his chest. Didn't seem to bother him that it was there. Wasn't he bleeding out? "And what do you hunt in these wee hours before dawn?"

"Coyote."

He gave a sudden snort and laughed out loud. "Bull's eye. Child, if you only knew. But of course, you just think I'm crazy. Maybe I would too if we switched places. Here's the thing: a *coyote* was what they used to call men long ago who'd take folks across the border for a hefty price. And back in the day, before the plagues, I was known in some circles as—"

"Don't care about your stories, old man. I want to talk to my mother." I stepped toward him, close enough I could see the glint of the fire in his eyes, the grizzled beard, could smell the odor on him—age and filth. He closed his hand over the shaft protruding from his chest and pulled. The arrowhead—not designed to reverse course—tore through him with a wet, meaty suction as he drew it out. He didn't even flinch at the pain.

I stood swaying on my feet, staring at the bloody arrow in his grasp.

"You'd best be on your way now." He remained seated. "You'll find your bike and your bow in the lean-to. That way." He pointed off to his right. "Sorry about the knock to your noggin. You'll need to put something on it. They still got ice in that compound?"

I nodded.

"Ice and alcohol—you're living in the lap of luxury, Maddie. Be careful. Carson's gonna want to try again. There can't be new life in this world. The human race has been given a death sentence. The plagues saw to that. But you'd best believe he'll keep at it. And after you and your baby die in the birthing, he'll find himself another Eve. Mark my words."

Mercer was a raving madman. I should've left. Yet my boots remained rooted to the floor.

I swallowed. "Aren't you bleeding to death?"

"I'm already dead, Maddie."

That did it. I high-tailed it out of there. Ginger and my bow were right were he said they'd be. Gunning the engine, I tore off back to the compound like a pack of marauders were after me.

☠

Doc frowned as he dabbed at my temple with a gauze pad dipped in alcohol. Jack Daniels' name was on the bottle. Mercer might've known who that was.

"Who did this to you?" Doc squinted in the candlelight thrown from my nightstand.

"Told you." I winced at the sting and glanced up at Hartley, leaning in the doorway with his arms crossed. I shifted on my cot. "I fell."

"Likely," Hartley muttered sarcastically. Doc only shook his head.

I had no idea how much medical training our doctor had received prior to the plagues, but the old man stitched us up and tended to us good. He'd cried almost as hard as I had when Mama passed on. He'd helped me bury both her and the baby.

"What were you doing out so late, Madeline?" Doc faced me squarely.

"Hunting."

"With Carson's blessing?"

I looked away.

"Didn't think so." He pivoted to face Hartley. "And you let her go?"

"Well-uh..."

Doc cursed. "You're both lucky. If anything had happened to this girl—" Doc shook his head and squeezed his temples with one hand. Then he blew out a sigh. "He'll want to know what really happened, when he sees that bruise on your face."

I had maybe two hours until dawn. Long enough to come up with a better story for the Boss Man.

"If he catches either one of you in a lie, there'll be hell to pay." Doc packed up his supplies in a duffle bag and shuffled out, pushing past Hartley. "Return to your post. And you—" He pointed at me. "Go with him. Can't have you sleeping on a head injury like that. Might never wake up again." Grumbling to himself, he returned to his quarters.

Hartley cursed under his breath as he looked down at me. "You sure went and stepped in it this time, Maddie," he said as quietly as he could. But he wouldn't stay mad at me for long. Never did. "C'mon." Shouldering his shotgun, he beckoned me to follow.

I retrieved my bow. "Hartley?" I whispered as we headed for the front of the compound.

"Yeah?"

"You think Boss Man loved my mama?"

His steps lost their rhythm. "Well-uh, we all did. You know that."

"Not what I asked."

He cleared his throat. "Sure." He paused. "She was carrying his baby, wasn't she? I'd say that's—"

"Was she the first?"

"How do you mean?"

"Were there others before her? Other women he got pregnant?"

"Hey now, Madeline, I don't know what you're—"

"Answer me." I placed a hand on his protruding gut. "How many others were there?"

"Doesn't seem all that appropriate to talk about. And besides, I wasn't around more than a few months before Boss Man took you in. It's not like I—"

"How many?" I stared him down.

He hung his head. "Maybe a couple. That I know of."

"Where were they from?"

He looked like he'd tasted something bad all of a sudden, and Hartley was no picky eater. "They were-uh...*marauders*."

My stomach squeezed in on itself, then went sideways. "He got them pregnant too."

Hartley winced and nodded, avoiding eye contact.

"And they died. Just like Mama."

"They...didn't make it. When it came time to give birth, I mean." He looked at me. "But your mama, she was healthy, and when you two showed up on our doorstep, Boss Man said you were a gift from—"

"You think he loves me?" I clenched my teeth. "Like a daughter? Or something else?"

Hartley's face muscles went slack, and his mouth hung open without any words. Then he said hoarsely, "I don't know what you're getting at, Maddie."

I pushed him away, but due to our weight difference, I was the one who stumbled back a step. Off in the distance, far beyond the compound gate, I thought I saw a trail of smoke curling into the black sky.

"I went to see him," I said at last. "That crazy hermit."

"What the hell? Did he do this to you?" Hartley's hand drifted toward my temple.

I batted him away. "He knew about Mama. How could he?"

"You know better than to go anywhere near that guy. He ain't right in the head. When Boss Man finds out—"

"He won't. Because you're not going to tell him." I patted his belly. "See you around."

"Where do you think you're going?" he hissed after me as I bolted into the front yard to round up Ginger. "What the *hell* is wrong with you, girl?"

I held up the bottle of alcohol I'd swiped from Doc, and without a care for Judah's or Carson's beauty sleep, I called over my shoulder, "Gonna talk to Mama!"

☠

This time, Mercer stood on his front stoop as I pulled up at the base of the hill.

"Didn't figure you for a fool," he said, his voice sailing down toward me in the stillness. He was out in the open, yet I still couldn't make out his face. "But I've been wrong before."

"Brought you something."

"Another arrow?"

I held up the alcohol. "Label says Jack Daniels. Barter?"

"Not my brand."

I propped Ginger on her kickstand and started up the grade, my boots sinking into the gravel without much in the way of purchase. I picked up my pace and was met with hard-packed earth that barely shifted under my soles. Any steeper, I might've slid right back down.

"You've got spunk, kid. I'll grant you that," Mercer said.

"Just because the marauders are scared of you don't mean I have to be."

"Never said they were scared. I'm not their type. They prefer fresh meat."

"Right," I grunted, catching myself with one hand as I lost my footing. "Because you're dead."

"I wear death like a trench coat, young Maddie."

More crazy talk. At least I was prepared for it this time—or so I thought. "How did you know about my mother?" I paused, halfway to his doorstep.

"I haven't always lived up here." He leaned back on his heels and surveyed the silent night, his hands deep in the pockets of his torn trousers. "Used to work for your Boss Man, truth be told. Before he killed me, that is."

"You want this or not?" I shook the bottle.

He shrugged. "Sure."

"Then no more madness."

He chuckled. "What do you believe about the dead, Maddie? Where's your mama right now?"

"Her spirit's always with me. I just can't get through to her without a—"

"I'm no medium. Just a coyote. I'll get you across the border, but then it'll be up to you to find her."

"Border?"

"Between this reality and the Afterlife. Or don't you believe in any of that?" I shook my head. "Yeah, well, most people don't these days. But that doesn't change the way of things."

"According to you."

"I suppose you'll see for yourself soon enough. You'll have to die, of course."

His hand gripped me by the throat, and I dropped the alcohol. He caught it as he lifted me off my feet. How had he moved so fast? He'd been over twenty yards away!

"What's wrong, Maddie?" He grinned as I fought against his hold on me, clawing at his hand, thrashing my legs. My boots made contact with his shins, but he didn't recoil. "You're bruising this fleshbag up real good. Might have to get me another one. Maybe yours, after I smuggle your sorry soul to the other side. You and your mama can catch up while I go back to Carson and kill him in his own bed. Fair's far, I say. This old hermit carcass doesn't agree with me anyway. Thing keeps leaking all over the place. Somebody shot it with an arrow—can you believe? "

It might've been the blow to my head earlier or the fact that he was strangling me, but my vision started going cloudy again, and I thought I could hear engines roaring in the distance.

"Let—me—go," I rasped.

"Clearly, you have no idea what's involved with a crossover." Mercer frowned. "Don't you want to see your mama? Need I remind you: barter has been made. I have my alcohol—"

A shot rang out and the bottle exploded, along with his hand. Mercer looked awful surprised, but not pained. He didn't let me go—not until the next shot took off half his head with a splatter of blood and brains. He toppled over backward then, and I went down with him. I tugged his death grip off my throat as we hit the ground.

"Madeline—you all right, child?" Carson called out from the base of the hillside. Judah stood beside him with his rifle shouldered, ready to fire again. Hartley stood wide-eyed on the other side. Behind the three of them, Judah's jeep idled next to Ginger.

"Fine," I managed, getting to my feet. Mercer didn't move. Not a single breath.

"Come down from there," Carson said. "We'll get you home."

I looked at him. An average-sized man, middle-aged, not handsome, not ugly. A forgettable face. But a voice that rang true with authority.

"Hurry now." He beckoned to me and cast Judah a withering look. "The marauders will have heard those shots."

Judah smirked. Bold and clean-shaven, he stood with his boots spread wide, his biceps bulging where they sprouted from a sleeveless shirt.

I looked out toward the city ruins and imagined the flesh-eaters devouring their latest victims, people like Mama and me but not as fortunate to have found Carson's compound first. But how fortunate were we, really? Would Mama still be alive if we'd passed by the Boss Man's gate that fateful day? Would I eventually die as Mama had—as those women had before her—with Carson's spawn erupting out of me, killing us both?

"Come now," Carson said, taking a step forward and reaching with one hand. "We have to go, Madeline."

"Do you love me?"

He blinked. "How's that?"

"You loved my mother, didn't you?"

Hartley squirmed. Judah scoffed. Carson nodded slowly.

"Of course," he said.

"You love me like a daughter?"

"You know I do, Madeline—"

"You're not getting me pregnant." Before I knew what I was doing, I'd whipped my crossbow into firing position and aimed it straight at him.

Judah was just as quick, training his rifle on my head. But Boss Man was fastest. He'd already pulled the revolver from his belt and fired a round into Judah's chest—right where his heart would've been. Hartley let out a sharp cry as Judah stared in silent disbelief and went over like he'd been hit by a bike at full throttle.

"No one points a gun at my girl!" Carson roared, his hair—usually combed so meticulously—flailing out of place.

Judah's rifle clattered down the rocks below, and he lay as still as Mercer, gazing up into the moonshine without blinking. Three shots fired in as many minutes—two from Judah, one from Carson. Marauders would soon be on their way to collect the fresh meat and maybe take down some more while they were at it.

Keeping my arrow aimed at Boss Man, I descended the hillside. I glanced at Hartley. Never seen him so pale. He hugged his shotgun across his chest like a toddler would a teddy bear. He didn't seem able to shake his gaze from Judah's body. So of course, he was the first to see—

"That's right, you come on down." Carson nodded. Jamming his gun back into his belt, he beckoned to me with both hands. Eager. Just as unblinking as Judah. "We'll get you home where it's safe."

"H-he's moving—he's still alive!" Hartley boomed, staring at Judah.

Judah sat up and stretched like he'd awoken from a long nap, never mind the bullet hole and crimson patch blossoming on his chest.

"Very nice," Judah said, admiring his muscled arms. "Definitely an upgrade."

Carson turned on him, reaching for his gun.

"Steady," I said.

"Go on, shoot me again. Won't do any good," Judah said to Carson. "Ask her. Got me with an arrow, nothing to show for it." Judah winked up at me and leapt to his feet. "Limber, too," he remarked, dusting himself off.

My legs stopped moving as I remembered something Mercer had said...about *wearing death like a coat*. Insane rambling at the time, but now—

I didn't know what to think.

"What is this abomination?" Carson stared hard at Judah. "You should be—"

"Dead. Right. I've been thinking the same thing for a couple millennia now—give or take a century. People have tried, believe me. But it never seems to stick. Death, that is." Judah strode toward Carson.

"Stay back!" Boss Man drew his revolver faster than I could blink. He'd already fired a round before my arrow caught him in the leg and brought him down.

Judah jerked back as the second bullet struck him in the chest. He laughed as Carson yelped, writhing and cursing in the gravel.

"You remember stabbing me in my sleep, Boss Man? Thought I was jonesing to take your place in the tribe? You sure had me wrong." Judah crouched in front of Carson. "Of course, I was wearing a different fleshbag back then. Damned inconvenient at the time. But lucky for me, this recently deceased hermit was up here—"

"You reanimate them." Before I knew it, my feet had taken me to the bottom of the hill. "The dead."

Judah glanced up at me and smiled. I'd never seen him do that before—at me or anybody. "I prefer the term *fleshbag*, but yeah, that's about the size of it, Maddie."

"Mercer." I blinked. My mouth had gone dry.

"What the hell is going on here, Madeline?" Carson demanded.

Engines sputtered and growled in the distance. From the direction of the city.

"We are." I pointed Hartley toward Boss Man. "Get him in the jeep."

"I'll take that." Judah/Mercer tugged Carson's revolver out of his hand and gestured at Hartley. "Go on. You heard the lady." Then he clubbed Carson over the head. Boss Man collapsed like a coyote on the receiving end of one of my arrows.

Muttering under his breath, Hartley hauled Carson's body into the back of the jeep, careful not to bump into his pierced leg. I approached Judah/Mercer with my crossbow taught but aimed at the ground between us.

"So what now?" I said.

"I get your doctor to stop this leaking." He dabbed at his chest with two fingers. "And I make sure that bastard doesn't try sowing any more of his seed."

I glanced at Boss Man, crumpled in the backseat. "I can take care of myself."

"No doubt about that." Mercer shrugged Judah's thick shoulders. "Not you I'm worried about. Just think of all those poor, defenseless flesh-eaters that just happen to be female. Somebody's got to protect them from this sex-crazed lunatic."

"And the whole strangling me thing? We're just gonna pretend that never happened?"

"Deal's off. No alcohol, no barter. But now you know what it means to cross the border."

"C'mon!" Hartley shouted from the jeep's passenger seat. "We gotta go!"

"Drive," I told Mercer. I climbed aboard Ginger and revved her up.

"And your mother?" Mercer paused before climbing behind the wheel.

"What about her?"

"You still want to see her?"

Stupid question. Of course I did. More than almost anything.

"I will someday," I said. "But I've still got plenty of living to do."

Ginger's rear tire spit gravel that pinged across the jeep's flank as I tore off into the night.

On the way back to the compound I got sidetracked by a coyote's silhouette on the northeast ridge. Yapping up at the moon or calling for a mate, I had no idea what it was doing. Seemed like a sign, though—if Mercer was what he said he was.

I shot the coyote and rode up to grab it by the hind legs, slinging it over Ginger's fuel tank as dawn glowed in the east. I could've ridden off solo and never looked back. Part of me wanted to. But I had a feeling things were going to be different at the compound from now on. Ginger and I would stick around for a while, see how things played out. Mama wouldn't have wanted me to go and leave Hartley anyway, not after the promise I'd made.

Breakfast was on me, after all.

C is for Coyote

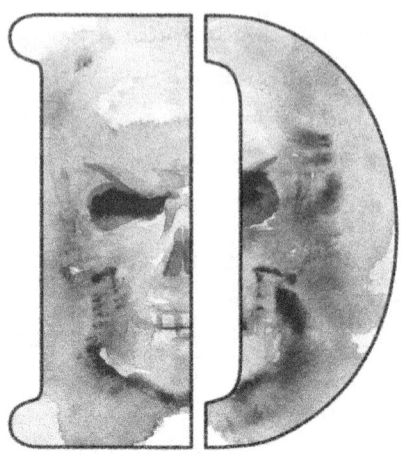

Beth Cato

The dosimeter is going to beep again. Rick is aware of it, the same way he's conscious of his own breaths. There are other beeps across the room, but otherwise it is quiet. The panels blink as they should. Emergency shutdown went according to procedure. A diesel generator keeps the electricity on and there's abundant food stashed away—ancient MREs— not that any of them are hungry.

Rick fidgets with his wedding ring, turns it clockwise. The skin beneath is a raw track of red. Sweat drenches his clothes. After a full day, the control room reeks of saltiness and unwashed bodies, the re-circulated air already foul.

It's Monday, just after seven in the morning. Neel and Lisa will be getting ready for school, arguing over which cartoon channel to watch while the dog whines at the door. The saintly cat is likely draping like a bean bag animal from Sean's arms. Priya will be doing a dozen things at once as she gets ready for work—making sure that homework is stuffed inside backpacks, that the crock pot is going, that online bill-pays went through overnight.

The dosimeter beeps. It jolts him, returns him to the control room with its tall walls of meters and switches.

Each beep is another tenth of a rem of radiation. It's a miniscule amount, but it adds up. He timed it a few hours ago—a beep about every ten minutes. His little Sean, eyes wide with delight, just last week said, "Math is everywhere, Daddy!"

Priya had given him that knowing look that said *like father, like son.*

Across the room, one of the big guys is sobbing again. The man is built like a linebacker, his shoulders heaving with each soft hiccup.

"My phone is dead," says one of the other men. "Can I use yours?"

"No. Phones have never worked in here, man. You know that. There's too much interference. No phone, no internet."

"I have to try. I have to." He rubs his face vigorously, as if he's trying to wake himself up. He looks toward Rick. "What about your phone?"

As if he has to ask. Everyone would know if that line rang.

"Not yet," says Rick. He feels the others' gazes slip away from him, back to the floor, the panels. He twists the ring again and stares at the landline phone, as if he could will it to make any sort of sound.

A day ago. A lifetime ago. Sunday. A boring, nothing Sunday. Outside, a crisp snow had fallen, though it wasn't terribly cold as he'd come into work at dawn. Rick knew it'd be the sort of day where the kids tumbled about the yard with red cheeks and runny noses. He had felt that stab of resentment at having to play the grown up and sit at a panel all day.

"Someone has to generate electricity," he told Priya, sighing.

About lunchtime, the blast jolted the building. The seismic alarm went off. The reactor tripped. Alarms wailed as the electrical grid failed. No time to think. Just react. Do what you've practiced in the simulator dozens of times over. Do the job.

Then he became aware of crying, screaming. Some operators staggered in carrying one of the guys who'd been outside on smoke break.

"I'm blind! I'm blind!" The man screamed, over and over. It was the kind of hysterical scream that cuts through the alarms, cuts through that almost cozy zone that's created by practice and training. Rick looked around the room to faces that were aghast for all of an instant before the questions poured out.

"A nuclear attack? It can't be."

"What else could blind a person like that?"

"How far away was it? What direction?"

A few people ran out. A few more people trickled in. Some returned with emergency dosimeters.

The Senior RO announced that he was locking down the room. A couple more folks left; the rest resumed their stations. The outside ventilation was closed off. They were sealed in.

Rick reached for the landline phone. It was standard operations when everything tripped offline that he had to call it in to the feds.

No one answered.

He dialed down the list. He hung up the phone.

It was like Washington D.C. no longer existed.

Another jolt shivered through the building. The seismic alarms went off again.

Five more seismic incidents had occurred. The dosimeters said the rest. The poured concrete walls of the control room shielded them more than the walls of a standard building, but it was all a matter of time.

Nothing had happened in the last two hours. Nothing but beeping, more beeping.

"We can't stay here forever," says one of the women.

"Sure we could. We just might not be alive—"

"Don't talk like that," snaps a man.

"It's weird. When I was in the Navy, I always knew that if something happened, I was going to go down with the ship. We were engineers. Stuck at the bottom. I was okay with that. This is the opposite. I don't like it so much."

"What other choice do you have, Gary? Really?"

"I could go outside with the satellite phone," says the first woman.

"As radioactive as it is out there?"

Arguments erupt all around, the dam bursting at last.

Stay. Go. Venture into the controlled area to get anti-contamination clothes—but what was the point, when you'd be contaminated by then? Just use the sat-phone and return. Just see what else is outside. Stay here. Be ready for a call, for whenever aid workers arrive. Aid workers, what aid workers?

Rick closes his eyes and twists his ring. It's almost eight o'clock in the morning. The kids will be packed up for school. Lisa will be double-checking her hair in the mirror yet again and probably dropping hints to her mom that she is almost ready for real lipstick, not lip balm. Neel will be grumbling as he picks up the last of his Legos from the floor. Sean's cheeks were probably smeared with grape jam or some other staining food that he would then share with the dog, the cat, and anyone else receptive of a hug. Thank God they didn't have white upholstery.

The dosimeter beeps.

"Listen, people." One of the men speaks up. "We've done our job. The reactor's cooled down. We know it's bad out there and it's only going to get worse in here. If you want to go home, I say, go home. We've done our job." He repeats it so softly that the words are almost obscured by the next beep of a dosimeter.

Rick opens his eyes. Everyone is looking around, gauging reactions. A couple head toward the door, murmuring as if in a church. One man cradles his cell phone within his palm and never looks up as he walks away. Others clap backs, hug, cry in quiet little groups. The stench of the room decreases by degrees.

His dosimeter beeps again. It's only been a few minutes.

"Rick?" One of the women rests a hand on his shoulder.

"I'm fine. I'll see you later," he says.

She gnaws at her lip, frowning. "What? No, listen to me, Rick. I have four-wheel drive. Your place would be on the way home. I can roll over anything in the way."

"I think I'll stay."

"Stay?" she echoes. "Here? But..." She studies his face for a moment and then nods. "Okay. Okay. I'll... it's been good knowing you, Rick." She pats his shoulder and then walks away.

A few others remain in the room, staring at meters. Rick twists his wedding ring. It's warm and sticky and seems to glide in place.

He looks at the clock and smiles. Priya will be driving the kids to school now. The crock pot will be warming up. The whole house must smell like roast beef.

His dosimeter beeps again.

Math. It's everywhere.

D is for Dosimeter

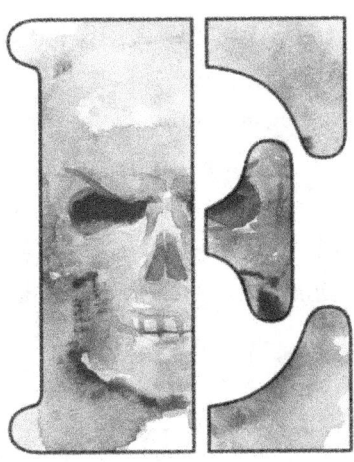

Simon Kewin

Commander Rosa Vishnu watched explosions flowering across the face of the Earth. London, Paris and Berlin in a neat triangle over in the east. Boston, New York and Washington directly below the station. Then LA, San Francisco and Vancouver on the western limb of the planet. She'd watched the recording so many times but still she picked out new details, like the way the cobweb of lights – highways and urban sprawl – flickered out just before each warhead struck. The power grids had been the first thing to go, plunging the Earth into its final darkness.

She thought, as she always did, about Ravi, her last sight of him waving goodbye at Kennedy as the transporter took her off to the rocket. Clever, handsome Ravi and the life they'd planned together. She'd wanted four children, two girls and two boys. He'd pitch them balls in the park while she showed them all the beauties of the mountains and the woods. Sometimes, in her dreams, her phantom family became real. They walked together down some trail, laughing and kidding around, talking about their lives. Their plans.

Those days, waking up to the reality of the cramped interior of Earth Station Six, were the worst.

She'd promised to wave to Ravi each day on one of their orbits. She still did sometimes, although the precise location of Michigan – of anything now – was hard to pin down. She just hoped the end, when it came, had been brief for him. Not some drawn-out, nightmarish battle for depleting supplies of food and water.

"Pretty lights."

Her crewmate – the one she called Zoe – had floated into the observation pod beside her. The familiar tang of the plasticizing resins that gave Zoe's skin its shiny glaze filled Rosa's nose. Of her five crewmates, Zoe was the most human, seemed the most alive. The other four barely spoke, but some fragment of the person Zoe had once been seemed to linger about her. Zoe gave Rosa hope. It was because of her that Rosa had decided on her course of action.

"Yes, Zoe. It's the Earth being destroyed by the nuclear holocaust."

Zoe nodded, accepting the news without reply. Just as she had done almost every day for five years now. Zoe and the others were programmed for simple tasks, nothing more. Rosa searched in vain for some look of understanding in those blank eyes. Their resurrected bodies were immune to radiation, oxygen starvation and all but extreme physical damage. They were also, as a by-product, immune to feelings of loss or sadness. Rosa found herself envying her five reanimated crewmates more and more. They went about their daily tasks, not knowing or caring that they were the last of humanity.

She wondered again who they'd been in life. Criminals given an alternative to the electric chair? Volunteers with some fatal disease contributing their bodies to science? Or even, as some had whispered, crazed science fiction fans prepared to go to any length to get into space on an actual spaceship? Whatever. She'd never know now. They were simply organic robots, corpses preserved by chemicals and animated by clever electronics.

Rosa switched off the recording. The screens returned to the true pictures of the planet below, relayed from the planetside cameras. The uniform grey shrouds of the nuclear winter filled the scene once more.

"Lights gone," said Zoe, sounding like a disappointed child.

"Yes, Zoe. All the lights have gone out now."

The decision to send reanimated corpses into space (only the press used the term zombies) had been a purely economic one. Her crewmates didn't require an oxygen supply, didn't sleep and could EVA to fix the station without even wearing a suit. They were machines, easier and cheaper to produce than anything artificial. It made sense.

But a living person had been needed to make the decisions. That was Rosa. She'd been reluctant to accept the mission: her life-long ambition to go into space tempered by the thought of spending a month cooped up with five reprogrammed corpses. Sometimes she still regretted it. Perhaps a swift end down on the surface would have been better.

Still, she was alive. She was *here*. And that was important. Precious. Perhaps, at the end, Ravi had enough warning to know what was coming. And perhaps the thought of her, safe up there in orbit, had been a comfort for him. So she liked to think.

But oxygen: that was the problem. Their reserves were now all-but depleted. The electrolysis units had been losing efficiency for months. The solar array gave them all the power they needed. They had supplies of dried food to last years and could probably eke out the recycled water that long, too. But the oxygen was running out. Which didn't affect Zoe and the rest, but it was a problem for Rosa. A big problem. That, in the end, had made her mind up for her.

Zoe was hauling herself away by the grip-handles now, to join Zed, Zeb, Zander and Zach – so Rosa had taken to calling them – in the science pod. They'd been instructed to carry out a series of zero-g physics experiments and they faithfully did so, even thought it was futile. Rosa didn't try to stop them. She liked the activity. The illusion of purpose.

"Zoe, before you go, I want to give you some new instructions later. When you're finished in the science pod. Is that OK?"

Zoe didn't reply. She had no views on whether it was OK or not. She hadn't been programmed to have views. She absorbed the information then waited to see if Rosa had finished. Her plasticized face gleamed from the internal lights of the station. Rosa wondered what it would be like to have a hide that tough. Nothing could hurt you.

"I'll have to upload some new routines and data into your chips," she said. "Do you understand, Zoe?"

Zoe still said nothing. Awaiting further instructions.

"Zoe, I'm going to become one of you," said Rosa. "Understand? Then we can all live together up here for as long as the sun gives us power. And I need you to perform the procedures. Do you see?"

Zoe looked at her but said nothing.

"Then we can sit here together and watch the Earth each day, you and I," said Rosa. "Would that be OK? Perhaps, one day in the future, the clouds will start to clear and we'll catch a glimpse of the surface again. Would you like that?"

Still Zoe didn't reply. With a sigh, Rosa turned away, back to the grey Earth and the blackness of space.

"Rosa ... like Zoe?"

Rosa turned back to see Zoe still floating in the O of the hatchway. The muscles beneath the plasticized skin on her face flexed and bunched as she struggled to form further words.

"Yes," said Rosa. "I'll become like you. Rosa and Zoe. We can sit here together."

Zoe looked down to her feet, then back up, still trying to get her mouth to work. Their faces didn't make expressions any more, but it seemed to Rosa there was something like puzzlement there, as if Zoe was grappling with some difficult concept. Perhaps she was imagining it.

Zoe's mouth worked some more before she spoke again. "We watch for Ravi. Watch Earth together. Until lights come back. Come back for *real*."

Rosa found sudden tears welling in her eyes. Now there was, clearly, an expression on Zoe's face. A longing. A desperation to be understood.

Rosa nodded. "Yes, Zoe. You and I. Yes. We'll wait here together for that day. For the day the lights start shining on the Earth again."

And something like a smile, or the thought of a smile, finally worked its way across Zoe's plastic features as she nodded in understanding.

E is for Earth Station Six

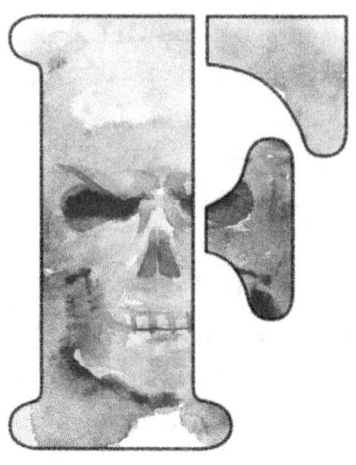

Suzanne van Rooyen

*The world will end in f minor, in dark red smudges of sound
that bleed into the hearts and minds of all who can hear
Earth's final lament.*

Sasha staggered through filth, kicking aside empty Ramen
packets and a moldy mound of forgotten pizza crusts. The
cracked handle of the screw-driver fit snug against the calluses
on his palm as he scratched at the flaking plaster of the wall.
He carved a diagonal line through four vertical ones – another
five days gone. Only ten left to complete the composition.

Gray sunlight filtered through the cracks in the boards
nailed across the windows. He dared not stray too close for fear
of the radiation corrupting his mind. His mind, his thoughts,
his music – it was all he had left as the world disintegrated,
succumbing to rot and ruin in the wake of the catastrophe.
Soon though, soon he'd end the suffering, end the long-slow
demise of humanity and wrap those clinging to life in a blanket
of sound to bear them into the afterlife. He owed them that

much, a last nod of appreciation for the years they'd filled the
halls and applauded his performances at Carnegie and Royal
Albert. If only he could've given a gentle death to his teachers
at Juilliard, to the maestro at La Scala who plucked him from
obscurity and made him a household name, to his fans and
lovers and parents who'd sacrificed so much. But for those still
left on the dying planet, he would play for them a grand finale.

Sasha knelt amidst the score. The pages fluttered like
broken dreams against the edges of his violin, which weighed
them down against the breeze seeping through the cracked
window panes. The laptop lay useless, the battery long since
dead and the wall sockets devoid of even a spark. Not that he
needed the files locked on his hard drive. He remembered every
note of the thousand page score by heart. He had almost
finished the transcription, only the last movement's
recapitulation and closing chords to go. The notes spilled across
the pages, across the floor and up the walls, blossoming across
the low sloping ceiling. He'd saved one precious piece of paper
for the ending, the staves neatly ruled in black ink completed
before the pen ran dry. The notes filling up the measures were
blue and green, black and red from the tips of a dozen different
biros scavenged from neighbors before the demons began to
stalk the corridors.

Although pen-less, Sasha was not deterred. Using the
jagged tip of the screwdriver, he slashed his wrist, careful to
catch every bead of blood in the chipped teacup turned ink-pot.
The scars on his arms were like the stripes on the walls – a
litany to the end of days. As blood ribboned from his veins, he
traced the ridges of scar tissue across his chest and thighs. For
months he'd been here while they'd been out there suffering,
waiting for the sweet sonorous release only he could provide.

He dipped the stump of a match-stick into the jar of blood
and began to write. The melody ran in triplets across the lines,

soaring into the upper octaves – the limit of the piccolo – while the tuba provided bass bombast beneath a sawing lament of the strings. F-sharp against B-flat – a burst of silver and blue. The woodwinds screamed yellow D and lime-green A as the trumpets blasted bright red C, the horns ululating pale blue E. The music danced behind his eyelids as the mystic chord thrummed to perfection and the orchestra stampeded towards the double bar lines. Too soon the blood dried up and he opened another vein. He was so close he could feel the energy of the universe rippling through his flesh, vibrating in the soft core of his bones. His heart pounded in time with the timpanis as they crashed towards a close.

Several bars from the end, a shadow passed across the page. Footsteps outside his door and the creaking of weathered floorboards. Sasha leaped to his feet, knocking the teacup in a burgundy sprawl, his blood soaking into the older stains mottling the blistered linoleum.

The line of salt at the threshold was undisturbed. The demons could not enter.

"Sasha? Sasha dear, it's Mrs. Turner." Devil voices floated through the door.

Sasha braced for attack, armed with the screwdriver in one hand and the remains of a splintered chair-leg in the other. The wood bit into his palm, finding the soft creases between calluses.

"You've got to eat. I've brought some rations." The demon pounded on the door, the voice a rasping soprano. "Sasha? Aren't you hungry? I'll just leave this here then."

"Waste of good food." Another demon grumbled. "That's all the soup we'll get this week."

"Poor thing's gone crazier than a coot. Don't blame him really, all alone in times like these and after the piano thing."

"We needed wood. He must be sick by now."

"I left him a mask." The demon wheezed. "Hasn't touched it, or the food. Such a waste."

"Him and his music."

Even the demons knew to fear his music, knew the end was near. For them, his composition would be the hammer of death, the divine mallet of justice sending the vermin scuttling back to the pits from which they crawled.

"Leave him be. No point anyway with the evacuation plans. Let the army sort him out. They're sending more troops next week. There's talk of moving us..." The demons slunk away and Sasha exhaled in relief, his weapons dropping from trembling hands as the shadows lengthened across his blood spattered pages. Night came too quickly, each day shorter than the last as dark clouds choked the sky.

He relieved himself in a bucket in the corner and slaked his thirst while it was still warm. His belly grumbled, a hollow groan of emptiness. There was nothing left to eat. He'd tried chewing on the wooden slats covering the windows, but they'd cracked his teeth and bloodied his tongue. Before, in days one through seventeen, he'd had food. He'd braved the rancid outdoors and joined the hordes searching for sustenance. That was before 'pathogen' punctuated every sentence and filled the air with more fear than ash. Sasha coughed, hugging his frail arms around his ribs that ran like ladders up his sides. He played his bones like he'd once played the keys, picking out the f-minor arpeggio along his ribs and intercostal muscles.

The slitted world beyond the grime-gunged windows sank into darkness and the sirens sounded, a wail to warn those lingering in the malignant air to barricade the doors and prepare for night. Outside, demons scuttled across the beige landscape, their bulbous eyes staring from grotesque faces. The siren sang in a spiral of rising augmented intervals, the overtones skewering Sasha's ears. He wrapped the moth-eaten blanket around his shoulders and curled into the corner where his piano once stood. Exhaustion tugged at every fiber of his being. He'd barely completed six bars today and still had so many to go. Only ten days until the solstice. After yet another coughing fit, Sasha succumbed to sleep and dreamed of being God, of sitting atop his throne in the snow-capped Himalayas with the music of the heavens spilling down the valleys, a great flood of celestial sound.

Sasha hurled the teacup at the wall, shattering porcelain and showering the plaster in a fine mist of blood. He couldn't remember the final chord progression. He'd done something clever, something transcendental before returning the listener to the comforting embrace of the tonic. He scratched at his head, gouging angry lines across his scalp and tugging at the matted thatch of hair turned dark by grit and grease. It was in the final chords that the power lay. The reams of music preceding this moment were rendered meaningless if he failed in the last bar to touch the divine.

He paced through the effluvium, kicking aside the remnants of Scandinavian furniture and Bohemian kitsch. He picked up the violin and spun in a circle, preparing to smash the instrument into concrete, but it was all he had left, a relic from his past life. It had been his mother's once and made in Moscow, just like him. Gently, he placed the violin atop the score. *Spi mladyenets, moi prekrasný, bayushki bayu,* Sasha remembered his mother's song as his fingers spun a melody from the air. He chased the imaginary refrain through the motes of dust floating in the squalid light. The light grew brighter and the wooden boards across the window peeled open as the black-tie audience began to clap.

Sasha bowed to the blood smeared wall, bathed in a blazing corona – the memory of spotlights. At the tap of the baton, the audience settled with bated breath as Sasha perched at the Steinway. The strings started with an ominous growl, building in intensity as the woodwinds blew dissonant. An orgy of sound assaulted his mind in a kaleidoscopic burst of neon. Just when the audience were close to blocking their ears, to shut out the pain of atonality, the piano cut through the riot of sound, weaving a lilting melody that subdued the chaos.

Sasha wiped his face and licked the salt from his fingers as the enraptured audience faded into the broken slats of reality. That life was gone, smothered in ash and buried in fear. There was only one way to escape it and freedom lay in the final notes of his masterpiece, and yet the final notes remained a mystery, taunting and spiteful.

He studied his hands as if the answers lay between the lines on his palms. Tiny hands that could barely reach a ninth, let alone master the works of Liszt or Rachmaninoff. A whole world of music lay beyond his grasp. He balled his fists and punched the wall, the pain ricocheting through his elbows and into his shoulders as he railed against fate. He smeared bloody knuckles across the wall adding a *tenuto* here and a *fermata* there: details, details, meaningless without the final progression.

Blood dripped down his finger, a scarlet ribbon from his sheared knuckle. Standing at the wall etched with the passage of time, Sasha began to write.

I am insane passion.

I am desire.

He paired back the skin of a second knuckle and continued writing.

I am a dream.

I am weariness.

41

Tears cut rivulets through the soot and scabs on his cheeks as he squeezed the last drops of blood from his wounded hands.

I am nothing, he wrote, the words dripping down the chiseled days, and he began to cough, each breath turned frothy and metallic. *I am nothing. I am nothing.*

☠

The demons were at his door again, spitting acid that fizzed against the wood. Too weak to stand, Sasha curled into a ball beneath the blanket and clasped the screwdriver close to his chest. He squeezed his eyes shut and wished them away, wished the din of their sibilant voices into silence. The noise corroded the music in his head. He was so close to those final chords. They dangled just beyond his reach in teasing shades of blue and green, if only the devils at his door would go back to hell.

"Sasha, it's Mrs. Turner. You have to come out now, sweetheart. Please Sasha!" The demon wailed.

"We can't force him."

"We can't leave him!"

"The evacuation is voluntary. And if he's sick, it's better for us this way."

"But he's all alone. Sasha, please, come with us. It'll be better at the camps in the north. They might even have a piano." Lies, lies, evil demon taunting.

"If you don't leave now, you'll die." The demon kicked his door. "Suit yourself, stay and..."

The words lost meaning, spinning syllables that provided the drone to the melody unwinding from Sasha's battered thoughts. He began to hum, the notes vibrating between his cracked lips – a prayer and a promise – and the demons hushed as Sasha's voice crawled free from his arid throat.

The music was not beautiful; it was raw, it was his soul spilling through his teeth. The shadows lingered at the door and he continued to sing, the song growing in intensity. He pounded the floor with heels and palms, a rhythmic accompaniment to his wordless tune. The building began to shake as Sasha increased the tempo. Sweat spilled between his shoulder-blades and pearled his chest as he beat his music into the shuddering floor. The demons screamed, forced into a retreat by the power of his melody.

A great roar accompanied Sasha's song as he surged towards the climax, palms red from slapping linoleum. The windows shook in their frames and plaster tumbled from the ceiling. The building swayed and juddered. As Sasha hummed the melody to a close, the building settled once more on its foundations and a pervasive silence laid a heavy shroud upon the world. The corners of his mouth cracked as he smiled, his lips splitting over teeth loose in their gums. He dipped his finger in a puddle of excrement and scrawled across the cut marks on the wall.

I am freedom. I am bliss.

This is the reckoning, the voice of a thousand angels screaming into the void, tearing souls from flesh as man becomes ghost becomes echo.

Sasha crawled towards the unfinished pages and unearthed his violin from beneath the second movement. His fingers brushed gently over the gnawed edges of the body. Maple should've tasted like waffles and syrup, like Sunday mornings and cozy days at home, but it had only tasted of failure and desperation and continued hunger. When Sasha was sixteen his father had asked how he planned to survive when being a musician would condemn him to a life of poverty. To being a starving artist. Sasha had replied with a smirk and the ego of one who knows no better, "I can survive on music alone." He fingered the strings of the violin salivating now at the thought of his mother's borscht and *pelmeni*.

He dragged the bow across the strings and winced at the pitch of the notes – muddy brown and gray. Holding the instrument snug beneath his chin, he turned the pegs until the instrument was in tune and the colors glowed clean. He hadn't played for six years, the piano his one true love and requiring total devotion, but his piano was gone, ripped from the apartment on day twenty-two. They'd torn her legs off, pulled out her innards and set her alight. Fuel, they'd said. Survival, they'd said. On day twenty-three, Sasha barricaded his windows and bolted the door, he'd laid down the salt and never again allowed the demons to step across the threshold. The violin he'd clung to, screamed and gnashed his teeth when they approached with their claws and distorted faces. He'd saved his mother's memory from the fire.

With brittle fingers he plucked *pizzicato*, the notes shimmering in the air: orange, yellow, green and baby blue. His left hand fingers changed position on the strings and the palette shifted into hues of purple and pink. With the last page of his composition lying at his feet, Sasha began to play the melody, picking out the theme with tentative bowing as the music turned into a rainbow mix he could almost taste.

He glanced at the wall, at the last set of days waiting for the final diagonal slice. Today was the solstice, the longest day of the year, not that the world would know with the sun struggling in a sky scarred by uranium. Today he would end their suffering, he would erase their pain and ease their journey into a better ever after.

Sasha played a *glissando*, sliding through violet and steel, circling the color wheel before coming to rest in the color of rust and blood. The music spun away from his fingers and the notes clashed as the orchestra joined *tutti*. The brass blasted harsh dissonance, the timpanis pounded out the beat, the woodwinds screamed at the heavens, and the strings sawed a violent *tremolo*. The music exploded in a myriad colors, colors Sasha could not name, colors never before seen. He had wrung something from nothing, he had pulled perfection from the ether and spilled it across the staves. The final chords floated towards him in swaths of neon. He slashed his wrist and, with trembling fingers, completed the last bars, tearing the page as he drew the double bar line.

With the red stained screwdriver, he turned to the sculpture on the wall and dragged one last line through the battery of days. Blood pooling in his hand and dripping puddles around his knees, Sasha slumped against the wall and scrawled three final words upon the crumbling surface. With the life dribbling from his wrist, he closed his eyes and curtains opened upon a grand vista, a stage set against the backdrop of the Himalayas – the seat of the divine. Seven billion people gathered to hear his music. Baton in hand, he gestured to the musicians and humanity fell into an expectant silence as the soundtrack to the apocalypse began to play.

F is for Finale

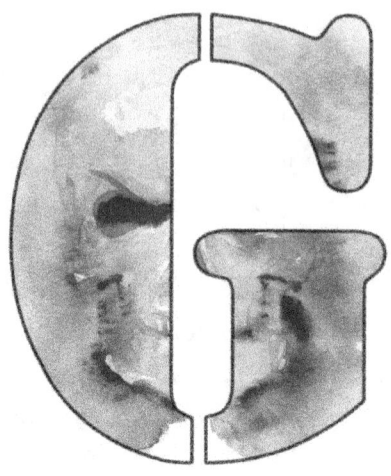

Alexandra Seidel

Even *before this, the world has ended, ended in intervals,*
yet completely. Everyone knows it, the drama of surviving
a child, the pain of watching someone you love die and know
that they are dying, the incredible emptiness of loss.

This time, the hands on Death's clock mark a different
hour.

The Lovers

The where was her room, second floor somewhere in
suburbia, windows facing east, which was ironic, but lovers
have no care for ironic, they only know truth. Her parents were
at work, they mostly were these days, because mom was a
doctor and dad an insurance investigator, and circumstances
demanded that they work long hours.

Her hair was straight, an ordinary brown shade, matching
her eyes just so. His dads thought that he was at school. When
things changed their every word and deed had become so
overcautious, and he was glad to be out of the house where

there was much more talk, much more fear and uncertainty. He had fallen for the earth-haired girl out of need, and she had fallen for his blue eyes because they reminded her of hope.

The room itself looked like childhood, a white mirror frame with pictures stuck to it, a few books, a few old toys in strategic places, a snow globe from a Paris vacation on her desk, a diary, hidden and blank-paged for months now. The room felt like it wanted to keep time inside and not let it go.

The lovers were on the bed, holding hands, locking eyes. She had a bottle of pills inside her left hand, hidden almost by the knot of fingers, but not quite. There was no second way, no other way between those two.

"Do you think it hurts at all?" I can take it, but not if I'm afraid of pain, he thought.

"It shouldn't. These are pretty much pain killers." Almost, I guess, or better; not that it matters, there is hurt all over, now, she thought.

"It will be better though, right? I mean, the, uhm, undeads... you sure your mom said they were alright?" I hope it still works with suicide, he thought.

"Serene was the word she actually used." That, and all the time she was looking at dad and me with a sheet white face, eyes looking like she was sleep walking, or high, the girl thought.

"Well, that's just like happy, right?" Happy is good, hell, serene could be even better, he thought.

"Yeah." I sure hope it does, for us anyway, she thought.

The brown-eyed girl opened the bottle, fed herself the tiny seeds of red, and then fed him. They ate without water, as if it were really food and not medicine to cure an ailment.

They slept. They slept for a long time, and then, they woke again.

The Hermit

I didn't think that Her horse would be this, well, fucking perfect. Beautiful, really, the kind of beauty that makes you cry because you realize: now that I have seen this nothing can ever compare, nothing will ever come close, and even if something did, you'd always just think of this one perfect thing and everything else would seem foul in comparison.

Craziness had been crawling the streets like the Spanish flu must have done back then. There were people shouting zombies, others were calling it a day of judgment and whatnot. Some folks were just having a hell of a party, and devil may care if they drank themselves into Death's dream kingdom, the place from which one might return after all.

You must see it as a picture: a busy street in a big city where anonymity makes everyone equal. In one corner, blood junkies, shooting or cutting themselves to come back and talk about it. In a different, shadowy corner those bigots who conspire to burn—themselves and everyone else with them— because they don't want to see the good in somebody else's pleasure while they won't even let themselves be happy for the space of just a thought. Smack in the middle, a helluva huge party; people were happy to be parted from loss and reunited with love. *Forever has real meaning now*, they would say. Sweet, salty, lipstick red, that's how they painted the streets.

I was just watching. Sure, I didn't believe that crazy zombie bullshit, but you know, they crossed a river. They may not moan for brains, but they crossed a river, and that would change anyone. And it changed them sure as bullets fly straight, though only few might admit that change can be worse than a thousand unfired pieces of lead.

I was watching this strange bacchanal, when somewhere out of the corner of my eye I saw this gray ripple, like a tear in the canvas. Did I hear the sound of hooves you ask. Nah, no sound at all, nothing strange, nothing wild or unnatural, just movement. Like an itch that wants scratching I had to check it out. The Labyrinth swallowed me rattlesnake quick. I took a corner, and there it was, the city gone, replaced by a riddle of walls. The strangest thing was this: I realized I wasn't too keen on getting out.

The Three of Swords

She hadn't wanted to breast feed at first, but the moment she held her girl, she changed her mind. *I would die for you;* this is the oath all mothers speak, if only to themselves or an empty room or a sleeping newborn. Even so, it is true.

The blade slipped in between the mother's ribs. And it was such a quiet blade. She remembered her own mother, long transcended to ash, telling her that her baby girl had her cinnamon earth hair. She saw the back of her girl's head, eyes facing the television, and despite the normalcy of the scene, there was wrongness all over.

Her daughter turned, her boyfriend's fingers threading through her hair, and when the mother saw her child like that, three sharp swords killed what no amount of breath or blood can keep alive.

Death

I did not find him at the center of the labyrinth. I just took a left and there he was, perfect like Aphrodite risen from the ocean deep. He did not breathe fire, and his hooves were softer than spring rain. I imagined how many souls had seen the Gray and his rider, and while they had always dreaded the sight, the reality of it all would have surprised them.

I imagine he didn't think it was proper for him to be without his rider, She who doesn't speak but listens. I know what you think is coming, me, getting up in that saddle and doing the job, but no; I wouldn't have been able to bear the thought of me touching any part of this creature. That wouldn't've been proper, no life is supposed to take the light out of a being that is the only one of its kind.

"Tell Her She is missed." I said instead, or I thought it maybe, I don't know. The Labyrinth was getting to me, after all. I'm not sure he even knows where his rider is, but the Gray looked at me, just for the length of one heartbeat, one breath then sure enough he vanished like a dream, and I felt his absence like salt in a gaping wound. When I took a step to where he had been standing, the Labyrinth vanished as well, left me shivering like a child who's had enough of building snowmen.

The city was still there, its noise, smell, feel, just like a semblance of home.

Even now, I can hear the sounds of life mixing with not-death seeping into my apartment through the open kitchen window. You know, I mind. Not the noise per se, the noise in and of itself weighs nothing, but I know, lying here and feeling time trickle by like heartbeats, that one of these days all this noise of never stopping hearts will weigh more than hope could ever lift. Without the Labyrinth we will be lost. Without the rider and the silken movement of Her steed, we will never be able to stop, yet stand still, forevermore.

G is for Gray Horse

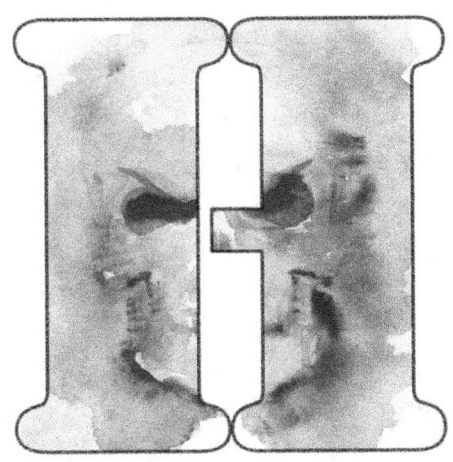

Sara Cleto

The Cold Time, Year 1001 of the Last Cycle (3015 CE)

The wind swung and pierced with the precision of a skinning knife the day the Lady fell. Neila did not see it happen. Crouched over a tumble of thin, damp twigs, she struck palm against fist. The hard crystal, nestled against the crease of her lifeline, and the oblong, black loop around her fingers shed sparks when they met, sparks that left lace traceries on her skin when they fell. Scars twined round her arms and hands like charms.

Her litany unfolded precisely, words falling in time with a curtain of sparks, words searing and sealing with heat. Her scars were thick with remembrance.

"Fortitude," Neila sang as sparks flared and died. "Honor. Resilience. Diligence. Supplication. Devotion. Revelation. Revelation. *Revelation*." The twigs quivered and caught, sparks kindling into wiry laps of flame. Neila bowed her head and spread her arms wide in the ritual gesture of welcome and thanksgiving.

The crack came first, then a long scream as metal parted from metal. A pause, as Neila and the world held their breath, and then the crash. Waves swelled high and surged across her threshold, slapping at her feet and washing away her small fire. Neila gazed intently to the west, but her nearsighted eyes could see nothing but twisting shadows. She retreated into her hollow for a moment, wrapping crystal and loop into her bedding, and rubbed sharply at the slits behind her ears before covering the small deformities with her long hair so as not to debase herself before the Lady. Shucking her ragged dress from her shoulders in one quick motion, she dove smoothly into the water at her doorstep.

Her long hands propelled her easily, the translucent webbing between her fingers adding extra power and fluency to each stroke, her flat feet kicking a graceful counterpoint. She shot past the bright fish, their aquamarine and canary stripes belying the cold, generating a visual heat that she could almost feel on her anemone-thick eyelashes, on her long, protruding nose, and in the infinite darkness of her black eyes, all blown pupil. She chanted as she swam—"Fortitude. Honor. Resilience. Diligence. Supplication. Devotion. Revelation."—her words escaping in bubbles that poured from her lips like silvered pearls.

At the foot of the Lady's pillar, a platform crowned with a propylaea and punctuated with an altar, rose from the waves. Neila had not been the one to build it, nor had the Priestess before her, nor the one before her. Legend said the first Priestess, Kassindra of Delfee, had wielded the strength of her immense tail to smash the bedrock into pieces and had gathered and arranged the resulting slabs, cementing them together with the kelp of her hair. As much as Neila liked the story, she had always suspected that the Lady had built her temple herself.

Neila pulled herself onto the platform, wringing water from her hair onto the altar in an offering of supplication before she raised her eyes. The Lady was gone, her pillar snapped. Neila ran to the edge of the platform, her feet unsteady on the hard stone, but the sky remained empty.

She was forsaken. But why? She had tended to the temple faithfully, swept the stones clean of salt, lit the small fires from dried kelp and twigs. She had sung prayers in her husky voice at dawn, high noon, dusk, and moonrise. The litany was a constant tattoo on her lips. She dropped to her knees, frost knitting across her damp skin, and wept.

Without the Lady, she was nothing. The rhythm of her days, the seasons of darkness and light, were bound to her service. And without the Lady, would the days, the seasons unravel? Her mother, the former Priestess, had spoken sometimes of a long-ago grey time when the air and the water were shrouded, when the Lady watched from behind a cloudy veil, her face unreadable. The grey choked those early Priestesses, and their songs were roughened—and eventually stifled—by the air's thickness. The Priestesses bred young, desperate to add new voices to their chorus before they succumbed to the grey, but the line had never been strong. Neila was the last.

Something flickered deep in the water.

Without pausing to sweep the platform or perform any other elements of the Ritual of Closure—how her heart clenched at the transgression—Neila tumbled into the water in a tangle of hair and limbs. One desperate gulp of air, and she surged downward, parting fish and weeds with reckless swipes of her hands. The water was heavy with sediment, blurring her vision, but Neila listened for the echoes and reverberations that painted the seascape's shape, felt the eddies that fringed the current tickle her skin.

She spiraled down and down. The bright fish darted overhead like stars, huddled into the warmer surface layer. In the dark, cold regions, stranger shapes undulated and clarified. A beast with many heads watched her from a dozen eyes, but dozens more studied a vast snake surging in the opposite direction, and she shot past its jaws unmolested. A school of seal men waved their tails hopefully at her, but she spared them only a quick, webbed salute without pausing, and they retreated gracefully into their cavern, pulling nets full of crabs with their strong hands.

Before the bedrock itself came into view, its agitation was visible—a cloud of sediment expanded up and outwards like a cloud, like the grey from her mother's stories. Neila checked her dive, hovering above the mushrooming sediment, searching for the Lady within its shroud, but the water was nearly opaque, reflecting light rather than illuminating the secret within.

Neila's lungs burned—she was a strong diver, but she had been under for too long. Her hands and feet felt numb, and her vision was spotting.

"Fortitude. Honor. Resilience. Diligence. Supplication. Devotion. Revelation," she said with the last of her air, watching the bubbles ascend. Her chest felt hollowed, hallowed, empty of all but the Lady.

Neila sank into the cloud, arms outstretched.

The Lady's face rose through the sediment, her smile warm as a benediction. Neila lifted her trembling arm, boldly caressed the star in the Lady's crown with her fingers.

An inscription ringed the Lady's face. Had it always been there, simply too small for the Preistesses' weak eyes to read from a distance? Or was it a final blessing from the fallen Lady to her last acolyte? The language was arcane, perhaps older than the grey time. Neila traced the letters, committing the shapes to memory.

The need for ascent racked Neila's failing body, but still she lingered, her hands on the Lady's face, her long hair. The image shifted and blurred, and Neila blinked the sediment from her eyes. When they were cleared once more, she half-believed that she was gazing into a mirror rather than a portrait. The long hair was much like the reflection she saw when gazing at the water's surface, as were the thin arms. But she had legs while the Lady's fins curled gloriously up to frame her face. When she looked down, they were kicking slowly beneath her. Catching one leg in each hand, she drew them up until she too was framed.

She gasped in surprise and recognition, and water poured into her defeated lungs. Water filled her, choked her, and Neila thought desperately of her predecessors who had strangled during the grey time. She waited for darkness to claim her, for the Lady to sweep her away.

Instead, she pushed water smoothly from the two small slits behind her ears, the slits that her mother had always bade her conceal behind her hair. Her vision cleared, and the Lady's smile seemed fractionally wider than before.

Revelation. Revelation. *Revelation.*

The Lady had not forsaken her. She had sacrificed her image to show Neila that she was within her—a mirror, a guide, a path. She had fallen to be reborn in her Priestess.

Neila would borrow a net from the seal men. She would cradle the Lady's medallion in its webbing and carry her through the waterways to the western coast—the Lady's birthplace. She would gather new followers, train new Priestesses, show them the mirror and teach them to see themselves in the Lady's smile. Pressing a kiss on the Lady's star-crown, Neila arced towards the light shining far above her.

2014 CE

Eric stepped from the dark warmth of Starbucks on 7th and Main St., a double soy latte in his hand, when the first explosion detonated. He looked up, saw the mushrooming pillar climbing higher and higher in the morning light. The Starbucks siren smiled down on him as he dropped his paper cup.

H is for Hieroglyph

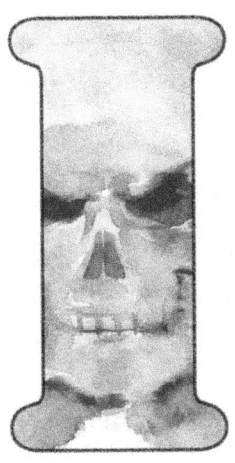

Kenneth Schneyer

The climb was Ameretat's idea. Budi never told her outright that it was pointless, but she knew that's what he thought. Zyan said it was sweet, but wouldn't have come if Ameretat hadn't wheedled and prodded em. Seanán — well, Seanán came along with the pleasant indifference he bestowed on every activity he encountered. Only Ameretat really cared. And that was the core of the crisis.

For the first hour or so Zyan held Ameretat's hand, murmuring comforting things, telling little jokes she'd heard five hundred times already. E meant well, but even Zyan, after all they'd been through, all the years and whispers and caresses and sorrow, didn't feel what Ameretat felt. Oh, e understood it, sympathized, wanted to help, but eir help was all about easing Ameretat's anguish, not the disaster that was causing it.

Now they couldn't even hold hands. The bumpy rock face scraped and sliced Ameretat's fingers and palms; her feet slipped and stuttered. The frozen wind slapped through her light clothes. The other three were shivering and blue, taking deep breaths to maintain their concentration. Seanán kept forgetting why they were there, summoning up furs that the Core obediently put on him — then he'd look again at the others, remember, and the warm clothes would vanish.

Budi slipped and slid a few meters back, landing on his bottom with a grunt. Ameretat and Zyan stopped and waited for him, Zyan with a patient smile, Ameretat with a worried frown. Seanán kept climbing.

Budi waved his fingers at them. "No repairs needed just now," he called. His voice was thin and breathy in the wind. "I'm bruised, but that probably helps." After a few minutes he'd climbed back up to them, wincing as he went.

The last few meters before the summit were steep. They crawled over the edge, then stood shakily, slapping their arms, then hugged each other, then slapped their arms again. Budi hobbled around the slippery hilltop. "I know I'm alive, because I hurt," he said to Ameretat. "Happy?"

Ameretat inhaled deeply, the icy air making her lungs feel as if they would solidify on the spot. She hurt too — her hands, her skin, her eyes where the wind still pricked them. She was definitely alive. "Yes, happy. And so are you."

"Maybe." He looked around at the clouds. "Enough to keep from turning into a tree, anyway. At least for today. Do you want to say something? Some sort of ceremony?"

Ameretat didn't. Now that she was here, standing on granite high in the air, she didn't know what to do. The climb had been an end in itself; the destination now seemed pointless.

Zyan lowered emself to eir knees, then ran eir already-scratched palms over the rocky surface. E patted the cold stone. "Hello, Osiris," e said.

"Don't call it that!" snapped Ameretat, banging her clenched knuckles together three, four times. "It's not Osiris. It's nothing like Osiris."

Zyan was still smiling, shaking eir head.

"It's what Osiris wanted to be," said Seanán in his usual placid way. He looked down at the ground and dug his toe into it.

"I don't care," said Ameretat. "This thing has no mind, no thoughts. If we didn't know that Osiris had dissolved, we'd never know there was ever anything remotely human about this. Ask the Core! Is there any trace, any glimmer, anything of Osiris in this?"

Silently the Core answered, "*The individual molecules that once composed Osiris are part of this formation, although it contains other matter transmuted from various other sources, primarily the nearby bedrock. The average distance between pairs of former-Osiris molecules is about 300 angstroms. You are correct to say that there is no cognition possible here.*"

Ameretat gazed down at the wooded plain at the foot of the hill that was once Osiris. She asked the Core, "*How many of the objects I can see from here were once people?*" She repeated the question aloud so that the others might pose it too.

It answered, "*One thousand, five hundred twenty-five. Six hundred forty-one trees of various species, 423 boulders, rocks, or geological features, 229 statutes or sculptures, 131 architectural structures. The remaining 101 are varied.*" There was a slight pause. "*This does not include the 462 individuals who interpolated into various species of flora and fauna and have since died, nor the 156 who remained in the form of homo sapiens but forbad any efforts to retard natural decline. It also does not include the 312 who elected, within sight of this spot, to distribute their molecules in the atmosphere at various altitudes.*"

"How long," Ameretat said aloud and to the Core. "Has it been since the first human being elected dissolution into a non-living or non-sentient object?"

"*One thousand, five hundred twenty-six years, 187 days, 34 minutes.*"

"And look how many of us are left," she said. The four of them looked around at each other, not speaking.

Seanán shrugged.

Ameretat remembered the day, more than 4,000 years ago, when eternity had been offered to her, when the matter-translation barrier had first been broken. She'd imagined century-long works of art, a millennium spent teasing out the more difficult bits of mathematics or philosophy, lovers devoting decades to exploring each detail of each other's bodies and minds.

And for a while, that's the way it had been. People went on walking tours of entire continents, conducted research into the behavior of elephants across multiple generations, built towers a mile high using nothing but toothpicks. One man wrote a poem about the first ten times he saw Halley's Comet. In a town in Vietnam, every occupant spent fifty years mastering a craft, trade, or profession, then switched to a new one for another fifty years, a game that lasted a millennium. In the mountains of North America, a group of twelve lived as six monogamous couples for a century at a time, rotating until every person had married every other person once.

But even the most obsessed, devoted mind tires of the search for wisdom. Given enough centuries, lovers get sick of each other.

Three days after the climb, Ameretat woke to scuffling and growling outside her window. She padded over to it, her bare feet touching the cold floor only at those places where she knew they would make no sound. In the indigo predawn light she saw a pair of male pumas, perhaps forty meters away. They circled each other, crouched and bristling, their teeth bared and their legs ready to spring. *My territory*, each said. She heard it as clearly as if she could really understand, as if the Core were speaking in her head. *My world, my freedom, mine. Me, not you. Me.*

She stood transfixed, her skin tightening into gooseflesh in the cool morning air, waiting to see the outcome.

Then, for no reason that she could see, the puma on the left turned and walked away, heading across the meadow to the woods on the farthest edge. The victor stared after his surrendered opponent until he vanished between the trees, then gave a satisfied *huff* and went about his own business.

One gives up, one doesn't, thought Ameretat. It's as simple as that. For a moment she wondered if one of them had once been human.

Then the Core really did speak to her. "*I have a message from Zyan*," it said.

"*Go ahead.*"

"*E suggests that you prepare yourself before hearing it.*"

Ameretat's heart (which still beat, still kept her alive under orders from the Core, although it was something like the 30th heart she'd had), jumped in her chest. She sat down on her floor, feeling tiny bits of grit under her legs, and took a few deep breaths, giving herself a space in which to hope, or to pretend, which was the same thing. There is no fact without observation, she told herself. Nothing has happened until I learn of it. I exist in the state of indeterminacy where the world may have changed, but has not. I could stay here forever, and we could go on forever, and there would always be a forever.

But she told the Core, "*I'm ready.*"

"*Zyan sends eir compliments and love, and wishes to let you know that e has spread emself among the grasses that live in all the meadows for a radius of a thousand kilometers from eir home. E asked me to tell you: I will lie beneath your feet and caress you as you tread on me. There is no parting.*"

Despite the warning, a gasp escaped her. She had known Zyan for more than a thousand years. They walked the sea floor together from one continent to another. They cried together when their friends dissolved into the air. They clasped their hands and held them first to one face, then the other, pledging that neither would ever leave the other alone. Zyan, O Zyan, never again.

Ameretat moaned aloud, wrapping her arms around herself. The world shrank. Shrank again. All her efforts for decades, all these desperate attempts, came to nothing, nothing. She would end as the last person on earth, walking alone until the end of time.

"*Do Budi and Seanán know?*"

"*I informed them of Zyan's dissolution at the same time I informed you.*"

"*Where are they?*" she asked.

"*Seanán is walking near his house. Budi was in his house when he received the message, but is now on his way to you. He should be here within twenty minutes.*"

"*Seanán is not on his way here? Nor to Budi's house?*"

"*No. He is continuing his walk.*"

Ameretat swallowed. It did not surprise her that Seanán had not reacted, any more than he'd reacted to Osiris's death, or to Panthera's or Hong Wei's or —

"*Please ask Seanán to come here as well.*"

"Done. Seanán says he will come. I estimate thirty minutes before his arrival."

Ameretat looked around the room, scratching her fingernails on the floor, trying to find something to concentrate on.

When Budi crossed her threshold she was nearly incoherent, throwing herself into his arms, grasping him so hard that he winced, whimpering over and over into his shoulder, "Don't leave me, don't leave me, don't leave me."

He was crying himself, but kept trying to say calming things. That lasted only a few moments; then she began shouting, still clutching him:

"No warning, no discussion, nothing! A nice climb, a nice little memorial, a nice little tiff about Osiris, and *Hello, I've decided to die now, so to hell with you and everything you care about; have a nice century!*"

She raged, cursed, used every foul word she could remember from the dozen or so languages she once cared about. Budi withstood it without speaking, without a change of expression, barely moving, giving back equal pressure to the pressure she exerted on him. Zyan was a hole in the air between them, a vacuum that pulled them together.

By the time Seanán walked in smiling, as calm as ever, Budi and Ameretat were standing still, holding each other silently. He gazed at them from the doorway for a moment, nodded, and said, "I will miss her. I'm sorry you're sad."

Ameretat felt another flash of rage and wanted to scream at him, but she caught herself. Seanán had always been this way: other people didn't leave any mark on his consciousness. He was pleasant with them and enjoyed himself in their company, but was just as happy without them. *I'm sorry you're sad* was a tremendous expression of sentiment for him.

(A few hundred years ago, Ameretat had consulted the Core about Seanán, asking whether neurological adjustments could alter this disturbing disconnection with others. It answered, "*Seanán has not authorized me to discuss any part of his medical or psychological condition with you. However, you are not the first to make the inquiry, and Seanán has recorded a response:* I like myself the way I am.")

"Thank you," she said. "It's come down to the three of us."

"Yes," said Seanán. Budi nodded.

"Let's stay together," Ameretat said. "Let's live in the same house, keep each other company, support each other."

"Why?" Seanán asked.

"So that we don't despair."

"I'm not in danger of despairing."

"I might be, though," said Budi. He squeezed Ameretat's hand.

Then she said, "Let's have children."

Budi frowned. "What?"

In hundreds of seasons among an ever-dwindling group of Perpetuals, everyone eventually drifted into everyone else's arms. But it was long since sex had been more than an aesthetic whim or barricade against loneliness, and no one had borne children for over 2,500 years: at first because a population of ageless, undying people made reproduction hazardous for the planet, but then — what need to leave a legacy when you yourself will be here forever? What urge to raise a child, to think constantly about the needs of another?

"Have children!" Ameretat continued. "Raise them. Give ourselves a new challenge."

"I've had children," said Budi. "So have you. What do you want, to recreate the race? Have a dozen, have the Core manipulate the genes on every fertilized egg for a hundred years until diversity is reestablished?"

"Why not? We could take turns being female, bear them in rotation. A new generation wouldn't be jaded and bored; they'd be seeing life for the first time, and they'd be full of wonder and excitement."

"And then?" asked Budi.

"What do you mean?"

"Sooner or later they'll get to the same stage we're at — "

"After another 4,000 years, maybe!"

"Sooner, I think," said Budi.

"And what of it? That's 4,000 more years than humanity would have had!"

"Ameretat..." He trailed off.

"What?"

He took her hand again, pulled her over to the pair of chairs that stood in the corner of the room. "Maybe this isn't the time to bring this up," he started.

"What? I want to hear it."

He sighed. "Do you think anything lasts forever?"

She set her teeth. "I thought we were going to."

"Why? Sooner or later every species goes extinct. Eventually the Earth dies, then then sun; someday, the Universe itself reaches a state of entropy. Maybe it's our time."

"That's so typical — we're the Perpetuals; we see things on the Grand Scale. Little things like the death of a planet or the disappearance of humanity mean nothing to us, in the Great Scheme of Things. We're so bloody *lofty.*"

"I can't help acting my age," said Budi.

There was a slight pause. Then from across the room, Seanán said, "I don't want children."

"What?" said Ameretat.

"I don't want children. I'm not interested."

"You wouldn't have to bear them if you didn't want to."

"I'm not interested in bearing them, or siring them, or raising them. I'm sorry."

Ameretat thought of arguing, of trying to persuade Seanán. But she knew it would be futile. She turned to Budi. "Would you at least donate some sperm?"

Budi shook his head. "There's no need for that. If you want to do this, you can generate the sperm yourself; the Core's going to modify the embryos anyway, so what's the difference?"

Ameretat said softly, "Just loneliness."

She did not try to have a baby. After talking to Budi and Seanán, the idea began to seem like nothing but vanity and desperation. Budi would drift away from her in any case; Seanán would never drift any nearer.

Over the next year, Budi came often to Ameretat's house, slowly explaining himself to her, preparing her for what was to come. At first she argued with him angrily, pled with him in tears, refused to speak to him at all. But gradually she listened, came to understand the calm relief, even joy, with which Budi contemplated his dissolution. "The ending of a beautiful song," he said.

But he didn't do it, not yet. He was waiting for her, waiting for her acquiescence and blessing. He would not leave her; he wanted her to release him.

At last, the night came when he sat cross-legged before her on her floor, smiling in the dim light the Core provided. He did not speak, just watched Ameretat.

Finally she said, "I'm ready."

Budi nodded and called the Core. Still smiling at her, his form blurred around the edges, then became smoke in the air, then faded altogether.

The Core said, "*Budi's molecules have been distributed throughout the structure of your house.*" She nodded, and patted the floor, and did not cry.

For a few months, Ameretat stayed in her house, trying to imagine Budi within the walls. Then she set out to walk around the world, wandering for three decades so that she reacquainted herself with each continent and ocean. Every place she went, she asked herself, *Could I be content for this to be the last time I ever see this?* Each time, the answer was the same.

When she returned home, she found Seanán much unchanged, pleased but not especially surprised to see her. She told him what she planned and asked him to attend.

"If you want," he said.

Seanán was relieved when Ameretat vanished. He didn't see why she'd decided to stay so long if she was so unhappy.

He understood what she'd said about "preserving the human race." But "human race" was just a collective noun used to refer to all the individuals of *homo sapiens*. Now that he was the last one, he supposed that he was the human race all by himself. The Core thought so too.

So preserving the human race now meant preserving Seanán, which was easy. He couldn't imagine wanting to vanish into the air, or turn into a hill, or anything like that. There were many, many things to do, and forever in which to do them.

He would miss Ameretat, of course. He would miss Budi, Zyan and Osiris too. Or he thought he would. He knew he'd remember that they weren't there anymore, and he supposed that occasionally he'd see something and want to tell Ameretat about it, and that would be sad. But Seanán liked his own thoughts best of all, and anyway, the Core was good company.

It would be easier to concentrate without all the distraction.

I is for Immortality

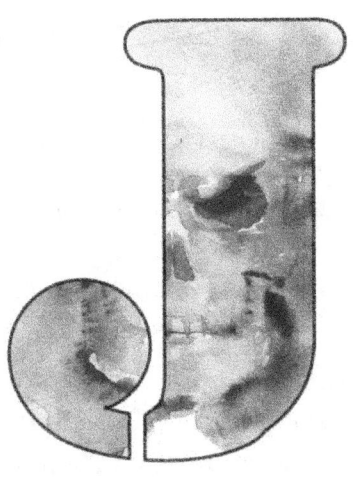

KV Taylor

The roads to Philadelphia were treacherous, but I made good time. The citizens here live in small, warring bunches, scattered throughout the city and its former suburbs. Oddly, in the city itself, it seems only the very large or the very old buildings have survived. The rest are rubble piles arranged in William Penn's neat little grids and squares.

A clan in what was once Society Hill have taken me in—I noted with interest the peeling sticker on their one unbroken windowpane that declared the home a historic landmark. The eldest member of the clan was old enough to tell me what that meant, and I confess to being impressed that he got it mostly right. It is a city that clings to its origins and therefore identity. It could be quite dangerous, if organization were ever achieved.

There's a boy here, Robin, not much younger than I. He's fascinated by me and my project. I hoped to taste at least one person in each new city; I think he will be the first.

-From the journal of Dr. Surya Johansson, August 3, 23 P.A.

☠

I've collected samples from several of the nearby friendly clans, most of whom are eager to help. Of course we learned all about it in school, but the human drive to survive, even when life is a misery, is truly awesome to see. The promise of a medical solution to their pathetic lifespan practically brings them to their knees. I don't know if this has something to do with the citizens of Philadelphia's odd connection to their own history—that they remember it was not always this way—or if it is a countrywide phenomenon. I look forward to exploring the idea further.

Robin is a very good boy. He's full of questions about the Authority and my work for them—both my journeyman year and what will come after—which I answer as I was taught. He knows he was named after a bird that disappeared in the Apocalypse; the citizens here call it the Antichrist Apocalypse, which I find charming.

I wonder if Johan would. I must remember to ask him.

After some observation, I am satisfied that his diet is very much like the other citizens. (Mainly root vegetables and stew made from every part of a given animal. With little grass available, the animals also eat a great deal of root veg. Wheat is at a premium, so very little bread is made except with potato flour.) I asked him tonight if he would like to feed me. His dull, human eyes—they are a deep brown, almost black—almost seemed to light up with real intelligence and excitement. He is keen for the experience. I am keen to taste him.

-From the journal of Dr. Surya Johansson, August 11, 23 P.A.

Robin lacks the sweetness of the humans in the employ of the Authority, but this is not surprising. He has a bitter taste, like carrot peels, underlying the natural succulence of his young blood.

-Note in the margins, dated 8/12

Richmond is a wasteland. I recall stories from Advanced Human History about the horrors they wrought on themselves with their American Civil War and find it sad how doomed humanity is to repeat its errors. After all, Johan and his lot hardly wrecked anything, physically speaking; If the clans here are any indication, they have no idea of the significance of their city in history—but they could be dangerous in other ways.

The humans are suspicious, but several clans with a loose alliance near the city center tolerate my presence without complaint. Yesterday an elder called Mariah came to me—old enough to have a few gray hairs and wrinkles about her dull eyes. She said if I wanted fed, I ought to come to her and leave her people be. I agreed, if she would round up a large sample to give blood for my project—under her supervision. I find her accent difficult to decipher, but I'm confident she's agreed. More or less.

-From the journal of Dr. Surya Johansson, September 29, 23 P.A.

In spite of myself and all of Johan's warnings about getting too close to the humans, Mariah interests me. She is protective of her clan *and* those she does not call hers, and speaks of a fellowship of humanity. "How can we trust an authority that must literally feed on us to survive?"

"All authority feeds on those it reigns over," I pointed out. "You survive because of the authority you have over them."

"I survive *in the style to which I am accustomed* because of the authority I have over them, but I won't cease to survive at all without it. I'm not desperate for it. Like *the* Authority."

For someone with very little understanding of history and no access to information infrastructures, I find her remarkably sharp-witted; as charming as my little Robin in some ways. I wanted to engage her further, but remembered what Johan always says about becoming too invested.

The diet here is greener due to the near-perpetual sweltering heat, but spare. Her blood was rich with a metallic tang, full of iron and salt. How someone so near to the death age for a human can taste so very, very full of life, I know not. I could survive on her for some time, but my little vials are full and my dietary survey complete, so I must go within the week. Lingering too long, when I've already become slightly interested in these people, would be ill-advised.

-From the journal of Dr. Surya Johansson, October 6, 23 P.A.

Savannah, I am told, was always a town full of ghosts. I have no real way of knowing if the stories about the old houses scattered over its many surviving squares have any basis in pre-Apocalypse history or if they're some new fetish of the scarred population, but I lean towards the latter explanation. Their clans are arranged in some kind of Byzantine class system, and like-minded clans meet at 'social clubs'.

These are places where fanciful stories are told of the Authority. They say Johan is a ghost, himself, and Mkembe and Derrick the vampires. My surname, they rightly take to mean I am of Johan's 'clan', and they are surprised to learn that I too drink blood. As taught, I tell them nothing of the Authority, even when they guess right.

I find it fascinating that, for all their tales, they have not yet realized that it was the Authority who crafted their little apocalypse. It would seem the obvious, considering their immediate rise to power. But then, humans are mostly slow creatures.

One or two shine, though, in every place. Here I have met a couple, Douglas and Thierry, who remark on the luminosity of my vampire eyes at length. Perhaps I might try two, in Savannah.

-From the journal of Dr. Surya Johansson, November 3, 23 P.A.

I could spend several months just chronicling the stories they tell here, but my vials are full and I must move on.

Thierry asked me to take them with me last night; I was surprised to find his request more poignant than amusing. "We can't afford horses or gasoline—you're our only chance to see the world"— by which he meant the US, as most evidence of the world beyond has been successfully purged to the point of fairy tale, now. They have little to know understanding even of the rest of North America.

Little to no threat of uprising here in the Old South, then, I think.

We went to a strange, almost macabre party where the humans danced in tatty old gowns and suits from the Before Apocalypse. era, sewed and refitted and remade over and over. It made me aware of a kind of inherent sadness in the human race, equally plagued by the past they've forgotten and the future they can't have.

It seems appropriate then that both Thierry and Douglas—
who consume the typical freshwater fish and ashy plant diet
here—taste particularly minerally. Like salt.

Humans cry salt. What a funny thing, really, seeing as they
are made of it. As if every time they lose something, they
sacrifice a little more in memory. Ridiculous creatures.

-From the journal of Dr. Surya Johansson, November 14,
23 P.A

How strange that I should miss them, especially Thierry
and, of all creatures, Mariah. Again remembering Johan's
lessons about how this sort of attachment leads to the
downward spiral, I steeled myself for Cincinnati. It is settled
on what was once the grand Ohio, now but a filthy creek bed.
Before leaving home, I read in the Authority Central Databank
that it used to be lovingly called 'Porkopolis'; I suppose I should
not be surprised, then, to find portions of it overrun by pigs.

As a result, they are oddly well-fed here, but I fear the
citizens will taste of fat and smoke and mud. I have yet to find
any with acceptable quarters, though several have offered to
house me for the sake of garnering favor with the Authority.
Instead, I took a vial from each of them and left.

It would be a shame not to taste for myself, though.

-From the journal of Dr. Surya Johansson, December18, 23
P.A.

There is some sort of winter festival now. People place odd
stocking caps on their pigs and make paper cut-outs that they
say look like snowflakes. I suppose they do, with some creative
license allowed. No doubt it has its roots in the old traditions of
the winter solstice and Christmas; no one here seems to know,

particularly. This is a good sign for the Authority. But, a bad sign for the people of Cincinnati.

Today I found several people huddled around a fire near the creek bed roasting lizards and singing old songs. They looked very small and strange in that flickering light, smiles on their faces and steam rising from their breath. Perhaps it sounds bestial, but that is merely my inability to communicate—in fact, I found it touching. In spite of knowing none of them by name, even by trade or some other form of usefulness, I was taken in. There were harmonies, simple but lush, that plucked at my heartstrings. There is no denying this is why these songs exist for them—they speak some universal language.

What does it say that it is one I too naturally understand?

I drank from one of them. I refused to know their name; they offered life, and I accepted. They tasted just as you'd expect someone eating lizards in a muddy creek bed to taste, I suppose: like dirt. No more like pig than the rest of the human race.

I wonder if my imagination influences the way they taste as much as anything. Can it really make such a difference, where someone lives? I suppose that's the point of my Masterpiece, in a way.

-From the journal of Dr. Surya Johansson, December 25, 23 P.A.

I originally thought Chicago desolate, but I couldn't have been more wrong. Today, I managed to convince the youngest daughter of my host family, Lani, to show me where it was people disappeared to at night, leaving the rubbled streets far more ghostly than any house in Savannah. She's about Robin's age, I think, and therefore near to mine; she looks at me with hope in her large, dull human eyes, and I feel a sense of responsibility for her, as if she might be a particularly clever pet instead of livestock. Dependent upon me and mine.

I recognize this as one of the signs of the downward spiral, but I have no will to stop it. Only a sense of curiosity that should, perhaps, disturb me more.

She took me into the tunnels, some forty feet beneath what's referred to as 'the loop' (though I doubt anyone recalls why). I read nothing of this place when perusing the Central Authority Databanks—they must've been forgotten by time, but not, it seems, by Chicago. I was astounded at the life that teemed so far beneath the surface of the city, safe from the biting wind and ash-snow. There, the citizens have built a world for themselves: miles and miles of bazaars, residential areas, workshops, storage.

They have replaced the infrastructures the Authority has destroyed and denied them with a strangely beautiful creature of their own creation. Multi-faceted, glittering underground, a small hidden jewel that pulses with light and life.

If the Authority finds it, it will be crushed.

-From the journal of Dr. Surya Johansson, January 31, 24 P.A.

My vials are full.

The diet in Chicago is remarkably varied for a place that spends much of its time in cold. I suspect there is a place in the underground where they grow some of their vegetables somehow, possibly with the help of ultraviolet lights run on what I suspect is water power... but I have not investigated. I ought to, for the sake of completeness. For the sake of scientific accuracy but instead, I will merely record that they eat a variety of root vegetables and small animals, especially poultry and small fowl, which exist in abundance here.

And yet, Lani tasted like ash and dirt. I recall reading in an old book that 'the food turned to ashes in her mouth' when a character was too upset or distracted to enjoy her senses. I begin to realize that my hypotheses maybe correct: my imagination must at least partially influence the way they taste. It has been since Savannah. At least.

-From the journal of Dr. Surya Johansson, February 3, 24 P.A.

"Surya," said Johan, "I wouldn't usually allow it. But your theories are sound, your methodology is tight, and you are a remarkably brilliant vampire. You may bring us to new heights of glory with your Masterpiece."

Now, I wish he had not allowed it. Six months into my journeyman year, six months of close contact with humans and almost no real vampire contact, and I am changed forever. Most doctors choose blood extraction, sunlight experiments, but I wanted to do something grand. I wanted to help my people. I wanted to categorize and cultivate our stock, our humans; I wanted to organize and streamline.

Instead I have made the world crumble. The world they so carefully built by tearing the humans' down; decades of planning for that one fell swoop that brought vampire rule. Taking down their political systems from the inside, kicking down their infrastructure, wiping out their resistance cells, feeding on the angry and claiming all the rest. It took less than a month of neverending blood sacrifice to change everything.

And six months for me to see how tragic it was.

The diet in Minneapolis is limited, but they do magnificent things with herbs and spices. The scents fill my head and make me dizzy, though I wouldn't think of touching their food.

-From the journal of Dr. Surya Johansson, March 1, 24 P.A.

This evening, I sat in on a prolonged debate on the subject of New Human Spirituality and whether or not vampires had a thing called a 'soul'. I kept my eyes down so my nature would not be noted, naturally, wanting to hear what human thinkers truly believed of us. I find it all to be absurd, but also touching in a way. They scrape and scratch for meaning no matter how swiftly and how often they're put in their place.

I spoke to one of the thinkers after, a young man called Hedrick, and when he saw my eyes he only drew himself up.

"You cannot deny that we are the natural authority," I said. This, at least, I still believe to be true. We are more powerful.

"You are. Doesn't that mean you should take care of us and lift us up, rather than stand on top of us in an attempt to reach higher?"

"We must feed," I pointed out.

"I'll feed you," he said, and tilted his head to offer his long neck. As if to make a point.

And so, he did. And he was delicious.

-From the journal of Dr. Surya Johansson, March 1, 24 P.A.

Dear Thierry,

In this book, you will find all of the data gathered for my Masterpiece, including but not limited to:

-The diets of the populations of over a dozen major once-metropolitan areas under Authority rule.

-A compositional breakdown of a large number of blood samples from each population.

-My own observations about the taste of one or two citizens from each population.

You may draw your own conclusions about the kinds of recommendations I meant to make in my final paper. However, I no longer wish to become a Master, and would now prefer that my findings, along with my other, far less academic observations about these dozen populations remain in human hands.

I also realize that my entries here reveal a great deal about the Authority, the trinity of vampires who comprise its highest echelon, their general methods and plans, and perhaps most importantly, a short history of the Apocalypse they so cleverly engineered. These also, I would like to commend to human hands; however, by now Johan, my sire, will have noted the absence of my weekly check-ins via Authority Central Comm, and will be looking for me.

Remembering what you said about wanting to see 'the world', I return briefly to Savannah to leave you my auto. You'll find it stocked with gasoline and provisions. I ask only that you find your way to Richmond and deliver my work to the woman called Mariah, described within its pages, who I think will make good use of it. After that, you and Douglas should go where you like and do what you will.

Please don't look for me. I won't be found.

Surya Johansson
May 3, 24 P.A.

J is for Journeyman

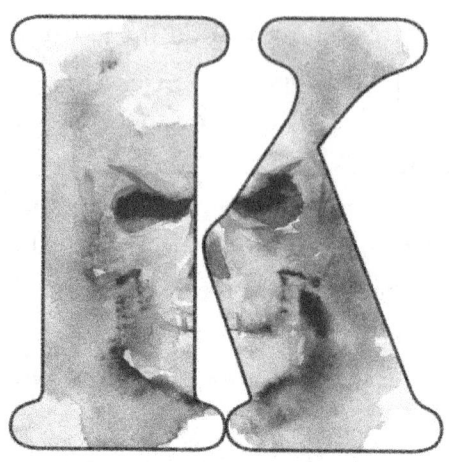

Gary B. Phillips

I think we can all agree that things are looking grim and have been for years. The war machine drones on, fueled by a faltering economy and the promises of governments that spy on and torture their own citizens. Religions preach and predict the end of the world, while cult leaders prophesy falsehoods to cash in on an impending apocalypse that never seems to show up. It's time to put our money where our mouth is. The end is nigh... *If you help us reach our funding goal!*

For a mere $16,980,667.97 we can end the world. Yes, that number is oddly specific, but it is correct. I have double and triple checked it with my accountant — and considering how much he charges, I trust that he is right. For his sake.

About Me

Who am I? To be honest, it's probably easier for me to tell you who I am not. I am not Satan, Lucifer, Baphomet, Beelzebub, Belial, Lilith, Iblīs, Shayṭān, Mara, or any incarnation or interpretation of the devil or a demon that you can think of. I am also not God, Jesus, Jehovah, YHVH, Elohim, Allah, or any other benevolent deity.

I am a commoner, one of the 99%, just like yourself. I am sick of what this world has become and I believe it is time to end it.

The Rewards

Personally, I think the end goal is its own reward, but apparently crowd funding backers expect a little more.

Pledge $1 or more

You'll get the smug satisfaction that comes with doing the right thing and ending this miserable existence for everyone.

Estimated delivery: As soon as your payment clears.

Pledge $10 or more

Congratulations! You're not as cheap as those other guys. Give yourself a pat on the back.

Estimated delivery: Immediate unless you have no arms, in which case you might need to find a friend, and even then, maybe never.

Pledge $100 or more

Now we're talking. I'd buy you a drink if we were in the same bar. Remember though, I'm just like you and your friends. We're all the same really, so go ahead and buy yourself that drink and we'll call it even.

Estimated delivery: Soon and via shot glass.

Pledge $1,000 or more

I can't believe you just blew $1,000 on ending the world! Pretty sure that's the kind of deed that gets you an express ticket to Hell. I'll put in a good word for you. (No worries if you don't believe in Hell, we can work something else out.)

Estimated delivery: Eternity-ish.

Pledge $1,000,000 or more

Limited (1 left of 1)

For pledging a cool million, you can be my lackey for a day. Fly yourself out to my place (at your own expense) and we'll make the world end together. *Maybe I'll even let you press the button!*

Estimated delivery: Right before the end of the world.

Risks and Challenges

An undertaking of this magnitude is not without risk. The chief concern among you will be a simple one: Trusting me. Trusting that I have the power, the connections, and the wherewithal to follow through and actually do the deed. I'm hurt that you *wouldn't* trust me, but I understand there are a lot of swindlers out there. I want your trust, your belief, so let me give you a token of good faith. On Saturday, November 20th look to the following sets of coordinates:

40°14'48"N, 82°42'02"W
52°21'43"N, 13°0'29"E
19°54'07"N, 75°05'56"W
47°9'0"S, 126°43'0"W
40°41'20"N, 73°52'41"W
36°13'34"N, 140°6'18"E

Then you will believe.

Frequently Asked Questions

Q: Are you insane?

A: Yes, thank you for noticing. But seriously, I am no more insane than anyone else that has dared crowdfund their dream. My dreams just happen to be a little bit more ambitious than a 90s adventure game or gimmicky science fiction anthology.

Q: I'm poor and can't afford to donate. What can I do to help?
A: Tell your rich friends. Also, get a job.

Q: Aren't you just like those wackos that predict the end of the world and then it never happens? Are we going to get our money back when you turn out to be wrong, too?
A: I appreciate the sentiment, but I've never been wrong before and I don't plan to start now.

Update #1 - Nov 19 2015
It Begins with a Whimper
A few pledges have trickled in, but we haven't even reached 1% of our goal. I'm not too worried though. I trust you will all keep spreading the word.

Comment by Joseph Hallerman
C-Bus is freaking out right now given the close proximity of one of the upcoming "events". The cops have issued a statement asking everyone to stay calm. They're assuring us there's nothing to worry about. But we'd never miss an opportunity to riot LOL!

Comment by Kitty Richards
I am disgusted that anyone is bothering to give this satanic wacko any credence. These are clearly the ramblings of a MADMAN. May you all repent and find Jesus!

Comment by Joseph Hallerman

Kitty: Did you seriously donate just so you could tell us to find Jesus? How precious!

Comment by Kitty Richards

I donated the smallest amount that it would let me, $1. I'll be canceling my donation and I urge you to do the same. 3 John 1:3-5, read it friends.

Comment by Joseph Hallerman

You're too cute, Kitty. I just want to take you home and chain you up in my basement.

Update #2 - Nov 20 2015
Happy Little Events

Things have really picked up now, as I suspected they would. The anomalies were a grand success and we're now 10% funded. I have no doubt that that we will reach our goal with time to spare. Keep on believing, friends.

Comment by Cutebookshopgrrl

Weird. I was at work late last night, stocking shelves, and I happened to open my favorite book but all the pages were completely blank. It was a new copy, so I just figured it was a printer error, but every other copy was the same way. Even our used copies! I tore through the store and every book I could find was like that. The only exceptions were the books in the Romance section.

My boss said I probably had a fever and sent me home. I passed out as soon as I got home. Now that I'm awake, my books seem okay. Thought I was in hell for a second there.

Comment by Jack Kline
I've been trying to call my mom and dad in Brandenburg
all day, but the lines are all engaged. Anyone have any luck?

Comment by xpiercex
near brandenburg. cant believe what i saw. gonna be sick.

Comment by Michelle G.
jack: i just talked to my brother in brandenburg. he is fine.
he lives about 30 miles out from where it was supposed to
happen and he didn't see anything. xpiercex: what did you see?

Comment by xpiercex
dont know how to explain. looked like some kind of orgy,
lots of writhing bodies. but then they began crying out in
terrible pain saying they were all stuck. just a mass of people. i
don't know what's happening.

Comment by Michelle G.
I'm hearing totally different reports over here. Definitely
not what you're describing.

Comment by Akiko Yamamoto
near the japan event. it is 1000s cats tumbling down
mountain.

Comment by Joseph Hallerman
LOL! Is Akiko serious or is that just bad engrish?

Comment by solidsnake
In Japan as well. She's not kidding... This is both adorable
and terrifying.

Comment by happygaijin

In japan as well but not seeing it. so some people see it but others don't? i don't get it.

Update #3 - Nov 26 2015
Thanks Mr. 1%

We have a lot more than just turkey to be thankful for today. Some one-percenter pledged $1,000,000 to the cause. He'll be flying down in a few hours to help me out in person. Should be fun. He has some... interesting ideas.

We should be breaking the 50% mark in the next few hours. Can't wait. I've got something special planned for when we do.

Comment by H. Truther

It's the government and nsa and the president and all those liars!! They've been poisoning us for years. Fluoride. Listening to our phone calls and web chats. This all makes sense. And you sheeples always act soooo surprised. Wake up!

Comment by Kitty Richards

I see nothing but God's beautiful earth. God has sent you all a strong DELUSION!

Comment by Admin

God has nothing to do with this. I ask you to kindly leave him out of it. He gets enough credit as it is, but this... this is my masterpiece.

Update #4 - Dec 15 2015
The Good and The Bad

Good: We reached 93% and have four days left.

Bad: I had some family matters to attend to which explains my absence. Fret not, believers, things are still on track. At this rate, I believe we will reach our goal with time to spare.

Comment by Cutebookshopgrrl
Anyone else really freaked out right now? I'm stuck at work. NYC traffic is a nightmare and yes, I realize how that sounds, but seriously, have you guys looked outside? I'll be sheltering in at work with a good book. (I'm thinking The Stand.)

Comment by M. Thomas
Cutebookshopgrrl: I swear I'm not a stalker but do you by chance work at Pequod Books on the Upper East Side?

Comment by Cutebookshopgrrl
As long as you swear you're not a serial killer then yes, I work there.

Comment by M. Thomas
Cutebookshopgrrl: You want some coffee? I'll bring my own copy of The Stand. ;)

Comment by Admin
The end of the world is nigh and M. Thomas is still trying to score. It cannot come soon enough.

Comment by Cutebookshopgrrl
Dark roast, room for cream and sugar please.

Comment by Kitty Richards
We can do it, brethren! Withdrawal your support from this PROJECT OF SIN and we can ensure it doesn't reach the goal!

Update #5 - Dec 19 2015
Believe!

Less than an hour to go and we have had a large number of canceled pledges. I am not a gambler, but I would bet that this is an attempt to bring the project to its knees at the last minute. Fear not! Keep spreading the word! Believe!

Comment by Joseph Hallerman
I think it may actually fail.

Comment by Kitty Richards
We did it! It did not reach its funding! PRAISE GOD!!

Comment by Joseph Hallerman
So was this all a hoax? Some sort of sick viral site? Have you seen what this has done? Looting and rioting and violence everywhere.

Comment by Jack Kline
Almost like it was its own self-fulfilling prophecy, right? I mean, look how bad things are. Reminds me of the old War of the Worlds radio show that had people killing themselves.

Comment by happygaijin
I admit it. i'm kind of sad this didn't pan out. i don't want to die, but would have loved to see the end of the world.

Comment by Cutebookshopgrrl
You can all say what you want, but I'm pretty happy with how it turned out for me. Love you M.

Comment by M. Thomas
Love you too, poppet. ;)

Comment by xpiercex
anyone else hearing that? like a low roar in the distance?

Comment by Akiko Yamamoto
yes in japan.

Comment by Joseph Hallerman
Sounds like a semi-truck engine idling in the distance, but it's been getting louder. Giving me a headache.

Comment by Jack Kline
Here too. This isn't right.

Comment by Kitty Richards
May God help us all!

Update #6 - Dec 20 2015
Final Update

This will be my final update. It will not answer all of your questions. I am a researcher with the Global Consciousness Initiative.

Our research involved the collection and analyzing of data that correlated with world events, to measure and study the global emotional responses to those events. At times this required staging events or anomalies. We wanted to prove that the sum of our existence was greater than its parts. Without a doubt, we were successful. I never imagined that I would not find myself celebrating the fruits of our research. Yet here I am.

I do not know how much time we have left. Find your family and friends and hold them close. Spend your last moments with them. Pray that we might be saved from whatever fate awaits us. Be good to one another. Whatever your compulsion, do it quickly. Make peace and find your salvation.

I am reminded of what Kenneth Bainbridge said to J. Robert Oppenheimer after the Trinity test: "Now we are all sons of bitches."

K is for Kickstarter

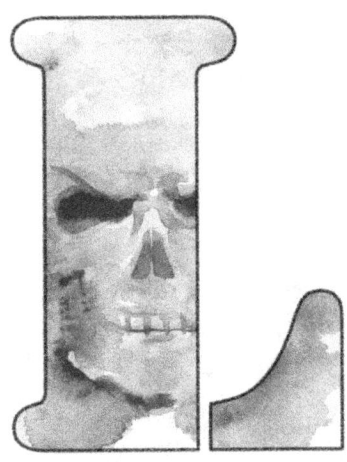

BD Wilson

Bairn crouched behind the entrance door, palm flat against the plastic of the ramp, feeling the vibrations of the crowd on the other side. The door wasn't thick enough to keep him from hearing the rumble of the crowd cheering for his competitor, but it was enough to keep him from hearing whose theme music was playing. He still didn't know who he was facing. There weren't many fighters left he hadn't beaten, and none he thought popular enough to earn so strong a response.

The heat backstage was like standing next to a blast furnace, and he could feel sweat building at his brows, threatening his face paint. It might not make it to the cage tonight, exposing the brown beneath the concealing grey. They needed to hit his cue soon. Bairn curled his fingers, scraping his nails against the ground. Impatience twitched through his shoulders, thighs, and forearms.

One more match.

He took a deep breath, held it for a three count, and then let it out. He made a fist, and tapped the surface once, again harder, and a final time to feel the sting. It didn't matter who was waiting for him. Freedom was close enough he could feel it tugging against his skin, urging him to run, to leave the damn arena forever, even burn it behind him. To go home.

Monsoon knelt, dropped by the unexpected cost of the loss. Wildfire kept one arm tight against her probably bruised ribs, the other clinging to their youngest children. Their eldest, the boy who would be called Bairn, stood apart from his family for the first time. His brother and sister were crying openly, and he struggled to share the stoic composure of their parents. He wouldn't cry, not in front of the audience.

In the centre of the ring, the Exhibition Chairman signed over a portion of the family debt: a lifetime contract, with Bairn to serve it. The arena filled with the sound of the audience's disapproval, but a deal was a deal.

"I bet on you," the Chairman had said to Bairn's parents, "and you lost."

The Chairman handed the contract to Samuel LeVarne, who shook his hand and thanked him for such an entertaining evening. LeVarne put his arm around his son Anton, and they exited the ring together. Bairn followed, alone. The audience united in a rising tide of boos, and though Anton glared at them, offended, the adults were unmoved.

Bairn clenched his fists at his side, and focused on keeping his feet moving, though they seemed heavier with each step. His vision blurred, but the aisle to entrance was clear. He didn't need to see where he was going. His sister called for him, too young to keep her fears to herself, and it almost shook the fragile grip he had on his tears.

When they reached the entrance, Samuel LeVine smiled and waved at the crowd, who had switched from boos to varied insults. Anton ground his teeth, and then gave a sideways look to Bairn before nodding at the ring. Bairn's muscles went tense, bracing for whatever was coming.

"I don't know why they're upset," Anton said, not quite pulling off the light tone he was trying for. "When you die in the pits, your debt is gone. They'll be ahead, but we'll be down the profits we'd have gotten from a real fighter. We're actually doing them a favor."

Bairn threw the punch in one smooth, practised motion. Anton's eyes grew wide before Bairn's fist hit the right one, but he didn't think to block. The impact shook all the way up to Bairn's shoulder, and a second later, the audience's cheer hit in a wave that sank right to his core.

Security guards in suits burst through the door, yanking Bairn's arms behind him before snapping cuffs on his wrists. Samuel was saying something about a contract clause, extended term, but Bairn couldn't make sense of it over the rush of the audience. He couldn't stop the grin it gave him.

At least, not until a guard threw him over a shoulder. The last thing he saw of his home was his family huddled in the centre of the ring, his father slumped and defeated.

"I'll come back," he shouted the promise, but if they heard, they didn't believe.

"To your mark," the stagehand said, and Bairn stood, taking his place. He tightened his fists as the door opened.

The sound of the crowd hit him with more force than the chill of the conditioned air. He let it hit him as he put on the emotionless affect and stepped forward to play his part. They screamed for the image, his painted death mask and show, and they screamed loud. Queens Arena was the largest left in any city and even it couldn't contain the sound. He'd been told it carried two streets over, even to the walls some days, but he credited that more to the promotion machine than the truth.

He stalked toward the ring, with a measured pace that didn't reveal his impatience. Beneath the noise of the crowd he could hear his own theme music, and he used it to time himself. He kept his entrance controlled, unconcerned, always the same.

Always, until reached the ring floor, and jerked to a stop. Anton was in the centre, tailored suit traded for a referee's T. His presence was different, and different was bad.

There was no lurch when the bullet train started moving. Bairn pressed himself into the corner, glaring at everyone around him and rubbing his wrists raw against the metal cuffs. Anton was the only one in the car paying him any attention, though the smug little prick was trying to appear as indifferent as his father and his entourage of suits. Samuel LeVarne was focused on the tablet in his hand and the corp-speech from his cronies. Now and again he cast a disapproving glare at the shiner swelling his son's right eye shut.

Bairn smirked, the rush from the ring briefly restored as he saw the progression of the bruising. He clung to it, used it to try and portray a strength he didn't feel.

Harsh red light replaced the darkness outside as the window revealed his first view of the land between the cities: a wasteland of dirt, sand, and rock. Rain hit the windows, sizzling even as the train's systems cleared it away. Away from the tracks it beat down on everything, punching holes in the ground and turning the rocks to dirt before his eyes.

"You're never getting back," Anton whispered, beside him now and still seething. "Even if you live through the pits and earn out, you'd still have to take my father's train, and there's no way he'll let you now."

Bairn looked back at the purple and blue bruise consuming Anton's eye and grinned. "Worth it."

Anton slammed his head into the window.

Nervous tension stole into Bairn's limbs, waiting for the strike of understanding, but Anton just smiled and smoothed out the front of his black shirt. He was smiling, as though there was nothing out of the ordinary, and Bairn couldn't do anything without breaking character, at least not now.

He entered the cage. There was nothing else he could do. The door closed behind him, lock clicking into place. He looked across the ring at his opponent and his tension broke as the strike landed.

Finley leaned against the cage wall, arms crossed in front of his chest. His bad eye was uncovered, grey and swimming. Bairn had never gotten used to that, not in twenty years of training, but the confidant smirk he knew all too well. It was the one that said he was too fucking stupid to live.

"What the hell is this?" the large Scottish man said. His pale skin was sunburnt, even in the underground training pits, and his bare shoulders were covered with freckles. There was a patch over his right eye, and scars damn near everywhere you looked. One of his wrapped hands pointed at where Bairn had been dropped on the floor in the corner.

"New transfer," the suit who brought him said. A surprisingly strong suit, who seemed like he was far more comfortable in the pits than he should have been. "Needs to be made into a fighter."

"No, that's a damn child," the Scottish man said. "What is he? Nine?"

"I'm already a fighter." Bairn rolled himself to a sitting position, the balance made difficult with his hands still cuffed behind his back. The Scottish man snorted and smirked. Bairn frowned, but the man just laughed at him.

"He's been doing Exhibition shows since he was four." The suit straightened his sleeves and folded his hands in front of him. "Dynasty. Boss wants you to show him how it's really done."

The Scottish man shook his head. "No. He won't live long enough to make it worth it."

"You'll get double the points as long as the boy's still breathing."

He stopped laughing. "Triple."

"Bargaining, Finley?" He held out his hand. "Like he knew you would. Done."

Finley shook it, and then pointed back the way they came in. "Now get out of here. I've got work to do. A lot of it." He turned his attention back to Bairn as the suit left, and pulled him the rest of the way to his feet. "Let's see how long you last."

"I'm not going to die here," Bairn said. "I'm going home."

"No one goes home, little bairn," Finley said. "Even if you get out, the Dead Lands keep you in Queens."

"I'm going back to my family," Bairn swore. "Whatever it takes."

"Introducing first," the announcer began, "fighting out of the red corner, with a professional record of 15 wins, 3 losses, and 3 kill shots, the Red Warrior." Finley held up his hands and stepped into the centre of the ring, playing to the crowd. There were signs with his name on it, shirts with his logo even after time out of the cage. With the warmth of his smile and wave, you could almost think he loved them as much as they loved him.

Bairn took advantage of the crowd's distraction. "What is this?" he demanded. Anton at least had the grace not to misunderstand.

"Your opponent, obviously. There aren't many left that can challenge you, and if things get too easy, the tickets don't move." He adjusted his gloves, and looked over the crowd. "But the Red Warrior returning to fight his protégée? That guarantees a sell out."

Bairn ground his teeth, but shucked his coat and took his place. Of course his last match would have to be something good. He should have expected this. Missing it was a mistake, and he couldn't afford to make another one.

Whatever it takes.

"And his opponent, fighting out of the blue corner, with a professional record of 18 wins, no losses, and 5 kill shots, our champion, the zombie, Bonne Nuit!" Scottish nickname, French ring name, and who the hell knew what for his real name? Something better suited to his skin tone, he assumed. Not that those designations mattered anymore. Not to the world, and not to the crowd. He stayed in his corner, hands at his side, letting the noise press down and ground him back in his persona.

Finley shook his head, entertainment tugging at his lips. Bairn had tried to make him understand what drew the crowds to him, other than the wins, but never could. It wasn't the warmth, it was the cold.

"This competition is one round for the Championship Belt, and can be won by knock out, limb destruction, or kill shot." The announcer stepped out of the ring, and the competitors stepped forward, Anton between them.

"If you're going to touch gloves," he said, with amused formality, "do so now."

Finley raised one hand. Bairn broke character long enough to tap his fist against that of his mentor, and the crowd loved it. Finley gave an approving nod, and Bairn rolled his eyes as he backed off.

"Are you ready?" Anton asked them each in turn, and at their assent, signaled for the bell.

☠

Bairn had Finley's arm trapped, and he knew from long practice how painful the lock was. Still, the Scottish man held on until Bairn gave up and released the arm lock.

"No! You don't let go." As soon as he was free, Finley smacked the back of his head.

"You should have tapped." He rubbed the sore spot. "It could've broken."

"That's the whole the point." Finley tugged at his red hair. "How stupid are you?"

"You want me to break it?" Bairn repeated. "To break you?"

"You're not in the Exhibition anymore, Bairn. There's no pin falls in the Dogfights, no submissions. You incapacitate them, you break them, or you kill them. That's how you win, and if you don't win, you never earn out."

The last part was familiar enough, contracts never fulfilled. His family was still trying to pay off their place in the Manhattan shelter. He could remember his parents talking about it even though the sounds of their voices were beginning to fade. "How long do you have?"

Finley rubbed the back of his neck. "Three lifetimes, which means I need to be more than just a fighter. I need to be a draw. You?"

"Earned a penalty, so two, and a train ride home."

Finley smirked at that, and the expression was already annoying as hell. "Then you'll have to make yourself a draw, too."

Finley attacked first, a jab to the head that hadn't lost any speed with age. Bairn dodged to the side, and aimed a kick at his knee. It didn't land, but he hadn't expected it to. They circled around each other, Finley's hands up, Bairn's down.

"Arrogant little punk, always have been." He jabbed again, Bairn stepped back. "Never should have survived this long."

Bairn tilted his head, and smirked at Finley's grimace as the lights hit the painted death mask.

"Right. Well, there is that. You and your theatrics." He shot forward suddenly, aimed low at Bairn's waist. The move took Bairn by surprise, and he stumbled until his back hit the cage. Finley worked to get the take down, leaving the back of his neck exposed.

It was an easy shot; Bairn could take it, try to make it a kill shot and end the fight now. Instead he shifted his stance and worked to free his leg. Anton watched from over Finley's shoulder, so fucking pleased with himself. Finley took Bairn's knee out, and they slid down the cage together, crashing into the mat.

This was not where he wanted to be. He raised his arms to protect his head, strikes already raining down. The Red Warrior was known for his ground and pound, and Bairn had forgotten just how hard he could hit.

"Damn it, where was his defence?" Finley had never sounded like that before. Like there was a crack running through every word.

Bairn wanted to ask what was wrong, but his throat felt tight and it was hard to get air into his lungs. His head was ringing, and he couldn't remember what they'd been working on. Couldn't remember what block he missed.

"So much for your bonus, Red. Should've been more careful."

"Fuck." There was the unmistakable sound of a fist hitting a jaw, followed by the vibration of a body hitting the mat. "That's not the problem. He's still just a kid." Finley was shouting. He never shouted. Insulted, cajoled, mocked, but anger wasn't his thing. Unflappability was.

"I'm not a kid," Bairn said, finally finding his breath. "I have my first match in two days." They'd been preparing. That's what it was, a final test. Which, he'd apparently failed.

The circle of people standing around him took a step back. One of the new guys even crossed himself, something Bairn had only ever seen in movies made before cities needed walls. The entire room was silent.

He looked to his mentor. "Finley?"

The Scottish man was paler than normal, jaw slack. He recovered before the others and swallowed hard. "You died Bairn, certified and everything."

One of the medics reached out a shaking hand to check his pulse. Bairn took in the information, and then shrugged. "That takes care of one lifetime, then."

"Try not to use this method to get out of the other, eh?" Finley pulled him back up to his feet. "Next time you may not come back."

Bairn nodded, but he was focused on the pair of suits who were already updating his forms. One lifetime left and he still needed to be a draw if he wanted to get back to his family before he died again. Finley was right. He needed to be more than just a fighter. He needed to be a superstar. Fortunately, that was the business he'd been born into.

The crowd was almost wailing. Finley was sitting too high up on his chest for him to just throw the other man off. Hammer-like blows struck his arms, but the pace was far too regular. He waited for the hand switch, and dropped his elbow into Finley's leg. He almost didn't get his arm back in place to block the next strike, but almost was good enough. They traded off as Bairn slowly inched Finley out of position and himself into a better one.

As soon as he had enough room, he bucked and caught Finley's leg with one of his own, tipping the Scottish man over. It shouldn't have worked as well as it did, but the crowd didn't care. They shouted Bairn's name as he took control, and dropped his own strikes down on Finley. He didn't stay there long, though. He worked better on his feet. As soon as he was standing, he stomped on Finley's stomach and then drove his boot into his kidneys. Finley cursed and rolled away, using the cage to get back on his feet as well.

They circled again, trading blows and working for any advantage, always with a smirking Anton nearby. Best seat in the house, and Bairn had never wanted to hit him more than he did now.

"Bonne Nuit, so good to see you," Anton said, voice dripping with false cheer. "Your next match has been arranged." He held out the tablet for Bairn's thumbprint on the contract.

"Final match," Bairn clarified, hand hovering over the surface.

"I thought you still wanted a ride on my train." Anton leaned back in his chair, and tilted his head. "Or did you decide you wanted to stay here after all."

"I know the points to credits conversion," Bairn said, "and the ticket prices."

"Of course you do." Anton smiled. "So there's nothing to worry about."

Bairn narrowed his eyes. This was off, but he couldn't tell what the trap was. "Who's my opponent?"

Anton snorted. "As if it matters."

It never did. If that was the trap, it was one he'd been in all his life. He shoved aside his reservations, pressed his thumb down, and signed the contract.

☠

Finley's confidence in his ground game did him in. He knew it was better than Bairn's, and he went back to it when it was clear he would lose if they stayed up-right and striking. It was a desperation move, made at the first opportunity without setting up the best position.

Bairn's back hit the mat again, but this time he wasn't trapped underneath, and Finley's wrist was in his grasp. He drove one foot into Finley's hip and swung the other into place before the older man could react. Finley struggled but his arm was trapped and he wasn't strong enough anymore to pull it free. Bairn extended, the arm lock sliding into place. He could feel the tension as Finley's elbow reached its limit. The Scottish man swore, striking at Bairn's legs with his free hand, face twisted in pain.

Tap, he thought even now, twenty years since it had been relevant. *Tap.*

But of course he couldn't. Bairn finished the move, pushing up with his hips. Finley's elbow gave to the pressure. The tension vanished as the arm broke, and Finley screamed.

Bairn let him go and stood, barely registering the bell as the match ended. He fought to keep the detachment of the character he'd played for all these years, but it wasn't just sweat that washed away the face paint now. All he could see was Finley huddled as he cradled the broken limb to his chest, slumped and defeated.

Anton stepped up beside Bairn, and looked around the crowd with approval. "Very nice. Kill shot would have gotten you closer, but they're eating this up."

"What do you mean, closer?" His reservations came back in a rush.

"Oh, didn't you see?" Anton shrugged. "Ticket prices went up again. Section of the system protections went down and the rain ate the track. Have to cover the costs, you know."

"Your systems don't just go down."

"Believe what you want. You're not under bond contract anymore. You're free to take your credits and try your luck walking back to Manhattan. Or, because I'm generous, I'll let you compete again. One more match should cover this change."

Bairn's hand clenched into a fist, and Anton's smirk dared him to land the blow that would prevent him from getting home forever. His shoulders sank and the anger drained into resignation. He watched the medics work on Finley's arm. Even if it healed well, he wasn't going to be able to compete again. He'd die teaching in the pits.

The announcer returned to the ring. "Your winner by limb destruction, and still champion, Bonne Nuit!"

Anton grabbed Bairn's wrist and raised his hand high above his head. The crowd screamed his name, the sounds of the full arena pouring down on him like acid rain.

One more match.

L is for Leverage

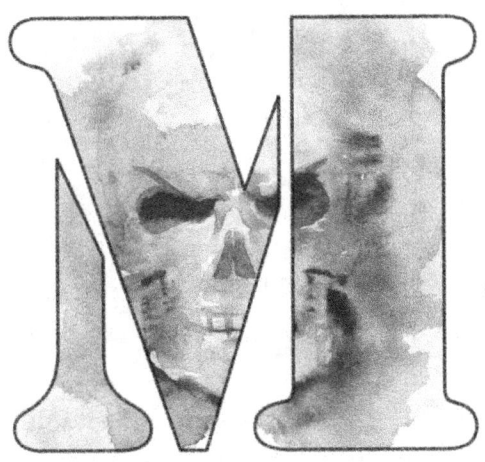

Ennis Drake

"Borrowed time and borrowed world and borrowed eyes with which to sorrow it."
—Cormac McCarthy

It's a new world. A world of empty skies and lifeless fields, still woodlands and dead cities. A world where life is lived on the literal bones of the old one.

When the pandemic started, by the time they realized they were dealing with a new mutation, there were three hundred dead in Asia, Russia, and the Middle East. When they recorded the first death in Europe, less than a month later, there were some 10,000 dead in China alone. The world was culling poultry by the millions. Then wild birds. Then pigs. Within sixteen weeks domestic swine and poultry had been culled almost to extinction. And two million people across Asia and Europe were dead. That was, what? Five years ago? Six? I used to try and keep track of the days...

...I stopped that first Christmas after the fall, after everything broke down.

What are they? Dayda asks. They're beautiful.

Robins, I say. You can tell by the color of their breasts.

We watch them for a bit, pecking and hopping and hunting grubs out of the March grass. They really are pretty little things, the males with their blue-black hoods and their chests the color of a wildfire; the females brown and gray and molten gold.

I unsling the shotgun from round my shoulders and pass it silently to Dayda. He only hesitates a second. Under his PVC hood and filtration mask, I can't make out his expression.

They don't look sick, Mom, Dayda whispers, but he shoulders the 20 gauge and sights in the largest cluster of the flock through the irons.

Don't call me that, I say, then: They're carriers. You know that. What do we do, Dayda?

He looks up at me, the sun and the trees a distorted ghost of a reflection in the plastic of his face shield.

We kill the living, Dayda. It's the only way to be sure.

The thunder of the gun. The flutter of wings. The shriek and shrill of death and surprise and fear.

They say there was a cataclysm. A die-out. About 70,000 BC. That humanity nearly went extinct. A super volcano was the chief suspect. They say humanity may have been reduced to as little as forty breeding couples. I think it must be like that now. Except Dayda's too young, and I'm too old, to breed. And the last living people we saw were infected. Seven of them, holed up in a nursing home. We killed all of them. Had to. That was three, maybe four years ago.

We've traveled the breadth of the Gulf coast and half back again in that time. It was only last year we decided to settle and started trying to grow crops; (re)domesticate the wild dogs. Dogs are the only animal we're sure don't get the flu.

I've tried to teach Dayda to read, but he has no enthusiasm for it and, truthfully, I've lost whatever verve I had for it, too.

"N-nobody w-wants to be ha-har-here and no-body wants to leeeve," he fumbles and throws the book into the yard, where it will presumably lay until eaten by earth and time.

I stare at the book, motionless, skewed in the dirt.

I'm sorry M...Alice, Dayda mumbles.

Don't be, I say. There are plenty more where that came from. Our treasures have outlasted their usefulness; they've outlasted their makers. What's a book without someone to read it? It's not even a curiosity.

"...[I] saw for a brief moment the absolute truth of the world. The cold relentless circling of the intestate earth. Darkness implacable. The crushing black vacuum of the universe."

What does it mean?

What does anything mean? I ask him.

I hear the gun, but can't get out of bed. My lungs are fire, my head a boiler. Everything aches, like I've got bone spurs in all my joints. I roll over, sit up on my elbow. I can hear the clomp of Dayda's boots on the floor. See his shadow under the bedroom door. He stands there for a long time.

It's dark when I wake up again. Candles flicker round the room, turning everything orange and black. There's a damp rag on my face, heated from fever. Dayda is sitting in a chair at the end of the bed. He's wearing his PVC hood and respirator, the youth shottie laid across his lap.

One of the dogs got sick, he says behind his mask.

I don't answer.

Mom...he begins, but I cut him off with a gesture.

Don't call me that, I say, trying poorly for a series of interminable moments to stifle a soul-cough.

I don't know what to do.

Did you put them down?

Yes.

I don't want to be alone, M...Alice.

What do we do, Dayda?

Please...

There's no one left but us, Dayda. The virus keeps mutating. It's outlasted us. Now, tell me, what do we do?

We kill the living.

M is for Mutation

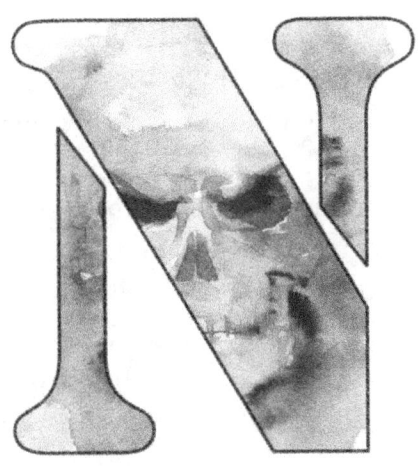

C.S. MacCath

VARDIGEN MEMORIAL ARCHIVE
ENTRY: Desans, Madame Chaell Gebares
COURIER: Gresetz, Jederen ID COU-045
CONTAINS: Text and Attachments

Dearest Readers,

There is magma in the music.

You will not understand this; the way it flows, bright and hot, through the cavern of the ear and settles in the hollow chambers of the mind. When my Opera 'Tribute To Her Excellency' (which earned an Obsidian Medal) premiered, not even the fathomless Dormissart Plance was ready to shape the viscous rock at the bottom of his aria. But I cannot blame him. He was poorly conducted, and there is a reason why President Incien called my work the bass of a people. I am igneous. I am of the deep inferno in the world.

Even my ballets have been called 'heavy', though I am not a serious writer of ballet. Still, the bourrée en couru of the

Vardigen Colonial Dancers must be mentioned. Such grace, the way they flickered across my music like flames over coal. I loved them for it, love them now, will love them wherever I am after I drink the death this handsome young courier has traded for my diaries and manuscripts. Do not ask your own dancers to perform my trifles; they will not know how to lift the mountain into fire, and it will only embarrass them.

We valued the fire and the mountain here; pyroclastic reminders that we were breaking the bones of this planet and distilling its marrow for you. It was the gift your predecessors augmented us to give. But the music, the dance, the art, those things we gave to one another, and they were exquisite. So you, whose skin has never silvered, hungry for an ash fall, who cannot bear the blessed heat your nanomachines have siphoned away, you will not understand them. Celebrate them anyway, remember that we *were*, and know that I forgive you.

- Madame Chae

2 ATTACHMENTS
* Madame CGD Diaries
* Madame CGD Manuscripts

VOICE MESSAGE via CHAMBRI PROVINCIAL GRID
FROM: Jederen Gresetz
TO: Rapho Langskraft
DATE: GCT 20:982:6:45:1:7:1

VIO ALERT: You are receiving an encrypted message from a secured sender on an unsecured grid. Please enter your password to continue.

It's me. Listen, do you mind...I need to talk...about what happened today. There's not enough space inside me to keep

breathing if I don't get this out. It was after we finished the
archive work, and Madame Desans was getting ready to...This
is insane. She's a world-famous composer, and I'm just
a...a...damn it. Her skin was peeling off in silver chunks, and
her eyes...They used to be brown, like mine, but now...She was
in a lot of pain, like most everyone else, I guess. Anyway, she
said, "I think you are probably a lover of men, but there is only
love now" and then asked me to help...it was so embarrassing
for her...I'm sorry. I shouldn't be crying. I can't afford to be
weak. Okay. There was an evening gown, hairpins, makeup
(you would have been better at all of it), and then she played
the piano awhile. I didn't know music could sound so...
Reminded me of the day you braided that copper ribbon into
my hair and then we...Oh, Raph. I miss you so much. At the
end I brought the mercy vial to her lips, and it was over. She
was over.

Nothing our ancestors did makes this right, makes any of it
right. So they chose augmentation over prison and came here
to mine. Great. Nobody told them the sludge from the fuel they
were sending off-world was nano food and...Think about that
for a minute. The Organics left us here to work for generations
until they could terraform the planet at our expense. We can't
even evacuate now because of the orbital barricade. Like we're
still a threat or something. We should blow this place...No. No.
We should hunker down, live lean on the ash we have left until
the new colonists come and then torture them all to death
while we recite the names of our children over their screams
and read them our books and...and...play them our music.

I can't do this anymore. I can't...Help me do this. Help me
give a few of our people a better death and send their life's
work out into the stars so it isn't lost.

There hasn't been an ash fall here in Touren Province for
over a month, now that all the volcanoes are quiet. I saw some

kids heading into Mount Sance to scavenge what they could, but the nanos have filtered too much carbon dioxide out of the air, and there isn't enough extremo...I can't remember what it's called, the bacteria that comes from lava and lives in our guts. So everyone is starving to death and short of breath and going crazy. But my meds are propping me up, and I have enough to keep going until this is done. The doctor made sure.

Wait for me. You promised we'd go together, remember? Don't let me down. Please.

VIO ALERT: End message.

VARDIGEN COLONIAL NEWS
BREAKING STORY: PRESIDENT ORIEU INCIEN
ADDRESSES UNION OF ALLIED PLANETS (UAP) IN Q-
NET COMMUNIQUÉ
ZURICE, VCN (Video by L. Fermet) —

Mister or Madame Secretary General,

As a mother, a wife, a woman of God and a president, I pray the UAP has received my previous messages and is currently preparing its reply. Indeed, I am not certain whether or not the Union remains in existence, since we have been forbidden from communicating with it except through Seron Energy, which holds the prison and resource contracts to this planet and has recently stopped corresponding with us. Nevertheless, I remain eager to discuss the present ecological crisis with any contemporary governing body or with Seron and come to an expedient solution that saves my people.

We are desperate here. As you can see from the footage on your screen, the remainder of our provinces are falling to nanotechnological terraforming and report clear skies, cooler temperatures and new greenery, ostensibly in preparation for

the arrival of Organic colonists. But I beg you: Look at my body
and the bodies of these young people standing behind me. Our
skin hungers for silica. Our eyes shine, resistant to heat. Our
hair is wiry and fire retardant. Our stomachs and lungs require
extremophiles and volcanic gases to function. We are Augments
designed for this world and cannot live in the one these
nanomachines are creating. Please do not abandon us in it to
die.

In the spirit of that plea, I would like you to meet these
brave, young souls; men and women determined to find a new
home where their unique physiology might be sustained. We
have upgraded two Seron Energy fuel carriers to serve their
immediate needs, and they plan to depart in one cesium week's
time on GCT: -45:1:8:2. In the history of Vardigen Colony, we
have never tested Seron's warning that the orbital barricade
would prohibit the passage of live cargo through it, but we
must do so now. On behalf of the families they leave behind, I
ask that you grant their freedom.

I understand that many centuries ago, ours was a prison
colony, but it is so much more than that now. Perhaps your
ancestors believed the augmentations they visited upon ours
were so extreme that none would survive to bear children.
Perhaps you forgot about us in the vagaries of time and
governance. But we are still here, and we are still what you
made us.

Our lives are in your hands.

VOICE MESSAGE via VARDIGEN INTELLIGENCE OFFICE
(VIO) GRID
FROM: Rapho Langskraft
TO: Jederen Gresetz
DATE: GCT 20:982:6:45:1:7:2

VIO ALERT: You are receiving an encrypted message from an unsecured sender on a secured grid. Please enter your password to continue.

I remember that ribbon; the way it shone in your hair, the way you chewed the tail to threads...I'm glad you were there for the great Madame Chae at the end. You must have been such a comfort to her, a boy so like the musicians she nurtured, embarrassment aside. And all that incredible music? It was for you; the humane courier who kept her from dying broken and forgotten.

Yes, the Organics are killing us to make room for more of their own, and yes, it looks deliberate to me. Seed the planet with dormant nanoterraformers, drop designer prisoners on it to mine, wait for the sludge to indicate a certain level of resource depletion, and boom. Activate the nanos and sweep it all away to make room for a new investment; the people, the environment, everything. There is no word for that but 'evil', and you're absolutely right to feel betrayed. I do too, but I refuse to die with a bitter heart. Your heart might hear a different call, but if there is any peace to be found in the time we have left, I hope you'll seek it with me.

I finally finished that portrait of us, and I'm sending a reproduction along. It isn't very good, professionally speaking, but there are things I love about it; your baby face and my laugh lines, your brown eyes and my green, your dark hair braided into my red...Be safe, beloved. Things are bad down in the capitol (despair makes people dangerous), and the provincial cities are...Well, I'm sure you saw the President's communiqué. Also, remember that Sulfabarbital isn't freely available yet, and your Fluorisone isn't even supposed to exist, so keep the pharmaceuticals hidden. And come home soon to your mountain, where I hope to be here waiting for you in the sanctuary we built.

Thank you for your strength. Thank you for your humanity. I love you.

ATTACHMENT
* R+J Portrait - Digital Reproduction

VIO ALERT: End message.

VARDIGEN MEMORIAL ARCHIVE
ENTRY: Purch, Thedral, Econdia Province Artist in Residence
COURIER: Gresetz, Jederen ID COU-045
CONTAINS: Text and Video

Curators and Others,

President Incien advised me to approach this introduction with a conciliatory tone in order to facilitate acceptance of the archive. In fact, my courier tells me that most of his artists have done the same and so have the scientists and philosophers his colleagues are helping to end their lives. When I'm finished here, I'll commit suicide too, but not before I've murdered my talented wife and beautiful five year-old daughter to spare them a harrowing death. This after having hidden in the locked attic of a university for nine days while the institution and the province it serves are destroyed by terrified mobs. So I have no patience today for your fragile, Organic egos.

My work is large-scale and kinetic; I sculpt the void, and lava fills it (see video attached). For all that Vardigenans are miners by design, we are a passive people, preferring to watch as the world shapes itself with heat and stone and time. This truth of our nature inspires me to create contemplative art that evolves over decades; hollow channels that fill with molten rock and later harden into permanence. Now that volcanic activity here has been quieted, the pieces will finish prematurely, but I choose to regard that change as a monument to genocide. May you look upon my work and never stop weeping with guilt.

And if you are an Augment reading my words, humanaformed for an exotic environment to avoid prison or pay a debt, remember that death is the only reward for trust in the Organics. Act accordingly.

- Thedral Purch

3 ATTACHMENTS

* Weave - A slender lava river looping back upon itself around an obsidian sphere.
* Flow - A system of lava tubes spilling into one another over a diorite channel.
* Sleep (Exhibition) - An artificial rhyolite caldera cradling a series of slow-cooling sculptures.

SEVTP MASTER CONTROL NODE CONNECTING... DONE!
Begin transmission of aggregated data...
   <Nanomachine Status Report>
       [Total Nanomachines Available]: 87%
       [Total Nanomachines Active]: 72%
       [Total Nanomachines In Reserve]: 15%
       [Total Nanomachines Defective/Policed]: 13%
   <Environmental Status Report>
       [Planetary Vulcanism]: Target +/- 15%
       [Atmosphere Conditioning]: 79%
       [H20 Conditioning]: 81%
       [Soil Conditioning]: 88%
       [Flora Germination]: 22%
   <Slave Control Node Report>
       [Vulcanism]: 100%

[Atmosphere]:
    Phase 1: 100%
    Phase 2: 58%
[H20]:
    Phase 1: 100%
    Phase 2: 63%
[Soil]:
    Phase 1: 100%
    Phase 2: 67%
[Floral]:
    Phase 1: 12%
    Phase 2: 0%
        Pending Phase 2 of [Atmosphere] [H20] [Soil]
SEVTP MASTER CONTROL NODE DISCONNECTING...
DONE!

VOICE MESSAGE via CHAMBRI PROVINCIAL GRID
FROM: Jederen Gresetz
TO: Rapho Langskraft
DATE: GCT 20:982:6:45:1:8:1

VIO ALERT: You are receiving an encrypted message from a secured sender on an unsecured grid. Please enter your password to continue.

I'm all-right. I wanted to say that first because the next thing I have to say will upset you. I'm in the Gouveau Provincial Hall basement, where there's a hospital set up for doctors, police and other people like me who have to stay alive longer to do their jobs. I was attacked on Z. Judicat's estate by her own staff and barely got away in the flier. They were after the drugs, just like you said. My arm is broken, and there are twenty-three stitches in my shoulder where I was stabbed, so the Governor is sending me home soon. Fluorisone is bad for healing injuries, and without it I'm sick as everyone else, so that's it for my body, I guess.

And I'm not the only one. Sixteen of the original hundred couriers have gone missing in the last two days, and three are confirmed dead. VIO thinks someone is sending private messages about us in the clear, and if that's true, it's really, really scary. When the President met with us, she said there probably wasn't any hope for Vardigen, but she wanted to be sure before making the Sulfabarbital available to the public, and that was supposed to give us time to finish our work. If it gets out she had a special steroid made for essential personnel, that we've been going around collecting bits of civilization and helping our most important people to die... Well, it'll rob everyone of the peace you talked about, and that's a serious understatement.

I'm glad we live on a mountain. Please keep the door locked when you're in the house. If my name is on somebody's unsecured list, then you're in danger too, and I can't... Just be safe, Raph.

Anyway, stop telling me your paintings aren't very good. They're works of art created by a last-generation Vardigenan, and they're perfect. In fact, I'm opening a new file tomorrow, and when I get home, we're going to catalog every one of them for inclusion in the archive. And I don't want to hear it, so you can stop protesting right now. I love you, and your portrait did what art is supposed to do. It made me better. It helped me go on.

Well, the nurse just stuck a needle in my arm, and I'm all of a sudden sleepy. They give us good pain meds here, so... I'm going to go to sleep and dream of what you did to make me chew that ribbon up. I want you to do it again when I come

home. Heh. And don't say you 'hope' you'll be waiting for me;
say you 'know'...'know'...

VIO ALERT: End message.

VARDIGEN MEMORIAL ARCHIVE
ENTRY: Trages, D. Reven, Vardigen Poet Laureate
COURIER: Gresetz, Jederen ID COU-045
CONTAINS: Text

Murderers, Bystanders and Innocents,
My courier cannot come to me because his body has been
crippled by terraforming and violence, so I am sending poetry
to him. If he were here, he would ask for all of my words, which
are many, but only a few of them matter now. These are my
contribution to the Vardigen Memorial Archive.
In exchange for my words, young Mister Gresetz would
offer my elderly body a merciful death, but I would refuse it.
Rather, let me live; raving, skeletal, agonized and look upon
the changing landscape of my home while I am able.
I remain,
Mister D. Reven Trages
Poet Laureate of Vardigen

Barricade

1. These Brave, Young Souls

They were already dying;
fiery coals before a deluge,
waiting for the wave -

when they rose to meet that terminus;
a holy, human flame -
casting light into the void.

How did they cross, we wonder;
embracing one another, eyes lifted up -
to see what lay beyond?

2. -45:1:8:2

There, at the border between two countries -
we watched them fall from the sky.

Behind, a high mountain in twilight -
clutching the sunset to its breast.

Ahead, a dark and implacable river -
tumbling stones toward an abyss.

3. Our lives are in your hands.

Where are your hands, your eyes, your ears?

Clenched around the pith of this world.
Averted for the killing blow.
Ringing with the clamor of those who will come -

when our flesh is gathered into the greening earth.
Will they bury the bones they find here,
the vacant cradles and empty shoes -
your surrogate butchers are leaving behind?

VOICE MESSAGE via VARDIGEN INTELLIGENCE OFFICE
(VIO) GRID
FROM: Rapho Langskraft
TO: Jederen Gresetz
DATE: GCT 20:982:6:45:1:8:2

VIO ALERT: You are receiving an encrypted message from an unsecured sender on a secured grid. Please enter your password to continue.

I love you. What do you need? Are you well enough to pilot the flier home? Is there someone in the provincial hall who might do it for you? We have room for another person here, and there are worse places to die. Ask around. I'll move my canvases out of the spare bedroom, just in case.

And Jed, hear me. Those people who attacked you were not themselves. I'm not excusing them; in fact, I'd like to take from them what they took from you, but they were hysterical in the face of an unspeakable thing. So please don't lose heart. Vardigen is still worth the effort you made to save it, even wearing its darkest, most desperate face.

Speaking of dark and desperate, I suppose we're certain now there isn't anyone coming to help us. The President never would have sent those fuel carriers up if she weren't grasping for hope, but what a gamble to lose. I feel guilty for saying this, but I almost envy the people who died in them. They don't have to watch what will happen to the world they left behind.

Yes, I'm keeping the door locked, but our neighbors are civil people, which is another reason I'm glad you're coming home. Minta Britic had the most wonderful idea this morning, that we should all gather here, share whatever ash we have left and tell the stories of our lives. She wants to do it in the next few days; none of us are looking well, and we might be housebound soon. I'm hoping you'll be home for the occasion, but don't rush your body. I...I understand if you can't make it in time.

Apart from that, things are quiet here. And I don't know what to say about your offer to archive my paintings, but if you think it's the right thing to do, then here is my introduction:

"My name is Rapho Langskraft, and my greatest work of art is the life I built with a beautiful young man who favored me with his affection, whose strength and commitment to Vardigen is finer than anything you will find in this archive.

"I also paint pictures, mostly landscapes. Here they are."
Will that do?

I'm off to my paints and canvas for awhile. I've been working on capturing the new colors of the sunset here. So vibrant without the ash clouds. I had no idea.

Did I mention that I love you?

VIO ALERT: End message.

VARDIGEN COLONIAL NEWS
PRESIDENT ORIEU INCIEN ADDRESSES VARDIGEN
FROM THE OBSIDIAN ROOM
ZURICE, VCN (Video by L. Fermet) —

My Beloved People,

The Union of Allied Planets has not responded to my repeated requests for intervention, though I continue to believe in the humanity of that governing body and remain eager to discuss the current crisis with it. Seron Energy has been silent for six months, and yesterday it murdered forty Vardigenans when they attempted to cross the orbital barricade. This means that we are presently alone in the face of a fatal terraforming protocol that our most gifted scientists are not able to mitigate.

So my heart is breaking today; for those who fell to that barricade, for you and for the Vardigen that may die with us all very soon. Because I am your president, in whom you have placed a sacred trust, I am responsible for that death no matter the circumstances. Therefore, in the days and weeks to come, I ask that you direct whatever negative emotion you might feel at me and not at your local governments, police, hospitals and emergency services, which will remain in operation for as long as there are people alive to staff them. Further, please know that while the Vardigen Colonial News is suspending operation after this broadcast, I will be here in Zurice conducting your business until I am unable to do so any longer. In that event, the constitutional line of succession will determine the president or presidents who follow me.

By now, many of you will have heard of the 'mercy vial', a lethal dose of Sulfabarbital taken by mouth. This morning, I issued a presidential decree making the drug freely available from physicians and pharmacists in every province. I waited to speak of it publicly because I would not trade your hope for despair, but my medical advisers now believe our children cannot develop into healthy adulthood on the planet we presently inhabit. So the time has come to tell you that there is a painless alternative to the suffering we will all face as this terraforming protocol reaches conclusion. I would not ask you to walk the path represented by this mercy vial, but it was your First Gentleman's last wish that you should know he...he walked it this morning when his lungs began to fail. In his memory, I am asking that you obtain enough Sulfabarbital to end your suffering and that of your dependents even if you do not plan to use it.

Finally I offer you a glimmer of light at this dark time. Three months ago, I commissioned a hundred couriers to travel throughout the colony, collecting the work of contemporary artists, scientists and thinkers for inclusion in a great memorial archive designed by the best engineers I could find. When they brought me several parallel repositories, I asked a team of miners to bury them at secret locations deep in the body of this world where they would be safe from tampering or extraction. This archive is now complete, in place and receiving the last of its data from couriers in the field. At the conclusion of my address, it will begin broadcasting on every frequency known to us, thereby filling the planet and nearby space with text, sound, images and video of our people in their final days. In time, this signal will whisper the tragedy of Vardigen to the farthest reaches of the galaxy, making our home a monument to its original inhabitants from now until every repository fails in the far distant future.

My beloved people; my heart to your hearts. My mind to your minds. My life to your lives. I remain your faithful servant, and I am proud beyond my capacity for speech to be counted among you, even now. Go in peace, and may God have mercy upon us, Her augmented creations.

Good night.

VARDIGEN MEMORIAL ARCHIVE
ENTRY: Langskraft, Rapho
COURIER: Gresetz, Jederen ID COU-045
CONTAINS: Text and Attachments

"My name is Rapho Langskraft, and my greatest work of art is the life I built with a beautiful young man who favored me with his affection, whose strength and commitment to Vardigen is finer than anything you will find in this archive.

"I also paint pictures, mostly landscapes. Here they are."
- Rapho Langskraft

Hello,

Rapho was my family, and I thought he deserved better than the introduction he gave, so here is the rest of it. I'm not a great writer, and it's hard to write anything at all when the sadness inside you is so much bigger than the words, but I'll do my best.

Raph did more than paint pictures. He found beauty nobody else could see and brought it to the canvas. I used to tell him that I was a selfish boy who only loved the money he was going to make on his art someday, and he used to laugh and say that I shouldn't get my hopes up. But I believed in him completely, and I knew there were days when that was the reason he kept going.

He even found beauty in the horrible thing the Organics have done here, or at least he found a way to keep it from cutting us both to pieces. He said, "I refuse to die with a bitter heart. Your heart might hear a different call, but if there is any peace to be found in the time we have left, I hope you'll seek it with me." I found him this morning when I finally came home from my courier work, slumped in front of his easel on the bench we made to watch the sunset together. Looking back, I should have known how sick he was by the tone of his voice and the things he said, but I wanted him to wait for me so much. Pretty stupid when you think about it.

I don't know how to die without my Raph. When he was still here, the end didn't seem so lonely or scary, and I could help other people meet it because there was someone who would do the same for me, when the time came. But where do you look for courage when there isn't anyone but your own, broken self to meet the dark place in front of you? I can't be like Madame Chae, all painted and dressed and full of music so she wouldn't forget who she was, or Thedral Purch, whose anger was hotter than anything he sculpted, or Mister Trages, who wanted to live as long as he could no matter how much it hurt. I'm not brave like the forty who tried the orbital barricade or steady, like President Incien, and I don't know where to look for the beauty Rapho Langskraft found so easily.

Me, I want my world back. I want to see the operas I didn't care about before. I want to learn what makes a president out of an ordinary woman. I want to say 'I told you so' at Rapho's first art show, because he would have made it, and I would have been there to see his face when it happened. And I'm not even angry at the Organics anymore, at least not like I was. I just want to go back, because forward is so unbelievably hard.

The sun is going down now, and Raph was right about that, too. It's clearer now that the ash is gone. I'm going to sit beside him awhile and watch the colors play across the sky. Maybe I'll find some courage in them and drink this mercy vial in my shirt pocket. Maybe I'm sick enough that I won't have to. But either way, the sunset is coming, and I plan to find something beautiful in it.

- Jederen Gresetz

ATTACHMENT
* Rapho Langskraft Paintings - Digital Reproductions

N is for Nanomachine

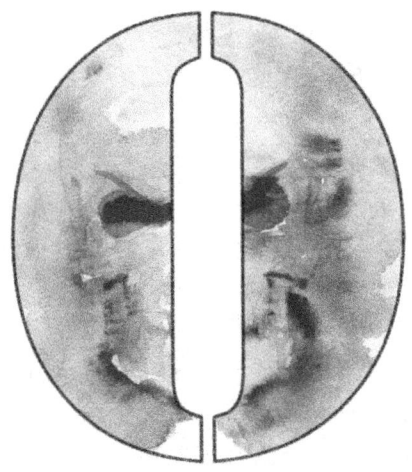

Michael Kellar

The moon was full.

Tonight it closely, although not completely, resembled a Harvest Moon. Rather than orange, it was more of an industrial rust-color. Having no light of its own, the image seemingly generated by the lunar orb is simply nothing more than the reflected light of the sun filtered through cold, sterile space. But now its persona also incorporated the scars and shadows of a dead world below.

It is in the nature of a doorway to be used long after its form or function has any traceable memory of origin or discernible purpose. Patterns imprinted and imposed from the distant past are merely a different type of ghostly manifestation. Habits linger. The actual portal had only accidental relevance. They were drawn to it more for the symbolism than the necessity.

In earlier times the point where the worlds touched might be a cave, a well, a darkened mirror, a particularly sensitive dreamer, or any of countless other conduits favored by a particular region or culture. Tonight, however, a dark nexus had appeared as a hollow space in the debris. From a few feet away, motes of dust seemed to be merely swirling about in the midst of a pile of twisted steel and concrete. That they settled into a distinctly geometrical pattern, and assumed vaguely runic shapes resembling inscriptions adorning a sorcerer's triangle of evocation may only have been a coincidence. Billions of random forms were constantly being generated by the interaction of the elements. Most – *but not all* – ultimately had no significant implication.

They easily crossed from the Other Side into the ring of fire. On this night of nights, the veil was lifted and passage required less effort than summoning a memory. Many of those who (or which) began to gather were quite capable of appreciating the irony: there *had* been a time when huge balefires had been erected on this evening to keep them *away*.

At more of a distance, that which had once been a city seemed to have degenerated into a deconstructed architecture of overlapping, crumbling masses of arches and columns. But it was from the viewpoint of the owl or the bat that true perspective was to be obtained. The huge, circular necropolis was nothing less than a post-modern monolith. A Stonehenge of the Apocalypse.

The lycanthropes were the earliest to arrive. Solid, powerful, eager. They were the first to respond to the lunar call, which drew them out in a swarming mass across the landscape and up the ruins, climbing over each other to reach the highest points possible, until finally issuing a collective harmonic group howl.

Almost a shadow, a proud figure with bold Slavic features was the next to emerge. The transition awakened in him a thirst which he knew would be unquenchable this night, but he had other distractions which drew his attention.

Selecting a particular configuration of rubble – a cubic slab with a slightly arched back – he gestured casually towards it, causing a miniature whirlwind to strip it clean of dust and ash and fragments of stone. He then seated himself, his presence completing the defining touch of what had unmistakably been formed into a makeshift throne.

Briefly casting a glance beyond the perimeters of the ruins, he took in the seemingly endless landscape of smoke and perpetually erupting jets of flame. Never having been of a scientific mind, he had no concept as to exactly what had been ignited so long ago under the surface, nor how deeply the fires roared or how long they might be expected to continue. He simply chose to regard them as the manifestation of Hell on Earth.

The more discernibly dead arrived in the next wave. Ghouls, skeletons, zombies, joined in on a march with reanimated corpses and other things having a more tenuous connection to either life or corporeal definition. All surged forward in a mad, misshapen mass.

The seated Count, for that had once been his designation, watched the proceedings with patience and something akin to a paternalistic sense of pride. They were *all* in a sense his children now, and for lengthy portion of the evening he was quite content to watch them shriek and snarl and shamble.

Finally, at the true mid-of-night, the moment exactly equidistant between the dusk and the dawn, he stood and issued a call for silence. While his words may not have been heard, or in many cases understood, a hush nevertheless passed through the otherworldly assembly. By now, this was deeply ingrained, conditioned response to both the time and the moment.

Presently a wind began to rise.

This was accompanied by a low whistle, joined by a barely audible rumble of moans and groans and world-weary sighs.

The most ethereal and gossamer manifestations of the night's magic began to wink into existence. White, wispy forms collectively rose in every direction. Transparent, translucent, cotton candy-like strands of silvered ectoplasm perversely wove together into an image Edward Munch might have drawn, just before stretching his canvas into the representation of an extreme parody of living beings. Twisted souls emerged from every possible crack, crevice or other point of egress, yet all were devoid of an air of torment. They writhed and swayed with an aura of weird intent.

The final remaining spirits of a dead and decaying world now gathered together into an ultimate Danse Macabre, a dark passion play of the damned, with the sole purpose of reenacting the last living memory of this doomed planet.

Up they rose into an ever-expanding vortex, until finally coalescing into the unmistakable form of a giant mushroom cloud.

This image imprinted itself upon the night sky, held together for a long moment by their determined preternatural force of will, before finally exploding into a cacophony of eerie laughter.

While it would have been impossible for the Count to have held his breath, he noted that he had reflexively held his chest muscles rigid in stunned silence.

Glancing down after having been caught up in a personal reverie, he happened to see a sun-bleached round object in the rubble near his feet. It was but one of thousands of skeletal remains that peppered the landscape, and would have escaped his notice had he not been struck with a flash of inspiration.

He grasped the skull and held it aloft as he remembered. "To be or not to be," the bard once queried.

Then, bearing a wry look upon his face, he proclaimed: "Not to be. That was their answer."

O is for October 31st

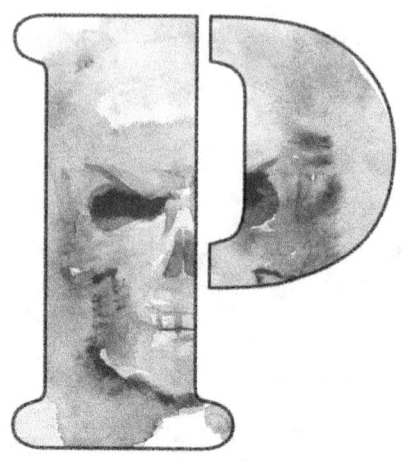

Cindy James

I was frying bacon when Hank stormed into the back porch, his thinning hair sticking straight out, face and hands ruddy from the cold.

"Get me the ammo, Myrna!" He yanked Grandpa's old twelve gauge from the walnut gun cabinet and looked down the barrel.

"What's going on? The coyotes after the chickens again?" I dropped the fork on the counter and opened the junk drawer next to the sink, rummaging for the box of Prairie Cloud. Hank danced impatiently on the muddied stairs, and when I pulled two shells from the box, he grabbed them and loaded the breach.

"If they think I'm going to roll over, they're dead wrong." He looked up at me, his pale blue eyes glinting with frenzied elation. "I knew the bastards would show up sooner or later."

"What are you talking about? Who showed up?" After twenty years of marriage, I was used to some level of paranoid hysterics from Hank, but this current display was far beyond his normal range of agitation.

"Department of Infectious Something or Other," he said. "They called yesterday."

"And you didn't tell me?"

"No point in gettin' you all worked up over nothing." He grabbed the box from my hand and stuffed a handful of shells into the pocket of his parka. He backed up against the screen door. "Stay here."

"Hold up one minute," I said, crossing my arms and pinning him with my best don't-you-dare-walk-out-that-door stare. "I'm damn well good and worked up already. What in God's name do you think you're going to do with that shotgun?"

"Same thing any self-respecting farmer would do." The door squeaked and slammed behind him, leaving me and my rising blood pressure alone in the kitchen.

I turned off the stove and hastened to the living room window to see Hank march resolutely down the gravel driveway, his long stride making his limp even more pronounced.

I shook my head, still incredulous that in my youth I had somehow seen fit to marry such an obstinate, argumentative, short-sighted pig farmer. I'd wanted to garden, have babies, play house and take care of my man. I'd thought we'd spend our evenings together, watching television and cuddling late into the night. I scoffed at the memory. We usually spent our evenings as far apart as possible, and when he finally did come in from the barn, more often than not I had to pry him out of his boots to tend to some sort of injury inflicted upon him by Old Betty, his prized sow. Even though she often hurt him, I was sure he loved her more than he did me. He denied it. Of course.

A flash of movement between the bared limbs of the aspens caught my attention, and my chest tightened mid-exhale.

"What in the name of Creation . . . ?" I trailed off as a convoy of police cars came around the corner of the dirt road, a shiny black Hummer in the lead.

"Don't you dare," I said, as the Hummer ploughed through the skiff of December snow and stopped just off the road in the middle of my prize-winning raspberry patch. I squinted into the sparkling sunlight reflecting off the fresh snow, my fists clenching involuntarily as the driver began a three-point turn, jeopardizing not only next year's blue ribbon jam production but my own precious reputation. The slender raspberry stalks folded under the knobby tires, and I sucked in an angry breath.

"Those fuckers," I said, and grabbed my coat.

With the shotgun dangling in his right hand, Hank had planted himself well back from the gate. I held my coat closed over my chest, my fingers hooked through the buttonholes in place of the missing buttons and shuffled quickly through the snow, my winter boots whisking against each other with each step.

The sheriff got out of his car and stood at the gate, his sunglasses perched on the top of his head. "Put the gun down, Hank," he said. "We came here to talk." He leaned against the chain link. His eyes flicked towards me and back.

Hank snorted. "Talk? Is that what you call it? You're here to cull the hogs, Ted. Tell it like it is. You probably got that fancy vet from upstate New York back there somewhere. And what's with the cavalry?"

"This?" Ted gestured towards the Hummer. "This is just a precaution. You made more than a few people a little nervous with those threats you made –"

"Threats? That I will defend what's mine? If anyone is being threatened, it's me. I worked hard for what I got, and I'm not going to stand by and let you take it all away." Hank hefted the shotgun and held it in both hands, across the front of his body.

"Hank," I said, huffing a little from my rush across the yard, "put it down before you get hurt." I tugged his coat sleeve to get his attention.

"They're bullies, Myrna." He wrenched his arm from my grasp. "I don't have to take their crap. Especially Ted's."

Ted rubbed a hand over his face. "Say what you want about me, Hank, but we have a warrant for an inspection. You're right. The vet is here. You've held out long enough. Every producer in the country is required to submit to review. This swine outbreak is spreading fast. Either you let us in, or we break down the gate, and I arrest you and Myrna. It's your choice."

"Me?" I asked.

Ted shrugged and nodded towards Hank. "What's it gonna be?"

"Some choice." Hank's breath plumed in the cold air, short rapid puffs of vapor that froze on his nose hairs and eyelashes. For just a second he closed his eyes and swayed against me. I frowned, leaned forward, and sniffed.

"You've been drinking?" I whispered. It was more of an accusation than a question. "Hank?"

Reluctantly he glanced down at me, and the guilt and remorse that momentarily softened his clenched jaw gave me the answer I needed. He was drunk. I looked up to the brilliant blue winter sky and silently asked for strength, yet again. Livin' the dream. Yes, I was.

"You promised." I gave Hank an exasperated look. "You promised, and now you're not thinking straight, and you're standing here in a showdown with the police. You are unbelievable, Henry. It's not even eight o'clock in the morning."

I closed my eyes and pinched the bridge of my nose, as the urge to slap his face nearly overwhelmed me. But, he was holding a gun, and violence was possibly not the best course of action in this situation.

"This is what you are going to do," I said. "You are going to quit being an ass. You are going to give me the damn shotgun. And then you are going to go over there, unlock the gate, and talk to your brother."

I looked up at him and held out my hand. Hank glowered, first at Ted and then at me. I could practically see him contemplating whether or not today would be the day he finally lived out his secret cowboy fantasy to go down in a blaze of glory.

"Hand it over," I said and swatted his arm. Playfully, of course.

"Myrna," he said, and I winced as he smacked the barrel of the gun into the palm of my open hand, "you're killing me."

I plucked the shells from the chamber and dropped them into my pocket. "Better me than them. Now go open the gate and bring your brother and this vet fellow up to the house. We'll sort this out over coffee."

The sheriff reached up and slid his sunglasses down over his eyes, his relief evident on his face. "Excellent idea, Myrna. Thank you."

I tilted my head and glared at my brother-in-law. We'd always got along, but that was beside the point. "I do have one condition, Ted."

"What is it?"

"Get that Hummer out of my raspberry patch, or I just might blow your brains out myself."

Hank unlocked the gate while I hurried back to the house. The coffee smelled burnt, so I propped the shotgun in the corner and started a fresh pot. The bacon was just starting to sizzle again when the three men crowded into the kitchen. The veterinarian, a young red-headed fellow with a pock-marked face, nodded at me, and I gestured towards the kitchen table.

"Take off your coats and sit down. Coffee will be done in a moment."

"My hogs are clean," Hank said as they settled around the table. "I've taken precautions."

The vet hung his coat on the back of his chair. "I'd love to take your word for it, Mr. Gallant," he said as he sat down, "but I can't."

"There's been calls to Town Council for a cull," Ted added. "Folks are scared this virus thing will start to infect people."

"A cull?" Hank's voice rose with resentment. "What a bunch of goddamn ingrates. I do my part around here. Every year we donate tons of pork to the needy. And they want a cull?"

The vet held up a hand. "There's a lot of fear, Mr. Gallant. Borderline panic. There's been no confirmed cases of swine-to-human transmission yet, but in rare instances –"

Hank interrupted. "I'd bet my life it's the other way around. It's the humans are the ones infecting the pigs." He leaned back in his chair. "That's why no one's been going in that barn but me."

The coffee finished perking. I set the pot and the bacon on the table before taking my place next to Hank.

"What about you, Myrna?" Ted asked. "Don't you help out in the barn?"

I shook my head. "I haven't set one foot in that sty for the past five years. Far as I'm concerned, those pigs would just as soon root out your eyeballs as look at you." I glanced at my husband. "Did Old Betty give you another go, Hank? I seen you were limping again."

"It's just my gout acting up." He glared at the vet. "You ever have gout?"

The vet shook his head.

"Goddamn painful." Hank reached for a slice of bacon. "Like a foot full of needles."

"Fact is," the vet said, "we need proof your operation hasn't been infected."

"Not once have I ever had any sign of disease. I know my hogs. Hell, Myrna always says I'm half pig."

"And that's not a compliment," I said. "Thank God we never had children."

"Never been sick a day in my life, because of this." Hank raised his bacon and waved it in the vet's face. "I eat it every day. Every single day. Keeps me healthy as a horse."

"Pretty hard to imagine life without bacon around this house." I offered the plate to the vet, but he shook his head and pushed a pen towards Hank.

"I'm a vegetarian," he said. "Just sign here. It gives me full access and the power to seize and dispose of any sick animals."

"You won't find no sick animals." Hank took a swig of his coffee. "Fine. You're the only one that goes in there with me. Let's get it over with."

It was near supper by the time they all cleared out, the vet promising to call with the results of the blood samples by the next day at the latest. He left a list of symptoms to watch for, and a warning to call instantly if anything showed up.

Hank disappeared back to the barn saying he'd eat a late supper, which was fine by me. I was still pissed at him for his antics of the morning. I could enjoy the evening to myself. I made a cup of tea and turned on the television for the first time in a long time and immediately turned it off.

That is exactly why I don't watch the news. What a horror show.

They were calling it a Porkpocalypse. I sat for a long time in the recliner with my feet up as I listened to the familiar creaks of the house as it shifted and settled on the frozen ground. Maybe I'd been too long on the farm. Who was I kidding? It was lonely and boring. To hell with peace and quiet. The pastoral life I'd dreamed of had never materialized. My husband preferred to spend his time with the swine rather than me.

Enough of that. I sighed and picked up a book from the side table. No point in dwelling on what wasn't.

I jerked awake, rocketing the recliner from prone to sitting and knocking the hardcover in my lap to the floor. I'd heard something. *A scream?* Or had it just been the dream I'd been having?

"Hank," I called out, but the house was silent. Everything was as I'd left it. He hadn't come in for dinner. No big surprise there.

I listened a moment to the wind as it whistled past the house, lifting the metal flap of one of the outside vents and dropping it against the siding with a muffled bang. It was a familiar noise that should have comforted me but didn't. I picked up the book and carried my empty teacup to the sink. The yard beyond the kitchen window was dark and deserted, but warm light from the barn illuminated the snow-covered ground. I pressed the intercom button next to the sink, watching the windows for movement. "Hank? You fall asleep out there?"

I waited for a full minute before trying again.

"Damn it, Hank," I said into the intercom, "you better not be passed out." I knew I should leave him out there, like usual, but instead I pulled on my coat and boots and reached into my pocket for my gloves. My fingers touched the shotgun shells.

It was right there, still propped in the corner. I'd never felt I needed it before, and yet... *Take it.* I loaded the gun.

The icy wind hit me full in the face, the cold sucking the breath from my lungs. Tugging my hood up with one hand, I hurried towards the barn under the hum and flicker of the yard lights. The wind teased the blowing snow into hard packed miniature grey, shadowy dunes.

I heard squealing halfway to the barn and broke into a run. "Hank?" I yelled as I pulled open the barn door.

A putrid stench punched me in the face, and I recoiled back into the open air, gagging as a heavy shadow knocked against my legs. I stumbled and fell against the outside barn wall to keep from hitting the ground. Hogs streamed from the barn in a flood, scrambling over one another as they escaped into the darkness. Pressed against the barn wall, I waited for the tide to subside. I covered my nose with my jacket and stepped inside.

Dead pigs littered the barn, every throat cut. Pools of shit and congealed blood blackened the floor. I stood in the doorway, confused. *What in God's name was he doing?* I uncovered my nose and tried to breathe shallow, but the foul air settled on the back of my tongue. "Hank?" I shouted. Careful not to slip in the muck on the floor, I picked my way through the landscape of pig carcasses towards the strip of light shining from under the office door. I called his name again, to no avail, and a tremor of cold ran through me. I hesitated with my hand on the doorknob. *I bet he gave himself another heart attack. I'm going to open this door and find him dead on the floor.*

He wasn't dead. Not quite.

Hank slumped in the corner on the floor, propped against the wall, covered in what I assumed was pig's blood. His eyes were open, an empty bottle of Jack Daniels gripped in his right hand. He wore nothing but his boxers. And then I noticed his leg.

"Myrna," he wheezed, "don't come near me." He nodded towards the blackened skin of his right foot and the dark lines that streaked up his thigh, over his belly, and towards his heart. "Guess my gout is worse than I thought."

"This is no time for jokes," I said, forcing my voice to sound calm and avoiding his eyes. I set the gun down and reached for the phone on the desk. "I'm calling an ambulance."

"Myrna." His voice broke, and I looked dispassionately at the man I had slept beside for the last twenty years. No doubt his own pig-headedness had brought us to this. He struggled to speak, but the effort made him cough, dark blood speckling his lips. "I can feel it," he said, once the spell passed. "It's like tar in my veins. If only –"

"Just you hold on," I said, and I picked up the phone.

A squeal of fury filled the room an instant before seven hundred pounds of lard slammed into me. My legs buckled, and I dropped to the floor, hitting my chin on the edge of the desk. Bright stars of pain shot through my neck and head as my mouth filled with blood. I gagged and pushed onto my hands and knees to spit out a tooth.

"Betty!" Hank rasped. The pictures on the wall of the office rattled, and I looked toward my husband. The sow stood guard in front of him, grunting and snuffling, glaring at me with her teeth bared. I didn't know a pig could snarl.

"She's protecting you from me?" I staggered to my feet and backed towards the door as I wiped the blood from my chin.

Hank smiled, a little too smugly for my liking. "She's always been a bit sweet on me."

"She's sick too." I pointed to a cluster of black streaks running up Betty's foreleg.

"I know. They probably all are. I tried to take care of it, but I couldn't do it. Not to her." His chest heaved as he lifted the bottle and waved it at me. "I was hoping for some courage." He patted Betty on the head, and she nuzzled her snout against his neck before turning her beady black eyes back on me.

"We have to put her down," I said. I picked up the gun.

"No!" Hank shouted, and he raised a weak hand in protest.

"She's a pig," I said, incredulous. Even now, he would choose her over me.

"Not just a pig. I can't explain it, but she understands me better than anyone."

"Better than me?"

He dropped his head. "You always said I was half pig. Maybe you were right."

Betty took a menacing step towards me.

I'd always hated pigs. Since day one. Mean critters. And they'd just as soon root your eyeballs out as look at you. Turns out I could imagine life without bacon after all.

I raised the shotgun.

"Don't," Hank said, and he wrapped his arms around Betty's neck. "If she goes, I go."

He said it like I wouldn't pull the trigger. Maybe he hadn't heard about the Porkpocalypse.

"Have it your way," I said.

I fired, and Old Betty's head exploded against the wall. As did Hank's.

P is for Porkpocalypse

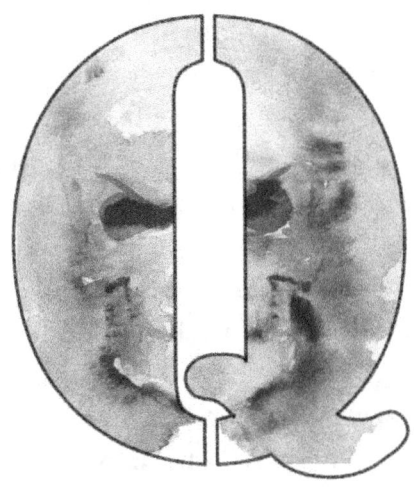

Brittany Warman

The night wind bows the trees to her as she begins her evening promenade. We are her attendants; we are her guards.

The queen is small, a pregnant bird in wrapped rags with knotted hands and sharp eyes. She wears a crown made up of dried leaves and twelve aluminum foil stars, her feet are bare and soaked with dirt. She walks with a limp, we don't know why, but there is something regal about her stance regardless. Her back is still straight, the movements of her hands are still graceful.

We are the only ones who know she is the queen.

Small, insignificant groups who call themselves gangs loot the stores behind the shabbily boarded up windows as she walks by. After the JDay — we call it that, we don't know what other people call it — a lot of people went crazy like that. They don't look at her. She says: "We are the people's spirit and we are the essence of survival. We cannot condone the actions of the small minded." She eats a discarded crust from an overturned trash receptacle and smiles in satisfaction.

We do not know if she refers to all of us, she and her child, or just herself – a queen may be plural, after all.

The streets are oddly quiet after JDay, even the gangs move without sound. Most of the people have gone – where we do not know. We, the chosen ones, remain. We serve, we defend – we will die for her. Did we once have families? Perhaps. We no longer remember. In this new world, all that matters is our queen. She walks slowly, weighed down by the child she carries. It will not be long now. The smoky sky above us seems to breathe – lightning flashes, the stars fall to earth. The sky is an angry red dragon.

Queen, we say, where were your armies at the end of the world? She does not reply.

When she falls, we are ready. The dragon is ready. We know instinctually that her child is coming and that her child's survival is the last hope of the world, if what we have now can even be called a world. The few of us who remain take our fated positions – we know the fight will come to us. Behind us, she screams and the labor begins – the heavens are the color of blood. We are not fit to look at her so we look instead at the blank city of silence. The ground shakes and hail beats down on us. We are nothing, nothing.

The queen howls to the moon at her feet.

The child is slow in coming and the queen presses her hands into the earth. She will not beg. We hear the thunder-laugh of the dragon and stand our ground – the determined faces of my companions form a stony wall around our sovereign savior and the rain begins. She says: "I will not yield to threats!" We say: "Amen." Two wings burst from the back of our queen, ripping her apart. We whisper: "Love for life will not deter us from death."

The child is born. She is alive.

Q is for Queen

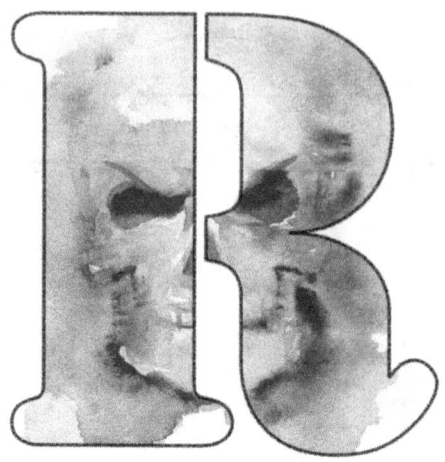

K.L. Young

Renee stood on the stage, unable to hear the screams and shouts of the crowd below. She thought a few of them – not many – were starting to get it. She looked at Zann, arms outstretched, head thrown back, his black greatcoat billowing in the winds that were starting to whip up. Finally, she looked over at Dave, bent over the guitar, a look of ecstasy frozen on his face. He looked happier than she had ever seen him before.

I did this, she thought.

Had it been only eighteen months earlier that she had strolled into that Portland pawn shop with Dave Evans – he of the long, greasy hair, the scruffy chin, the piercing blue eyes – and been sucked into this nightmare of madness, misery and death?

The road trip to Oregon had gone as well as it could, considering that Renee's beater hadn't been asked to drive

more than the twelve miles to work and back since she had
started working at the theater two years ago.

Well, and that she and Dave hadn't so much as kissed or
even held hands the entire time. Not surprising – they weren't
a couple by anybody's definition of the word, she had just been
nursing this crush for the last year or so, since just before they
graduated. Dragging him down to see Fenris during their
"Ragnarok and Roll" tour at the Rose Center was just the latest
in a series of attempts to show him how perfect they were for
each other.

And so, with plenty of time to spare before the concert, they
found themselves wandering aimlessly, enjoying the general
weirdness of Portland, and debating the idea that Norse-
rockers Fenris had surpassed the achievements of Led
Zeppelin, KISS or Erik Zann.

And as they entered the pawn shop, lured in by the sight of
several guitars hanging in the windows, had she felt a chill
pass over her? Had she experienced a moment of dread, as
quick and light as the flutter of a moth's wing in the dark?
Looking back, she realized she had.

The old man at the counter grinned through picket fence-
like teeth, noting their attention to the guitars.

"Buying or looking?"

"Just looking, right now," Renee said, almost apologizing.
She knew what they looked like; Dave's jeans showed more
skin than denim, and she had spiked her platinum blonde
pixie-cut into a faux-hawk for the show.

"But buying, if there's something interesting enough," Dave
said, surprising her. Dave had a cheap acoustic at home that he
could play three chords on, but he'd never expressed any
interest in getting any more serious than that.

The old man nodded, an action that pained Renee to watch.
He was ancient, the slightest movement enough to send his

bones into an epic Jenga-collapse. But he got off his stool and creaked towards them, past the old records and toys and computers, his head continuing to bob slightly.

"You look like a rock-roller," the old guy said. It sounded insulting.

Dave surprised Renee again. "I guess I am," he said, smiling. Dave avoided talking to people in general, and wouldn't say a word to someone if he thought he was being teased. This playfulness was definitely not normal, and she smiled to see him come out of his shell a bit.

"The Led Zeppelin," the old man said. "The Rolling Stone. The Who. You like them?"

"Sure," Dave said. "I like The Led Zeppelin."

"'bout Erik Zann? You like him?"

Dave's smile was blinding and genuine. "I love Erik Zann." Renee felt a twinge of jealousy. Had he ever smiled like that at her? She didn't think so.

The old man turned and motioned them to follow, his feet shuffling along the concrete floor. *This guy has a top speed of just over zero miles per hour*, Renee thought, as they followed him to a back corner shrouded in shadows.

He flipped a light switch that looked as old as he was, and a little lamp on a table turned on, coating the darkness with a sick, yellow film. He motioned to the wall, where an old guitar of polished cherry wood hung, almost ceremoniously. Near the neck, the guitar's body swooped gracefully into a devil-horned shape. The instrument had definitely seen better days, its finish scratched and scarred and cloudy. Underneath the guitar, a framed photo of Erik Zann during a live performance. He was on his knees, back arched, playing what looked to be the exact guitar hanging above.

"No way," Dave said.

"1962 Gibson SG," the old man croaked. "The Super Gibson."

"This is Erik Zann's?" Dave asked incredulously.

"One of them," the old man said. "But this is the one that he played during his final concert."

"Bullshit," Renee said. "The whole place burned down. We're supposed to believe that this guitar survived somehow?"

The old man shrugged indifferently, as if to say *I don't give a rat's ass what you believe*. He pulled the guitar carefully off the wall, handing it to Dave, who held it reverentially.

"Feels good, don't it?"

Dave strummed a few chords on the old electric, the sound tinny and ugly on the unpowered guitar.

"How much?" Dave said.

"Twelve hunnert," the old man replied. He stared at Renee when he said it.

A large TWANG exploded as one of the strings broke, and Dave jerked his hand back, his index finger sliced near the tip. The blood beaded up on his finger and then dropped to the guitar, once, twice.

"Shit," he said, using his sleeve to wipe at the mess.

The old man pulled Dave's sleeve away, and smiled in what Renee suspected he thought was a kindly manner. It sent a shiver of uncomfortableness through her.

"The cost," said the old man, "is unimportant. All that really matters is that it gets into the right hands. Your hands, I think. With that in mind... nine hunnert."

Dave looked at the guitar wistfully. "It's a great price. But it's a little out of my range. The highest I can go is five hundred. That's all the money I have in the world."

The old man smiled sadly, looking at Renee. "That is unfortunate, my friend. But I certainly can't let it go for less than eight hunnert."

Dave turned to Renee. "What do you think? Loan me three hundred until next week?"

"Next week," she said. "What happens next week? You won't have three hundred bucks by then."

"Come on. I know you've got it."

"What do you think's paying for our hotel room tonight?"

"Renee, it's Erik Zann's guitar! We don't need to stay in a hotel. We can head home right after the concert!"

Renee's heart dropped as she realized that her plans for the two of them were unraveling quickly.

"We don't even know if it's really Zann's guitar in the first place," she said.

Dave turned to the old man, who put one hand on his heart and raised the other in the air, nodding solemnly.

Renee sighed. "Fine. Yes, okay."

Dave beamed at her and gave her a ferocious hug. "Thank you! Thank you!"

And hadn't she almost felt that that hug had been worth it? Yes. At the time, she really had.

As they rang up the sale, Renee looked at the guitar tucked into the case the old man had supplied. It was battered and beaten for sure, but it looked a little nicer out in the light streaming through the shop's windows. The cherry wood held such a beautiful tint; she couldn't even see where Dave's blood had dripped onto it.

Everything had gone downhill from that moment on. Dave was terrified of leaving the guitar in the car while they went to the concert – "Somebody will steal it!" – and so she had allowed herself to be convinced that the best course of action was to simply turn around and drive back home to Seattle.

Even that would have been fine under regular circumstances. Three-plus hours of one-on-one conversation time with Dave was something she would normally kill for. But Dave was fixated on the damn guitar the entire time, running his hands over the fret, his pupils big and black and dazed the few times he turned to acknowledge her — always in response to some question she had repeated for the third or fourth time.

About half-way home, she noticed that his fingers were bleeding, speared and sliced by the broken string, and he was unconsciously smearing the blood all over the instrument.

"Jesus, Dave." When he looked dreamily at her, she tilted her chin at the guitar. "You're getting blood all over it."

He looked down stupidly at the guitar and his fingers, then gave her a goofy smile. "Don't worry. It'll be fine."

And when Renee pulled up in front of the dumpy house that he rented with Catfish and Johnny, it was. In the glare of the ugly yellow sodium lamp that illuminated the entire street, she couldn't see a smudge of blood on the guitar as he placed it back in the case.

She walked silently with him up the weedy, cracked concrete that led to the door, then stood there dumbfounded as he walked right in, strolled past Catfish and Johnny and into his bedroom, closing his door without a word to her.

"The fuck?" Catfish said, putting down his Xbox controller and stroking the ridiculous almost-mustache that was the source of his nickname. "Did the concert get canceled?"

Johnny gave her a courtesy head-nod to acknowledge her, but refused to stop playing the game.

She could feel the tears burning in her eyes, wanted to leave before they started to spill. "Yeah," she said, and left.

☠

Her anger and hurt feelings lasted a little over a week, when – because she hadn't heard at all from Dave – the hurt slowly morphed into a fear that he was angry at her, and then finally into a worry that something was seriously wrong. They never went two weeks without talking. They hardly went two days without talking, fer chrissakes.

Phone calls went unanswered, messages were not returned. More than slightly alarmed, she made the decision to end the self-imposed break, jumped into her beater, rattled across town and pulled up to Dave's place as the sun was dipping below the horizon. The rock music inside the house was loud enough to vibrate the windows as she made her way to the stoop. Already she was feeling foolish for worrying – things were obviously fine. It sounded like the house was in full-on party mode, and she hadn't been invited.

Her knock was answered by Catfish on the second attempt.

"Renee!" he exclaimed around a dangling cigarette. His whisker quivered as he grinned and gave her a hug, dragging her into the house so he could shut the door. "What's up, Chiquita? Where have you been hiding?"

She had to scream above the din coming from Dave's room. "I hadn't heard from Dave in a while! I was starting to get worried!"

They retreated to the kitchen, where the volume dropped a few decibels.

"Yeah, it's been a little crazy here," Catfish said. "Johnny just up and left last weekend, kind of screwed us over on rent and bills."

"That's shitty," Renee said, not really caring. "Did he say where he was going?"

"Didn't say shit. He and Dave got in some kind of fight one night, and when I woke up he was already gone."

This brought her back to the conversation. "What were they fighting about?"

"I dunno. Probably about Dave practicing constantly," Catfish said, nodding towards the source of the music. "He's getting pretty good, right? We're talking about putting a band together."

Renee blinked a couple times, trying to process what he was telling her, finally understanding that the music she was hearing wasn't some Jimmy Page clone, but Three-Chord Dave himself, bending and twisting notes like he'd been at it for years.

"You're shitting me."

"Right?" Catfish nodded wisely. "I never knew he was this good!"

Renee pushed her way through the wall of sound. "He wasn't."

At first, she almost didn't recognize him. His greasy hair hung in sweaty strings as his fingers, covered in band-aids, slid over the beautiful, inlaid fret board like an old pro. His face looked different, withdrawn almost, as if the skin had decided it needed to be that much closer to his skull. The dark half-moons under his eyes told her that he hadn't been sleeping.

When he looked up at her, it was as if he was gazing beyond, to something far in the distance, something miles past the old Erik Zann poster on the wall behind her. What are you seeing, she had time to wonder, and then the music abruptly stopped.

"What do you want?" he said simply, his eyes finally focused on her.

She was so taken aback by the question that her mind shut down for a moment, leaving her mouth working up and down and no sound coming out. Finally, "I was worried about you. I hadn't heard from you." She hated how stupid she sounded.

"I've been busy. I'm fine."

She pointed to his fingers, which were starting to bleed through the band-aids. "You're getting blood all over the guitar," she said weakly.

"Look, I'm fine. Okay?"

"Jesus, Dave. What the fuck? You've been acting like a complete asshole ever since Portland." Fuck. She was going to cry if she didn't get control of this conversation somehow. "And you still owe me three hundred bucks." Oh. Way to go.

He just looked at her for a moment, as if the words she said had to trudge through a mile of mud to reach his brain. Then he got up, walked past her to the dented and scratched dresser under the Erik Zann poster – another angle of him on his knees, his back nearly touching the stage – and pulled open a top drawer, removing a roll of bills. He peeled off three hundred-dollar bills and handed them to her, his face clearly indicating that the visit was at an end.

But she didn't notice at first. It took her a full five seconds to pull her eyes away from the poster, and Erik Zann's gaunt, sickly visage. When she finally did, she snatched the blood-stained money out of his hands and walked out of the room, past Catfish in the living room, and out the door to her car without another word.

Renee wasn't the Erik Zann fan that Dave was. Where Dave could list all of his albums in order and their respective release dates, Renee knew the few hit songs he'd had, and owned only one Zann album, his last. She also knew, of course, of the infamous Final Concert, where the rock star had burned to death along with several hundred of his fans. VH-1 had placed it at number one in their list of Top 100 Tragedies in Rock, but the details of the event had never been that important to her.

She pulled into her driveway next to her dad's pickup truck, breezed through the door and raced up the stairs to her room, closing and locking the door while her tired old laptop hummed and buzzed to life.

She searched "Erik Zann" online and came up with nearly two million hits, decided to just Wiki him. The entry was gigantic, and filled in the gaps in her knowledge.

She'd known that he'd risen to fame with the British prog-rock band Arkham, but didn't realize he was only fifteen when he'd joined. She'd known that he'd struck out on his own in the early '80s, recording three instrumental "concept albums" that were considered masterpieces in the genre, but hadn't known that his first album came just two months after surviving the infamous tour bus accident that had killed the other members of Arkham.

She glanced at the thumbnails of the cover art for his solo albums. The first, titled "The Music of Erik Zann" had a backdrop of a vast cosmos with a small window floating in it. In the window, Zann seemed to be playing his instrument furiously, his face a grimace of agony... or ecstasy. The second, "Cry Horror!" had some kind of Frazetta-like demon ape bearing down on a Viking warrior wielding a glinting and apparently razor-sharp Gibson. And the third, "Burn the Universe", showed a strangely unsettling likeness of Zann upon a great altar of some kind, guitar held high like mighty Mjolnir, while below him a pit filled with a thousand souls in some kind of humanary stew writhed and grasped towards him. He was flanked by two giant tuning forks that were lit up like a Tesla coil. Above him, a tear in reality revealed an alien entity made of various eyeballs, screaming mouths and whipping tentacles. This cover she was familiar with, having inherited the album from her dad, and finally purchasing her own CD when it was re-released and remastered. That particular album told a story (decipherable only from the liner notes, in Renee's opinion) of a hero sacrificing his own, mundane world so that its rightful rulers, The Old Ones, could return and lay claim.

Accompanying all of this were a half dozen photos of Zann, which convinced her that Dave's new resemblance to him was actually very slight, and made her feel a little foolish for running out the way she had. The last photo was a live shot, one of the very few that had survived the Final Concert, and showed Zann on a stage constructed to look just like the altar on his album cover, right down to the tuning forks. Eerily, the writhing audience below filled in as a perfect mirror to the damned souls in the artwork.

Except for Catfish's casual mention of putting a band together, Renee might have passed by the playbill taped to the power pole near the theater's parking lot without a second glance. Her brain caught up with her eyes three steps later, and she backtracked to take a closer look.

"BURNING UNIVERSE", the text screamed, was apparently the finest Erik Zann tribute band on the West Coast, and right there in the live-staged photo of the band was Dave, performing what one would believe must be a blistering solo of epic proportions. He wore Zann's trademark greatcoat and puffy white sleeves, and with his newfound gauntness made for a passable Zann impersonator, at least in photos. Playing bass in the background was Catfish, looking very Catfish-like, and then some guy she didn't know behind the drum kit.

They would be playing at The Central on Friday at 9, an all-ages show with Led Zepagain and The Atomic Punks in a night of Tribute Madness, apparently.

Renee hadn't quite gotten over their last discussion and her subsequent weird feelings after, but she thought this might be the way to test the waters. Besides, they were going to need a friendly face. Although Dave's prowess was impressive when she last heard him, it was doubtful that he had become the next Erik Zann in the three weeks since then. They would likely be laughed off the stage by the fans that showed up at these kinds of gigs.

After paying her fifteen-dollar cover charge and heading into the bar, she was glad she'd taken the time to spike her faux-hawk up and put a little thought into her wardrobe – the place was jam-packed with people dressed in classic rock attire. Oddly, there was no real clash with the time frames; the music may change, but denim and leather were still the standard uniform.

She had only just made it to the bar for a Coke – there was no way the bartender was falling for her fake ID – when the lights went down and Burning Universe took the stage.

Dave looked good, she thought, despite his newly-gaunt features. Sexy, even. He absolutely rocked the black greatcoat, frilly white shirt and tight leather pants. The drummer seemed to be going for some kind of '70s-rock look too, but Catfish was always just going to be plain, old Catfish: wrinkled shirt, dirty jeans, Chuck Taylors.

The drummer raised his sticks over his head and clicked a four-count, and they came screaming out of the starting gate with "The Most Merciful Thing", the first track from Zann's final album. Three songs later it was obvious they were going to play the Burn The Universe album in its entirety.

And... they were good. Really good.

Scary good.

She didn't know the drummer, so it was no surprise that he knew what he was doing. And Catfish had at least been in other bands, so there was some kind of pedigree there. But Dave... she knew what Dave was capable of a month ago. What she heard at his house three weeks ago was pretty damn impressive. But this was almost unbelievable.

Every note, from the shrillest highs to the lowest lows, was spot-on. He seemed to breeze effortlessly through Zann's neo-classical guitar solos, shredding through song after song, until even the band members from the other bands were standing open-mouthed up front with the rest of the crowd.

And as they dipped into the penultimate song on the album, "Love Kills", with its weeping chorus and heartbreaking bridge, she knew there was no way she'd get to say any words to Dave tonight, kind or otherwise. The crowd was jammed against the stage, and she thought if he wasn't careful, he might be hoisted on audience members' shoulders and paraded around the bar at the end of the show.

And so she weaved her way through the crowd towards the exit, swiping at a renegade tear that was going to have its way with her mascara no matter what, and bolted into the night.

Which made Catfish's funeral six months later even harder, knowing that she had missed out on speaking to him one last time because she had been so stupid about her feelings for Dave.

The beautiful, crisp Autumn-in-Seattle day mocked the mourners in black at the service. Afterward, she found herself bee-lining toward Dave, who had come alone and stood at the back of the mourners while the eulogy had been read graveside.

"Dave," she called out, then again when he didn't seem to hear her the first time.

He turned and looked at her, his eyes swimming in tears. She was relieved to see that although he was still a little too skinny, he looked more like the Dave she remembered than he had in the last several months.

His face started to crumple a bit as she came in close and hugged him, the feel of his body against hers bringing back all those old feelings she had thought she had successfully gotten past.

"You okay?"

He pinched his eyes, gave her a rough smile. "Yeah."

They started walking towards the road, avoiding headstones and markers as other mourners begin to pass them.

"I don't even know what happened," she said. "I just found out that today was the funeral."

Dave just nodded, his head hanging low.

"So... what happened?"

He looked up sharply at her. "Well, how would I know? They just found him dead in his car, okay?"

She stopped, startled by the outburst. And had she thought then that he sounded like he was a step from losing it all? Like he sounded just a tad, I don't know... guilty? Yes. She had.

"I just meant..." she started to say, but was cut off.

"They don't know who did it or why. Nobody knows."

She stopped walking then, but Dave... Dave just kept moving on.

Two weeks later he had signed with Carcosa Music, just about the best one could hope for in the genre. Renee heard about it second hand, of course. Dave wasn't speaking to her.

The night that Renee heard the single from Dave's first studio release, she had a dream. The song was called "Love Never Dies", a pretty instrumental that began with a catchy acoustic sound and morphed into a crazy guitar anthem by the end. It seemed to permeate the entirety of her dreamscape.

In her dream she was standing in one corner of Dave's living room, in the crummy rental he had shared with Catfish. In fact, Catfish was there, alive and well, and apparently very angry. He was pacing around the room, gesturing wildly, occasionally pointing an accusing finger at Dave's guitar - Zann's guitar – which stood on display in the living room, leaning in a guitar stand.

Dave sat on the couch, his eyes hooded, cheekbones sharp against his skin. He watched Catfish stride back and forth, his head never moving. Predatory. Dangerous. A snake watching a mouse.

There was a third person in the room. Perched on the back of the couch was a man, old and shriveled and scarred. He crouched imp-like next to Dave, softly whispering into his ear as Catfish wore a path into the carpeting. Despite the heavy, ropy scarring covering the man's face, Renee had no trouble identifying him as Erik Zann, his piercing eyes staring out at Catfish through bottomless pits of hatred and misery.

Catfish's volume rose, although she could not make out the words he was spitting out. It was obvious that he was not happy with Dave, and that he was oblivious to the ghost in the room. Dave's response, though calm and measured, sounded equally murky to her, though he seemed to be trying to reason with his angry friend.

In fact the only words she could hear clearly were the dark whispers that the shade on the couch was pouring into Dave's ear. They slid into her own ears like a thick snake, sinewy and pulsing, moving deeper and deeper into her brain.

killhimkillhimkillhimkillhimkillhimkillhimkillhimkillhimk illhimNOW

She used her fists to plug her ears, but the volume of Zann's whispers rose and rose to the point where she thought she might kill Catfish herself if it would make the sound go away.

And that's when Catfish grabbed the guitar just below the headstock, raising it high and bringing it down in an arc that would have made Townshend proud. Dave jumped up, his mouth an O of shock and fear, but the only sound Renee could hear was the unearthly wailing from the ghost of Erik Zann, a sound that threatened to rip the Universe in half.

Dave dropped to his knees next to the guitar, broken now where the neck met the body, the two pieces held together only by its strings.

Zann knelt next to him, whispering furiously, his shark eyes fixed balefully on Catfish, who seemed shocked and sorry and mortified at his own behavior.

And then Renee was begging to wake up, screaming at herself to close her eyes, to open her eyes, to do anything so she couldn't see Dave take that jagged, broken guitar neck and slam it into Catfish's soft throat, destroying his friend's neck in eye-for-an-eye-retribution that seemed to have its own soundtrack; a moaning, wailing noise that Renee finally realized was coming from Dave's guitar, Zann's guitar, which was not plugged in but was somehow sustaining a sound that was no musical note that had ever been heard on this Earth.

And as Catfish lay dying just a few feet away, his blood pumping and pouring and cascading over his shirt, Zann's lips were glued to Dave's ear, instructing him, teaching him, showing him that what he had to do was take the guitar's broken neck, slick and stained and almost sizzling, and press it back against the beautiful wooden body as if Catfish's blood could act like some kind of horrible, nightmarish super-glue.

Because, in this awful, impossible dream she was having, it absolutely could. The two pieces fused together with a horrific cry of agony, and Dave started to weep. Not tears of horror at what he had done to his best friend in the whole world, but of joy that the guitar was safe and whole again.

She was startled awake when the shade's eyes suddenly moved from Dave's ear to stare directly at her, its mouth stretching wide and grinning at her even as it continued to whisper to him, and she knew one thing: That wasn't even Dave anymore.

"Love Never Dies" became a minor hit for Dave, selling several thousand copies in its first month of release – fairly impressive for a rock instrumental from an unknown artist. It was nothing compared to the millions that Erik Zann had sold thirty years earlier, but the musical landscape had changed drastically since then.

Renee checked the safety on the Beretta 9mm she had taken from her father's nightstand, just as he'd taught her years ago. He'd flip when he'd find it missing tonight, but she'd be long gone by then.

She glanced at the newspaper article about Dave's sold out show tonight, and chuckled dryly at Dave crediting Erik Zann as the biggest influence on his sound.

"No shit."

☠

Selling 20,000 copies of a single might not qualify Dave Evans as an overnight success, but it did mean that his first solo gig in his hometown had him packing Rawker's 1,500 seats.

Renee had been to the club a dozen times before, making friends with everyone from the promoters to the light and sound techs to the cooks and servers. It took her a couple of calls to finally secure the hottest ticket in town, stopping short of outright agreeing to sleep with one of the bartenders, but she knew the score.

Who knows, Renee thought, standing in line underneath Rawkers' neon star. *Given enough time, I might be looking forward to a conjugal visit from just about anyone.*

Getting through the door was worrisome. If they were checking bags, the Beretta in her purse would end her night awfully quick. But they were just taking tickets, and her uniform – leather jacket, tight jeans, black t-shirt with band logo, heels - was correct. She was waved through without a second glance.

As the lights began to dim, she felt herself beginning to hyperventilate, her breaths coming in shorter and shorter gasps.

The rock queen next to her noticed and grinned through blood red lips. "I know," she said to Renee, as the first whistles and cheers started up. "It's awesome, isn't it!"

Renee nodded, forcing a smile. "Rock and roll," she said, throwing weak devil horns.

The rock queen laughed, then cupped her hands around her mouth and let out an ear-piercing scream as Dave and his band members strolled out on stage.

She didn't recognize the drummer or bass player - studio cats, most likely, hired by the label to accompany Dave for this show — but she recognized the weird, eight-foot tall tuning forks standing behind the drummer's kit, and that was when she realized just what was going down tonight.

The forks were perfect replicas of the ones Zann used in his final concert, down to the dull, brushed-steel finish. Hell, they might actually be the same forks for all she knew. It seemed pretty obvious that Zann was calling the shots these days, and if her suspicions were correct, he was going to attempt to recreate that final concert in this tiny venue tonight.

Dave blasted through his set, looking every inch the rock star he was turning out to be. He pinwheeled his arms, he propped a foot on the amp, he posed and preened his way through one song after another, and Renee found herself mesmerized, watching the man she still loved transforming himself into a bonafide Rock God in front of her eyes.

She had lost track of time and purpose and was suddenly jostled back to reality when Dave began playing the opening notes of "Love Never Dies", and the crowd, patient up to this point, finally left their seats and pushed up against the stage, cell phones and lighters held high. She was surprised that it had taken nearly the entire show for the audience to get to their feet, and then wondered if they had been lulled into the same dream-like state she had found herself in.

She moved through the swaying, writhing crowd, reminded of the image from Zann's final concert, finally parking herself at the front of the stage.

Here, she could see Dave up close and personal, and was shocked by how much he now resembled Zann in his early days. His fingers danced over the frets like lightning, confident and sure. His hair hung in sweaty curls, his face scrunching and relaxing with the notes.

And next to him, an almost imperceptible smudge on reality. At first, it seemed a trick of the light, but then she saw it grow thicker, more solid – the shade of Erik Zann, a wicked puppet master pulling the tendons in Dave's arms and fingers, manipulating his music and his life for the last year and a half.

She felt for the gun in her handbag, closed her hand around the stock, her finger slipping into the trigger guard. Could she do it? Could she actually kill Dave before he completed Zann's ritual? Was there even anything left of Dave in there anymore?

In her mind's eye, she saw herself pulling the weapon and pointing it at Dave, saw the reactions of the crowd around her, some screaming, some ducking; and inevitably, some attacking her and stripping her of the weapon before she could do anything with it.

No, she couldn't do it from the crowd. She had to get on stage. Craning her neck to either side, it was apparent there were no easy ways to climb the four-foot high stage, no steps at either end. It had to be accessed from backstage.

She pushed her way back through the crowd, enduring the angry faces and pervy gropes, then found herself in front of the swinging door to the kitchen. She nudged it open, wondering if she'd have to make a break for the backstage.

But the kitchen was deserted, and from here she could see the hallway to the green room and stage entrance.

Still waiting for a hand to fall on her shoulder and escort her out, she eased through the darkened kitchen into the hallway, and listened as the crowd cheered after Dave finished his hit song. He followed it up with the beginning notes of Zann's "Burning Universe". There were a few moments of silence, and then the crowd roared its approval.

This is when it will happen, Renee thought. *Whatever "it" is.*

She quickly climbed the steps to the side of the stage, then stopped in wonder.

On stage, Dave and his band were doing justice to Zann's most famous number, and the tuning forks were beginning their Tesla-coil arcing. She could taste the charge in the air as the hairs on her arms began to rise.

She saw a few people near the front of the stage start pointing towards the roof, and she followed their gaze, her mouth dropping open and her mind reeling at the sight.

Near the ceiling of the concert hall, something was happening. A tear in reality, spilling alien colors and lights through, widening slowly at first, then faster and faster. A window was opening onto an alien vista, a world so unlike our own as to be terrifying in its sheer fundamental difference. A bizarre sky filled with stars and worlds so old that our own cosmos seemed newborn in comparison.

And in the middle of this starscape, a nightmarish creature of epic proportions, writhing appendages and blinking, rolling eyes; mouths and teeth and tongues; arms and legs and legs and legs as it reared up, perhaps sensing the tiny human eyes that were viewing it for the first time.

Renee tore her own eyes away from the thing, feeling the edges of her vision starting to dim, her mind trying to shut down from the impossibility of the being, shut down or go stark, raving mad.

Through all of this, Dave's rendition of Zann's masterpiece built and built, until he was on his knees, leaning back so far that his head nearly touched the stage. His eyes were glued to the rift that was growing in the air above him, his face bursting with joy. Standing next to him, as solid now as anyone else in the hall, was Erik Zann, urging him on.

His drummer and bass player had long since stopped playing, their eyes turned towards the creature that filled the alien sky that had taken over the concert hall. Renee saw that the drummer's mouth was hanging open stupidly, and that his eyes had begun to bleed, running down his cheeks like scarlet tears.

Which was when Dave hit the final note of the song, sustaining it longer and longer and longer, the tuning forks vibrating like crazy, shattering stage lights and glasses and cell phone screens.

It has to be now, she thought, striding out on the stage, pulling the Beretta out of her purse and firing it point blank into Dave's chest, emptying the clip without even being able to hear it over the musical note and tuning forks.

But instead of ending, the note seemed to bend and twist of its own volition, turning into something louder, harder, madder. Renee cupped her hands over her ears, looked down to see the guitar greedily sucking up Dave's spilled blood like a horrific sponge and spewing it back out in the form of an alien symphony.

An interstellar breeze blew through the concert hall, and as the note continued to grow louder and louder, she looked over to see Zann grinning maniacally, staring up at The Old One that was finally taking notice of the tiny organisms that had summoned it.

Her mind began to crack then, as she realized that this was the end; that this thing, this hateful, malevolent entity, would usher in the final chapter in the history of the human race with its very first step in our reality.

She stood on the stage, unable to hear the screams and shouts of the crowd below. She thought a few of them – not many – were starting to get it. She looked at Zann, arms outstretched, head thrown back, his black greatcoat billowing in the winds that were starting to whip up. Finally, she looked over at Dave, bent over the guitar, a look of ecstasy frozen on his face. He looked happier than she had ever seen him before. And isn't that what she'd always wanted, anyway? It was.

I did this, she thought. *Cool.*

R is for Rock N' Roll

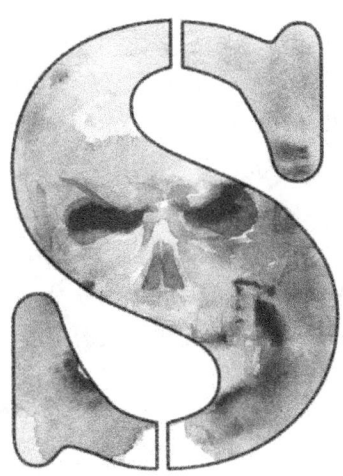

Pete Aldin

i

Day 751

"There are no monsters in your cupboard."

Mommy used to tell me this whenever I was afraid to enter my room.

"There's no monster beneath your bed, son."

Daddy used to say this whenever I had nightmares.

They both told me there's *no such thing* as monsters. Over and over.

Idiots.

Monsters ate them both.

ii

Dear Fellow Survivor,

I'm not sure why I'm writing to you.

That's a lie.

I'm writing because you're the only human being I've seen in two years, even though it's at a distance.

I'm writing because I want you to find this note and write back, or better yet wait for me.

I saw you in the market, scavenging for scraps, for cans and bottles and packets. I watched you from the department store roof. You looked like I must when I'm scavenging: desperate, desolate, terrified that a monster will come get you. I haven't seen one in nine, ten months.

But I saw you.

And when you saw me – galloping across the car park like some rabid racehorse – you fled. What the hell was I thinking, running at a woman like that? Already tired, I couldn't keep up with you. God, you were fast. I don't blame you; if I saw me, I'd run too. Who's to say I'm not a monster?

Except I'm not. I'm just me. My name is Eric, by the way.

Eric hopes you'll find this. Eric hopes you'll meet him here at midday next Wednesday.

Eric hopes you still keep track of days the way he does.

iii

Day 751 (continued)

All the people. All the pets. All the cattle, all the sheep. They ate everyone and everything.

They even feasted at the zoo. God, that must have been a sight to behold: monsters versus lions, tigers, polar bears, elephants. I hope the animals took a whole lot of the bastards with 'em when they died.

And then with all the live food gone, they turned on each other until most of them were gone too.

At least, that's my guess. It's the only sense I could make of the carnage I found when I emerged from my neighbor's shelter.

Yeah, they killed everybody and then they killed each other. Leaving me with nothing. Leaving me with silence.

iv

Dear Friend,

You didn't collect my last note so I worried that I'd imagined you. I didn't think I was having a Crazy Day that day, but it's possible. So when I came back, I checked around. I remembered I'd seen you put down a backpack and yep, there it was, exactly where you'd left it. Wet of course, since it's rained a couple of times this week. But proof you're real. You're alive.

Geez, I hope you're alive.

Are you? Anything could have happened in the last few days.

I used to think I was the only one left. Just me. Me and the silence. One Crazy Day – well, maybe more than one – I spent hours walking around my burb, shouting. Shouting at geese. Shouting at ravens. Shouting at walls. Shouting down the road and up the road. Shouting in through windows and up at the sky. Shouting at God. Shouting at the devil. I even shouted at Buddha, just for good measure. And while I shouted, the world was full of noise again, of people-noise, voices.

But when my throat finally went hoarse, the echoes quickly faded. And the pressure of no-noise pressed back in on me. Frigging emptiness. Who'd have thought nothing would be so tangible, so oppressive?

I used to think I was the only one left. If you've died, then I'm back to square one. Just me and my new BFF, Silence.

I'll leave this inside your backpack, hoping you come back for it.

Please be here next Wednesday.

I'll come Thursday too, just to make sure.

v

Day 766

The world's not totally silent, of course.

There's still the birds. Thank God the monsters couldn't get all of them. There'd have been nothing left to clean up the mess they left.

And there's still thunder occasionally.

There's the creak of old buildings. The occasional crash of something falling, humanity's structures breaking down.

Last summer there was the fire. I can't believe the ruckus *that* made: took out an entire estate not far from my place. I'm just lucky the estate boundaries contained it. But the noise was glorious.

What else?

Oh, yeah, there's still the wind – or as I call it on my Crazy Days: the Breath of God. I like to imagine it's a sign of an all-powerful Being keeping me alive, keeping me strong, keeping me going. I might have got this idea from the start of the Bible. I read the first twenty pages or so down in the shelter. Thought it might bring me peace. Thought I might find answers. *And the Lord God formed man of the dust of the ground, and breathed into his nostrils the breath of life; and man became a living being.* That was kind of gentle of God. Parental. A couple of chapters later the same God is banishing this other guy, Cain, condemning him to walk the Earth alone for the rest of his life, to live in silence. Cain deserved it for what he did.

But what did *I* do?

vi

Dear Friend,

Thank God, I saw you again. I know you're real now. Totally know it.

What were you doing in the library anyway? What were you looking for before I scared you off? Again. I hope my sudden appearance doesn't stop you going back there. Books are important. Books are essential if we're going to stay human, stay civilized, rebuild.

Rebuild? What the hell am I thinking? (Notice the way I'm not swearing. See, I still have self-control. That's a good sign, right?)

How are we going to rebuild? If the possibly last two people on earth can't even connect, if one can't even trust the other enough to come talk to him, or at least leave him a note, what hope does the human race have?

So, anyway, the library. I'm writing two copies of this now, one for the library and one for the market. Doubling my chances of communicating with you. Maybe.

What is it about me you don't like anyway? My hair? I'm not very good with scissors and the shaved head look never suited me. At least I still shave my face; that's a sign I've kept my civility, isn't it? I'm not a total animal. I'm not a Wildman.

I'm not a monster.

vii

Day 789

I've seen a total of three since I came out of old man Thompson's shelter sixteen months and three days ago.

Three living ones.

The first two were a day apart, a month after I emerged.

One was waiting for me down the street the very first time I left the house to go foraging. The air was all staticky with snow, the last fall of that winter. The thing had been standing there all night judging from the drifts on its shoulders, piles like mega-dandruff. It snarled and tried to hurdle a mess of corpses, but caught a leg in them and went down hard. I shuffled closer through the snow and popped it twice in the head before it had a chance to recover. Blood. Brains. All of a color that seemed too dark to be "right". I poured petrol over it and burnt it where it lay, left it there for the day while I went on my merry way, gave it another dose of fire that night and the day after until it was nothing more than a pile of wet ash that would wash away with the thaw.

The second one lunged at me from the carpark stairwell on Third Street. Much more dangerous. I was about ten feet away from it and it scared the bejesus out of me.

I don't know if it had been waiting in ambush or hibernating...

I went down, tripped backwards down the gutter, sprawled on the street. I was lucky I didn't crack my head open, luckier the thing had a busted leg and couldn't move fast. It was nearly on me before I got the Glock out of my holster. The first bullet went wide. The second took it in the shoulder, the third in the other leg and then it hit asphalt, still scrabbling and snapping at me. I pulled my legs up, got to my feet, my heart hammering so hard I thought my chest would explode. I steadied my aim and shot the mother in the eye.

Booyah!

That one still feels good!

viii

Dear Girl,

Why the hell won't you trust me? I know you read my letters I left at the market. They were gone last time I went back, along with your backpack. So I know you'll read this too.

And the question still stands. Why don't you trust me? Why don't you wait for me? Do you have other people with you? Are you already in a com-mun-it-y? Then for God's sake let me in!

Or would I be a fifth wheel, is that it?

Sonofabitchshitdick. There I'm swearing now. Happy? You've made me really angry!

Look...

You've got nothing to fear from me. Nothing. I am not a mugger. I am not a rapist. I was a student before the world ended, studying to be a Pharmacist. Mild-mannered. Decent. I've never hurt a fly. I've never so much as killed a bird for food. I grow strawberries and carrots and celery and tomatoes in my neighbor's back yard, lettuce and spuds and pumpkins in mine. I raid a nearby farm for apples and pears and plums. I eat out of tins. Like you do. I'm like you. I'm not a threat. I'm a good person.

A lonely good person.

A lonely grieving good person.

A lonely grieving rejected good person.

A lonely

Screw it

ix

Day 789 (continued)

The third monster was just last month, right when I was beginning to think I could stop lugging three handguns around with me. Right when I was thinking I was finally safe. Safe from *them* at least.

Where the hell did it come from? Where'd they all come from anyway (oh, there's an original thought; bet no one ever wondered that before!)? Virus? Lab? The ocean? Outer space? Inner space?

Inner space. What the hell's inner space? The center of the Earth?

So I shot it too. Killed it dead. Killed it before it could get anywhere near me. And I enjoyed it, I'm happy to admit. That's not wrong, that's not bad. Surviving is *good*. Living is *good*. It was him or me.

Anyway.

Three monsters, thirteen bullets. That's more than four bullets per monster. Not that all my shots hit home. If I had to estimate, I'd say I fired thirteen, hit them with nine. So an average of three bullets per monster with an accuracy rate of approximately seventy percent – at that rate, with the bullets I still have, I can safely kill another sixty-seven monsters. If I'm attacked by an average of two a year, that's thirty-three and a half years I can be safe from them.

Thirty-three and a half more years that the monsters can't get me.

Yep, that should be enough.

x

You crazy bitch!

You could have killed me! Even with the ricochet!

I've just finished picking a bullet fragment out of my left pec. You have no idea how hard that was, how much it HURT*!!!*

I think my rib stopped it or I would have joined the other seven billion members of the human race in the afterlife. If there is one.

And it'd be your fault. Bitch.

Don't you realize how valuable I am? I might be the only man left alive. I might be the only person who'll talk to you, listen to you, play cards with you. Or checkers. I know medicine and science. I could stop you dying of the flu. And you shot at me? What the hell is wrong with you?

Maybe it's me who should be scared of you. Maybe you're my greatest threat, not the monsters. Not even the silence.

Maybe I should be saving all these bullets for you!

xi

Day 796

The fourth monster came for me today, came right to my goddamn house like it knew I was there. Keeping up the averages, the sonofabitch was. Two last year. Two this year.

And when I shot it through the head, I saw her face. The face I'd seen through my binoculars at the market that day. The face of an angel. An evil angel. I *wanted* it to be her. I wanted to punish her for what she'd done, for what she *does*, taking my letters without replying. Scorning me. Shooting at me.

I shot the thing through the forehead, then walked in close and shot it again and again and again, four shots in total: forehead, sternum, left lung, right lung. The sign of the cross.

And then I took my machete and I hacked off its head. (Took longer than I expected, blood stank like sewage). Dragged the body into the street and leant it up against a trash can as a warning to others: "Come mess with me and this is what you'll get!" Stuck its head on a star picket. Took the picket to the market and jammed it into a drain grate. That'll show her when she comes back. I'm not out to get her. I'm her ally, not her enemy. We have a common enemy. We can be friends. I can protect her.

Bitch.

xii

Dear Friend,

Okay. I'm sorry. I shouldn't have written those things. In the last letter. Which you collected. (When the hell are you taking them anyway? I'm here at the market all the time and I never see you). The things I said? That was just pain talking. Pain and anger.

But you can understand my rage, can't you? You get shot in the boob and see if you aren't more than a little pissed.

Yesterday was a Crazy Day. Do you have them too? Days when you can't take it. Smoking pot to make it all go away – dumb thing for a chemist to do. I'm not dying of cancer after all. I'm dying of loneliness. Of silence.

That Crazy Day came in handy. Sometimes craziness breeds creativity. I have an idea. It's an answer to my problem. My problem and yours. I read it once in a survivalist book and the phrase came back to me yesterday: Position your snares where you find strong signs of animals passing through...

xiii

Day 811

I am a genius.

Rohypnol's a cinch to make. Crashing the truck into the lamppost by the market, slashing the two front tires: great fun! Leaving the rear doors swinging open with the single packet of

178

Twinkies lying just inside (my last pack, but worth it for this!)–
as I say: genius. Who can resist a Twinkie or six? Especially
when they're much *much* rarer now than the hypodermic I
used to lace them.

All I need do now is settle in to wait. This roof's secure. The
weather's fine. I have supplies (sans Twinkies of course). Gives
me time to read. After the story of Cain, the Bible gets pretty
boring, but those first few pages – whew! Well worth a second
read. And a third.

xiv

*...I'm not saying you're an animal. Far from it. But the
principle's the same. I know where you'll be, if not when.*
And if you're reading this, you know it worked.

xv

Day 818.

I have her now.

She's here. With me. Down in the shelter where she's safe.
Where I can protect her.

Her tantrums make me miss the silence – just a little.
Well, that's nothing a little more rohypnol won't fix. She has to
eat sometime.

The important thing is we're together.

She might not like it. But she'll come round. She'll play
cards with me, one day. She'll play checkers. She'll thank me.
She'll recognize the good I've done – for her, for the human
race. She'll realize who I am and love me for it. She must feel
something for me already; she did keep my notes after all. If
that doesn't count for something, I don't know what will. They

were meant to be kept, a record of our undeniable connection and of my vision for the future.

I've had time and space to see the signs and understand them. I was an educated man and now I am more – a man reborn of silence and solitude. She and I, we have a purpose. We have an opportunity. We are a civilization in the making, the beginning of a new beginning.

I get it now. I get God's plan. Or Buddha's, hah. A cleansed world. A sanitized receptacle. The empty Earth is ready for a new creation, a rebooted Eden.

No more chaos.

No more solitude.

No more monsters.

S is for Silence

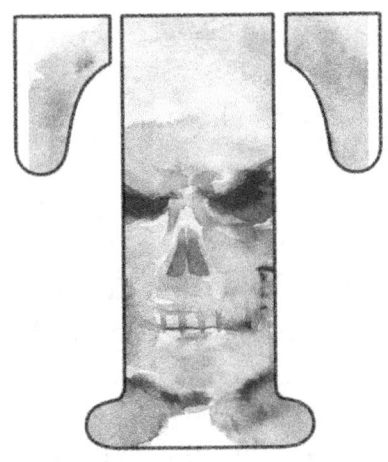

Cory Cone

1

Maxwell Lake walked the city streets with a leathery bouquet of rat tails sprouting from his fist, and a crescent moon accompanied him. The remains of human life whimpered within crumbling row homes like lonely, forgotten dogs; the sounds of sorrow mingling with the shrieks of rooftop crows and the scuttling paws of alley rats—a chaotic urban symphony. *It's beautiful*, he thought, *but it ain't Beethoven.*

When he reached his house he opened each of the five locks with a different key and stepped inside. His studio was in the back, and he made his way through the dark to set the bundle of rodents on his work table. There were six tonight.

He plucked one from the group and took it to the living room. There he lit two candles and switched on one of his last remaining generators. A CD player hummed to life. From the speakers mounted around the room came the opening notes of Beethoven's *Piano Sonata No. 14, in C-sharp minor, "Quasi una fantasia":* the *Moonlight Sonata*—a suitably somber selection for cooking rat.

Three dozen sets of eyes shimmered in the candle light, watching.

Maxwell retrieved a knife and took it and the rat out back. He placed them on the picnic table and started a fire in the small round pit just outside his door. The chain links of the barbed wire fence surrounding his backyard flickered from the firelight, but otherwise he was bordered by darkness. He suspended the rat over the flames by snout and tail and twisted his fingers to rotate it, filling the air with the sour stench of burning rat hair and revealing the skin. Once the hair was gone he transferred it back to the table and took the knife in hand.

He opened the stomach with a quick and precise incision, then proceeded to gut the corpse. The innards he placed onto the floor of a rusty steel cage near the fence. It was rigged to shut on entry, and lured mostly skunks, raccoons or rats, but occasionally a fox or dog, the meat of which was, in Maxwell's opinion, far superior to rodent. He returned to the fire and once more held the rat over the flames, now to cook. Five minutes at most, or until the flesh turned from pinkish gray to black, then he set it down on the table. It was then, as he prepared to kick dirt onto the fire, that he saw movement out of the corner of his eye, and a young woman detached herself from the shadows.

"I can pay you," she said.

Maxwell kept a gun in his pocket at all times—a small yet effective Smith & Wesson pistol stolen during the early days of the end of the world—and he took it into his hands now, but didn't point it at her. Not yet. He could see she was weak and in poor health. Her coat and pants were filthy, hung loosely from her flesh. A green glove on her left hand seemed to hover in the firelight. Her right hand was bare. Maxwell took a single step in her direction. "How did you get in here?" he said. She lifted an arm and he saw where her jacket was torn at the elbow. Blood stained the fabric. "You climbed my fence? What did you think would happen?"

She clasped her hands as if in prayer. "Please," she said. "For some rat, I can pay."

"With what? Your jacket is ruined and I have no need for half a pair of gloves. I wouldn't take them anyway, considering the diseases you might have."

"I'm not sick," she said.

"And I'm to take your word?"

"I...." Tears glistened under her eyes. Her face softened in defeat. Maxwell had seen that look so often from the desperate. She began to unzip her coat.

"Stop that," said Maxwell.

"Please," she said, and with her coat unzipped began to work at the button on her pants, fumbling pathetically. "I have nothing else to give."

"Christ's sake, stop. It's cold enough out here as it is."

She paused, and then zipped the coat back up. Maxwell had not missed the purple bruises briefly exposed on her neck. "I have nothing else to give," she repeated.

Maxwell sighed, returned the gun to his pocket, and rubbed his face with his hands. The woman watched as he kicked dirt onto the fire until it was only embers. He lifted the rat from the table by the tail and it swung like a pendulum from his fingers. With a nod of his head he indicated the back door to his house. "Come in," he said.

2

After washing the wound on her arm and wrapping it with gauze, they ate the rat underneath the watchful eyes of the animals, in silence and by candlelight. She ate timidly, her arms and legs pulled in close and her head leaned forward to bite at the meat, like a squirrel with an acorn.

He'd lit a small fire in the fireplace with twigs collected around the city. They fizzed and popped and filled the room with the faint scent of sewage. But the fire was warm.

When all that remained was bone and sinew, Maxwell asked, "Do you like Beethoven?"

"Is that what's playing?" She gestured to one of the speakers, but didn't lift her eyes much further than the floor. She had yet to acknowledge the dead things in the room, and Maxwell was content to let it lie in the back of her mind until she remarked upon them on her own. He had given her fresh clothes from his dead wife's closet. Already the wound had bled through the gauze onto the fabric of the blue sweater.

"His fifth symphony. It's quite famous." He poured more water for them both from a dirty pitcher.

"I recognize it," she said. She closed her eyes. "A movie I saw when I was a kid, I think."

"*Fantasia 2000*, maybe," said Maxwell. "The film opened with it."

"Yes," she said, quietly. "That was it."

He closed his own eyes now, allowing the symphony to enrapture him. Oh, how dearly Maxwell loved Beethoven. He loved to share the music with others, to watch it transform them. But more than anything Maxwell loved to perform Beethoven's piano sonatas. To give the gift of such beautiful music, such human music, back when there were people to appreciate it. Now the world was too lost or hungry or feral to care. He sighed longingly and, remembering his guest, opened his eyes. She was staring at him. Her figure flickered in firelight. He said, "Beethoven described the first movement of this symphony as fate knocking at your door."

She turned away. "You have generators."

"Not many more," he said. "Just the one here, and another in my studio. I scavenged them when this all began. The initial looting was madness—"

"I remember."

"—and rather than focus on televisions or cars or whatever it was most idiots went for, I hoarded essentials. Food, supplies, and of course, generators." He sighed. "Seems so long ago now ... but they lasted this long. That much I'm thankful for." Maxwell rose from his chair and tossed more sticks onto the fire. "What is your name?" he asked.

"Amelia."

"Maxwell." He returned to his chair, sat, and gazed at the woman seated across from him. A dark purple bruise stained her neck. "Why did you climb into my yard?"

"I'm sorry," she said. Her eyes traced the intricate pattern of Maxwell's rug. "I didn't know what else to do. I'd been staying in the third floor of the textile mill—on Sixteenth Street—but two days ago everyone died. Just like that. It was like those first days all over again, when everyone was just ... dead." She looked up. "I was attacked earlier tonight." She pointed to the bruise on her neck. "They wanted my jacket, I think, but I managed to get away. I'd seen your fire before, in the night, and I...I was desperate."

"It's all right," he said. "You're safe here."

She leaned back in the chair. Maxwell noticed her shoes. The soles were worn thin but otherwise they were in decent condition. If he were to chase her he had no doubt she would outrun him. A gold wedding band twinkled on her ring finger.

"Were you married?" he asked.

She was caught off guard. He wondered when she had last been asked such a personal question. When, even, had she last had a normal conversation? She regarded Maxwell with a look of uncertainty, as if it were by some mystical force that he should know of her marriage, like he were a psychic being, but blinked and then covered the ring with her other hand. "I am," she said. "Was. Before."

"He didn't make it?"

And it was that question that forced her to look somewhere new, to escape, and to focus on, at last, Maxwell's work. She wiped at her nose, pointed to a red-haired fox posed on a stand atop one of several bookcases that flanked the room. "Is it real?"

"Of course it is."

"I mean," she said, "is it a real animal?"

"Yes." Maxwell stood and walked to the bookcase. He lit a candle to give them a better view of the fox. Its shadow strobed and stretched along the wall. "I caught this one in the trap out back."

She put a hand over her mouth. "You stuffed it?"

"And most of the rest." He lifted the candle and walked about the room. Animals of all types were scattered throughout. Near one wall was an African Genet Cat, another a Corsican Sheep. Along the windows were a handful of separate owl breeds. And rats. The rats were everywhere. Black beady eyes shined out of the spaces between books, the shadows beneath chairs; all of them watching.

"It's unsettling," she said, and stood.

"They're very dead, I assure you. It's just the skin. The older ones—the sheep, for instance—have a higher quality stuffing than the others, but these days I make due with what I have."

Amelia stepped over to the CD player and admired a spotted cheetah. "This one is beautiful," she said. "I prefer it much more than that." She pointed with disgust to a Russian Hog's head where it was mounted above a brown leather couch.

"The cheetah was a gift from a collector," said Maxwell. "The hog, however, I made in 1997."

"Were you a hunter?"

"Not then. But I knew many, and have always found myself drawn to the art—taxidermy I mean. Now more than ever we must preserve the beauty of life even after death. I do that for them much the way a recording holds still the musician's creation long after he is gone."

Amelia nodded, though Maxwell believed the connection was lost on her. No one ever saw it the way he did. She walked the length of the room and arrived at Maxwell's piano. "Do you play?" she asked.

Maxwell smiled. "Wonderfully," he said without modesty.

Amelia betrayed the tiniest hint of laughter, and in the light of the fire suddenly looked quite pretty, and Maxwell thought that with time and rest the bruise on her neck might heal nicely.

Amelia tugged up the neck of the sweater, hiding most of the bruise. She stepped away from the piano to sit on the couch below the hog's head, her face now tight, the laughter gone. She had let herself grow comfortable, and to do that in a stranger's home was a deadly thing. Maxwell couldn't blame her.

He switched off the record player, sat at the piano and performed for Amelia Beethoven's 8th piano sonata, *Pathétique*. He performed it with verve and excitement, looking, digging, clawing for that old feeling. The hush of a thousand voices. The eyes, human eyes, watching him from the seats of a packed concert hall. It wasn't the same here, even if he had someone living to perform for. As he played, he felt the weight of how very long it had been.

3

Maxwell brought a CD of Beethoven's piano sonatas, as performed by the great Alfred Brendel, to his studio. There was a second generator in the studio, and he switched it on, then shut the door. He preferred to work in solitude. Amelia had seemed tired after he'd performed for her, and so he'd offered her his bed for the night. He would sleep on the couch. She accepted the kindness without argument and was now asleep in Maxwell's room.

Where he was frugal with the candles elsewhere, in the studio he lit several—five on the tool shelves, six on the work table, and four taller ones set on pedestals at each corner of the room. He never used batteries or the generators for light, only for music. The fireplace and a few sparse candles suited him well in the living room.

He separated one of the remaining rats from the pack and made an incision down the length of the its spine with a scalpel. The skin from neck to hip split like a parting eyelid. He eased two fingers into the wound and maneuvered them around the torso, and with one quick hooking motion popped the torso from the skin. It fell to the table. The legs required the flesh to be rolled down to the ankles, like removing a sock, before snipping the leg bones at the hip joint, maintaining a skin connection while only severing the bone. The foot bones he kept inside for extra support when displayed. Next, he peeled the stomach from the body, working down to the tail first. Removing the tail was not unlike removing one's arm from a sweater; go too fast and it might turn inside out. Maxwell, by now, was an expert, and he guided the bone out with ease, then began to pull the skin up toward the head. The ears he detached with the scalpel, cutting them away and leaving behind only the round holes of the ear canal. Then he cut away the eyelids, which allowed him to peel the skin even further, at last exposing the snout all the way to the tip. The snout was detached by breaking it at the nose, freeing the skin entirely from the body. With his thumb he rubbed the remaining nose bones from the soft skin of the snout, and then placed the skin flat beside the remains of the body.

The final movement of Beethoven's sonata, "*Appassionata*", in F minor, began to play.

Maxwell leaned back on his stool and heaved a sigh of satisfaction. He sipped water, smearing blood along the glass, and then repeated the procedure four more times.

4

He watched Amelia sleep from the darkness of his doorway. Her face sunk into the pillows, accented in cool moonlight. In the morning he would ask her to stay. She had nowhere else to go. He quietly eased the door shut, put on his coat, and left the house.

It was past midnight, the air considerably colder now. He kept his hands shoved deep into his pockets, the right hand caressing the muzzle of his gun, until he arrived at the large cracked doors of the Jonathan Louis Symphony Hall. Once—in a heyday that ended long before the world did—Maxwell had performed here to a sold out crowd of the dignified. This sanctuary of the arts now lay unappreciated by all but him. Inside he found a man sprawled on the floor. The man saw him, and Maxwell stopped and took out his gun. "This place belongs to me," he said to the man.

"There are people in there," the man whispered. He made no move to get up. "So many people."

"There are no more people," said Maxwell, "only humans," and he shot the man through the teeth.

On a ticket counter he found the candle he'd left behind on his last visit and lighted it. Two large oak doors separated the atrium and main auditorium, and Maxwell stepped through them into utter darkness, save for the orange orb of his candle. Eyes forward, he walked carefully down the incline of the stadium seats and then up the polished wood stairs to the stage. His footsteps echoed as he walked to the grand piano at center stage. The sound made it feel as if the room stretched on forever. He placed the candle on the floor.

The auditorium was black. Some time ago he had placed candles along all of the balconies and in all of the walkways, but he would not light them tonight. He wasn't ready. The crowd was not complete, but in the darkness around him his mind could see it all; the faces tight with anticipation, many of them here—he was sure—for the first time in their lives. Neophytes deserving of a perfect performance, a performance to be remembered long after the final note was played, that rang eternally in their minds. *A night of Beethoven's Sonatas, as performed by Maxwell Lake.*

He lifted the fallboard. The clack of wood on wood was sharp and satisfying. He lowered his fingers to the keys blindly, ran them gently back and forth, compressed each key lightly, but not far enough to strike. He thought that maybe he could perform tonight, at long last, he could, and his heart beat quickly, wildly. His hands twitched—but no; from the corner of his eye he saw the hint of bare red at the end of the front row. The mocking gaze of that remaining empty seat. He turned his head to confront it but the candle dimmed and it was gone.

He shined alone on the stage, and all around him was black.

Maxwell lowered the fallboard. He took the candle into his hands and stepped down from the stage.

A thousand eyes watched him impatiently.

"I regret to inform you," he whispered, "that I must delay my performance once more." He held the candle so that he could not see any of the seats. Shame washed over him. "I—" The candle blew out and Maxwell shrieked.

He fled from the auditorium, feeling his way along the walkways in the dark, careful not to trip over anyone's feet.

5

"I believe," she said one evening, interrupting Maxwell's piano practice by leaning against the keys and talking straight into his face, "that one day things will go back to normal."

She had been with him for a week. The morning after she first arrived Maxwell had awakened to find her gone, and, certain she had foolishly returned to the mill on Sixteenth Street, was about to go out and look for her when she returned, informing him she had only gone out for fresh air. He accepted her story readily, but knew that fear had driven her to flee. She had returned because she realized that if she did not she would die. Everyone she once knew was gone, and there would almost certainly not be any others to take her in.

Only him.

His concentration destroyed, Maxwell left the piano and sunk into a chair. "I completely disagree," he said. "We—you and I—may very well be the last two *sane* humans alive. When we die, that's it. It's over."

She paced the room, occasionally running a hand along one of the animals, though never the rats. If she had taken notice of the new one that Maxwell had placed beside the bed in his room, she'd not yet mentioned it. "I can't afford to think that way. There must be other people out there. But if there aren't—and I mean this in a purely survival sense—I think it falls on us to consider repopulation strategies."

Maxwell, having taken a glass of water to his lips, choked. "You can't be serious?"

She looked down at him. "Why wouldn't I be?"

Maxwell fumbled, then said, "You're married!"

"To a dead man." She twirled the ring on her finger. "Can a dead man repopulate the world?"

"Maybe I was mistaken," said Maxwell. "Perhaps *I* am the only sane human left alive."

"If there are others with even half a brain left they'll be doing the same thing. I don't care if you find me repulsive. Honestly, I find *you* repulsive, you and all your disgusting dead animals all over your house. It sickens me. It worries me. You worry me. But there's no one else, and we can—"

Maxwell held up a finger. "I do not find you repulsive," he said. "I think you are a fine, beautiful young woman. But I must listen to the voice of reality here. It would be useless. Our child would be born here in the house—unsafely, I might add—and when we died, because we *will* die, who would take care of it? It would starve to death or be eaten by stray dogs in days."

The conversation continued in much that way for over an hour, until Maxwell prepared a rabbit from the cage out back for dinner. They ate in silence before retiring to bed: her to his room, he to the couch.

From his doorway, in a long purple robe that once belonged to his wife in a time that, perhaps, had never existed, Amelia beckoned him. "It's cold tonight," she said. "Sleep in here with me."

Maxwell held a candle to her face. "Your neck is looking better," was all he said before turning his back on her and walking to the couch.

6

He dreamed of his wife, of the morning he found her dead in the kitchen, the French press shattered on the porcelain, her pale legs sprawled from her robe in a broken V. In the dream he stared at her, frozen in time, and the first thought to swim through his mind was of the children they never had. They'd waited too long. He got a broom and swept up the glass around her face robotically, and then he sat beside her, holding her hand until he could summon the courage to call an ambulance. He knew that when he did there would be no turning back. It would be real.

As he picked up the receiver to dial (a call that would yield no answer, though when this first occurred he could not know that) that the dream diverged; there was Amelia stepping into the kitchen, naked except for a single green glove. She looked down at the body and then up at him. Her eyes pooled with pity. Then, crouching, she began to work his wife's body from the robe. She stood, covered herself with it, and, weeping, left the room.

No one was answering the other end of the phone. Maxwell hung up, then scooped his wife into his arms. He felt a presence at his back. He looked over his shoulder—

—and woke.

He was on the couch. Gauzy moonlight filled the room.

His body ached. It creaked and popped as he twisted himself to his feet.

Why dream of Amelia? Why her? She was, of course, the only woman he'd spoken with for any length of time in years, and possibly her presence here in the house was affecting him in ways he hadn't been prepared for. He feared that perhaps he might come to rely on her being there. It would do him no good to rely on another human. The only way to survive in the new world was on your own, doing what you love for as long as you could. To remember what it was like to live before.

Anything else could get you killed.

He walked down the hall and looked into his room. Amelia was awake, sitting up on the bed—a phantom in sparse moonlight. Her head turned.

"I was an artist, before," she said.

Maxwell stood unmoving in the doorway.

"A painter."

"Portraits?"

"Sometimes," she said. "Mostly landscapes, still lifes."

"Do you miss it?"

"I miss having beautiful things to paint. Where are the beautiful things now?"

Maxwell stepped softly into the room and over to the window. Her eyes followed him. Outside the moon was bright and the world had taken on the color and consistency of chalk. "You, Amelia. You are a beautiful thing," he said.

They were silent for a while, Maxwell watching the city, Amelia watching him. She spoke first. "I was at the airport the first day," she said. "I remember eating crappy fast food and thinking about how much I hated airport food, of all things, when everyone started falling over. I watched from one of the windows as a plane that had just taken off fell straight down again. It wasn't until I saw the flames on the runway that it all began to click, and I tried to find Ray—my husband. He was at our gate. He..." She was crying. "I had to leave him there. People were running out of the airport. Where did they think they were going? I didn't want to leave him, but someone grabbed me and told me to run. They thought it was a terrorist attack. So I did. I left him there." She wiped at her face with the duvet. "Made my way back to the city with some guy who didn't even speak English. I was terrified." She got out of the bed and stood behind Maxwell at the window. "Where were you?"

Maxwell's breath fogged on the pane. "Performing," he said. "It happened sometime in the middle. When I'd finished there was the softest whisper of applause, and I looked into the crowd to find my wife there, clapping. She had a look on her face of absolute fury. I'd never seen her so mad. Why was no one else clapping, she was thinking. How could they be so rude? There were maybe a hundred people clapping throughout the hall, and slowly they all stopped. That was when it began to sink in for us, when we knew something was wrong."

Amelia pressed her body against his. He felt her breasts against his back. "I wanted to apologize," she said, "for what I said about your animals. It's not repulsive. It's just ... different, but isn't everything? I can respect it." She paused. "I can respect you. You've taken me in, given me shelter. I shouldn't have gotten upset. It's just ... I don't know how much more of this I can take. The not knowing. What happened? What's happening? Are people out there, beyond the city, making progress and bringing everything back to normal?"

Maxwell stepped back from the window, not forcefully, and left her there. He crossed the room to the door. Her phantom shape now glowed before the window, her arms outstretched just a little, silently asking him to return. "There are no people anymore," he said. "Only humans."

Then he left the room.

7

He woke to the hammering of rain. The house was dim. Clouds suffocated the daylight, muting it to gray. He sat up. On the table near the couch there was a drawing on a scrap of paper. Amelia, in the night, had sketched him as he slept. It was quite good, expressive and quick, and caught his likeness well. He took the sketch into his hands.

"Amelia?" he called to an empty house. He knew it was empty the moment the words left his mouth. After setting the drawing on the bookshelf, near the fox, he walked down to her room.

No, his room.

She wasn't there.

Maxwell checked the bathroom, his studio, and the living room again before taking a look in the kitchen, and through the door to the backyard.

She was there, standing naked in the rain, scrubbing her flesh with a bar of soap she'd taken from a closet. Maxwell watched her. She was, as he'd told her, very beautiful. Her skin had gained new color, and the bruise on her neck was gone, replaced by lush white skin. Amelia shivered in the deluge as she worked the soap through her hair.

She wouldn't want to be out in the cold rain too long, so Maxwell assumed she had only just begun her shower, and perhaps the sound of the closing door was what had stirred him from sleep. She would return soon, after a quick wash, to get dry.

From his coat where it was draped over a chair, Maxwell took his gun into his hands and stepped out into the rain. He was soaked through in an instant.

She saw him come outside and, despite the cold, a playful smile spread across her face. "No peeking!" she cried, laughing. This woman has grown used to me, he realized. The patina of caution was now entirely gone. "I hope you don't mind! I borrowed some soap!" She had to shout to be heard over the downfall.

Long rivers of soap suds spread through the yard like veins.

Maxwell had showered in the rain whenever possible. It was a terrible experience in the colder months, but necessary. Amelia had set the bar of soap onto the grass, and was squeezing the remaining suds from her hair. He thought, watching her bathe before him without a hint of shame, that there was a mystical quality to the scene. Like he'd stumbled upon a rare and precious treasure.

Something squealed from the steel cage in the yard. A raccoon. Amelia wiped water and soap from her eyes and looked to the cage.

Maxwell stepped forward. His foot sank into muddy earth. Rain battered his head, thundered within his skull.

Amelia brushed slick hair from her face, and saw the gun in Maxwell's hand. "Maxwell?" she shouted.

He pointed it at her.

She didn't move. Her lips trembled. Rain drops burst on her body.

"Maxwell," she said, this time a whisper. "Please..."

He shot her twice in the stomach. She curled forward, wrapped her arms across herself, and fell to her knees. Her eyes never left his. She toppled sideways and lay with her knees pressed up toward her chest, like an infant.

Maxwell set the gun down and went to her. He knelt and took her hand into his. Her mouth widened to an O, then clasped tight, pressing the color from her lips, then widened again. It did this over and over. She extended her legs, then brought them up tight to her chest. She tried to pull her hand from his, but Maxwell's grip was tight.

The veins of sudsy water turned red as Amelia bled out in the rain, and died.

He carried her limp body into the house to his studio and lowered it gently onto the work table. Her arms bobbed over the edge.

With a flip of the switch the generator hummed to life; *Pathétique* filled the studio.

Tenderly, Maxwell Lake ran a towel over her flesh until it was dry, the last spots of blood wiped away. Then he gathered his tools and set them out beside her body.

T is for Taxidermy

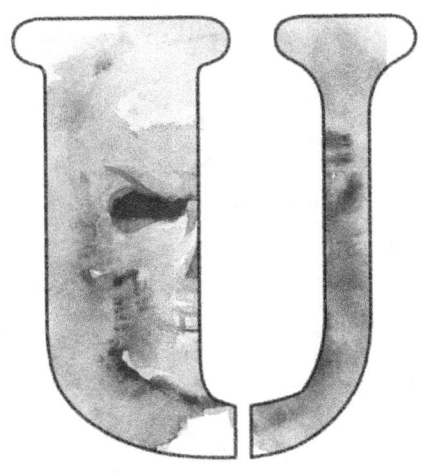

Damien Angelica Walters

"Motherhood: All love begins and ends there."
Robert Browning

Fourteen days until impact:

I can't stop watching the clock. It's stupid, I know.
Nothing's going to happen tonight, but still I find my eyes
drawn to the clock again and again. I'm trying to keep a brave
face for Millie, trying to pretend everything is fine and normal,
but she knows *something* is wrong. She may only be five, but
she's far from stupid.

Does it make me cruel, does it make me a bad mother to
want to make these last weeks for Millie something close to
normal? Something peaceful?

If we lived in a big city, it would be impossible. The news is
full of reports on the riots, the looting, the panic, the people
who are trying to run away, but this thing is too big to run
from. There is no running, no moving anywhere that's safe.

We're all in a future dead zone. All of us. The end. Extinction. Just like the dinosaurs.

Trust me. If any of the research I'd done had given me even the slightest bit of hope that someplace was safe, I would've done whatever I had to do to get us there, even if I'd had to plan on going to Antarctica.

But that's the worst part of this whole thing. I can't do anything. The clock keeps ticking and every second is a second less that we have.

☠

Millie and I take our morning walk a little after breakfast—me, toast and coffee; she, waffles smothered in maple syrup. Our closest neighbor, a quarter mile away, Mr. Theodore James, a cranky old bastard if I ever met one, is sitting and smoking on his porch as always, his mutt, Trixie, by his side. Trixie gets up, does her crazy shake, and pads down to the end of driveway to smother Millie in sloppy kisses.

"Mommy, we can still get a dog when I start school, can't we?"

I try to reply, feel the catch in my throat, and swallow hard. "Uh-huh." I blink back tears, hating this momentary weakness. Millie doesn't notice, thankfully; she's too busy rubbing Trixie behind the ears and burying her face in the dog's black and white fur.

"Crying over things you can't change is for fools," my mother always said. I hated hearing those words each and every time, but lately they keep running through my head, and sometimes I think they're the only things holding me together. The words and Millie. Always Millie.

"I want a dog just like you, Trixie," Millie whispers.

I wave our goodbyes (no reason to be rude on account of not liking someone; another one of my mother's sayings) and we walk on down to the end of the road. It almost feels like a normal morning in our little speck of a town here in the Midwest. And yes, the town is that small. We have one gas station, no traffic lights, and you have to drive over an hour just to get to the Interstate.

Millie and I live in the house I grew up in, a house I inherited from my parents after they were killed by a drunk driver while visiting my mother's sister in Tulsa. I wish they'd had a chance to meet Millie, but she didn't come around until I turned twenty-nine; by then they'd been in their graves for seven years.

Millie and I get to the end of the road and turn around. Mr. James and Trixie are already inside when we pass their house again.

Ten days until impact:

On the outside, I'm all smiles as I cut the crusts from Millie's grilled cheese sandwiches, all hugs when I dry her off after her bath.

Inside, I feel like I'm melting, like my puzzle pieces are falling apart and there isn't enough glue in the world to hold them together, but I'm trying.

I'm trying so hard.

And the clock keeps ticking.

Seven days until impact:

The days pass slowly, but still they go too fast. I've kept Millie occupied with books and crayons and walks up and down our street, but it's all like a dream, one of those dreams where everything is perfectly fine, but you know something bad is waiting right around the corner.

There's a part of me that wants desperately to cling to a miracle, a maybe it won't really happen, a maybe it will somehow pass us by, no matter how many calculations have been done.

I think about all the disaster movies, how there's always a master plan or a lottery, something that gives people hope. Real life isn't like that. There are lots of people who claim they'll survive in their underground shelters, and there's a big conspiracy theorist who claims the government has built something and only a handful of people know about it, the same people, presumably, who are going to spend the rest of their lives there.

Maybe it's true. Who knows? For the rest of us, though? There is no rest of our lives. There are only days. Take shelter (as if a roof can protect anyone from what's going to happen or what's going to happen *after*), have a surplus of food, and pray. That's the prevailing message. And all the while, they talk about the stages of impact: contact and compression, excavation, and modification and collapse.

Crying over things you can't change is for fools.

"Mommy?"

I look up from the book we were reading, realizing I stopped, lost in my tangle of thoughts.

"I'm sorry, babygirl. Mommy was woolgathering."

She giggles. "You're silly sometimes."

"I'm silly? Nope, nope, nope, you're silly."

I tickle her sides until she's giggling and twisting in my arms, then I tickle her feet and she shrieks with laughter. I want to capture the sound and hold it forever, no matter how short that forever is. When she finally wriggles free from my grasp, she plops onto her stomach and props her chin in her palms.

"Can we go to the grocery store tomorrow?"

I laugh, but it feels like broken glass in my throat.

"We could if we needed anything, but we don't. Remember how Mommy bought extra food?"

"Uh-huh."

"We have enough so we don't need to go to the store for a while."

She quirks up her face. "Can we go visit Miss Karen?"

I take a deep breath. Too smart; she's too smart. When I speak, I force my voice to stay even. Controlled. "Don't you remember? Miss Karen went to visit her daughter. That's why Mommy took off work."

"Will she be back soon?"

"Pretty soon. Hey, how about we finish this book?"

"O-kay."

She crawls up into my lap and I hold her close.

After I've tucked her into bed, I step out into the backyard. My father and I used to stargaze when I was only a few years older than Millie. He taught me the constellations, patiently pointing at each one until I could recognize the shapes without his help.

They were a link to something bigger, something *more*, but no longer. Now Orion's Belt mocks me with its precision; Cassiopeia with her beauty, a beauty that will remain even when no one's left to see.

Once a comfort, all of them, now my enemy.

Why, why, why?

I bite the inside of my cheek until I taste the coppery slickness of blood. I won't cry. I can't. If I start, I'm not sure I'll be able to stop and there's not enough time left for tears.

If not for Millie, I'd let them fall; I'd rage and scream and tear out my hair; I'd roll around and punch and kick like a toddler in the throes of a tantrum.

For the first time in a long time I think of Jack, my ex-husband. He left when I found out I was pregnant. His wish to have kids had turned out to be nothing more than hot air, like all the other promises he made. I shove the thoughts away hard and go back inside, careful not to slam the door.

Five days until impact:

I'm stirring cheese into the macaroni—funny how we haven't lost power; I thought for sure we would've by now—and staring at the clock when Millie tugs my sleeve.

"What's up, buttercup?"

She gives me a half-smile.

"Are you okay, Mommy?"

"Of course I am. Why?"

"You seem sad."

I force a smile on my face, but my fingers tighten around the handle of the wooden spoon. "I'm perfectly fine, just a little tired. How about you?"

"I'm okay."

"Hungry?"

She smiles then, a real smile. "Uh-*huh*."

"Good, because there's too much here for me to eat by myself."

My gaze flicks to the clock again and even when I turn away, I feel it counting down the seconds, the minutes, the hours, the *lives*.

I'm almost asleep when I hear the sound, something sharp and quick that echoes itself away, and I know exactly what it is—a gunshot. I'm out of the bed in a flash. I peek in on Millie, but she's still sleeping. My heart races when I run downstairs to check the locks on the windows and doors. Funny, I never worried about that before. I don't think anyone here will do anything and it's not like we're on the way to anywhere, but better safe than sorry.

I stay up for a long time, but I don't hear anything other than the steady hum of the refrigerator and the creak of the house settling deeper into its bones.

Four days until impact:

"Mommy, it's Trixie! Trixie's here!"

"What?"

"Trixie is here on the porch."

Sure enough, Mr. James' dog is on our front porch, pacing in strange erratic circles, her tongue hanging from her mouth; then I see the blood on her front paw, and my mouth goes dry.

I crouch down, put my hands on Millie's shoulders, and look her in the eyes. "Honey, I need you to stay inside for a few minutes while I go check on Mr. James, okay?"

"Can't I come with you?"

"No, because I can go faster by myself."

"But I can be fast, too."

"No." The word comes out sharper than I wanted it to, and her face twists. I take a deep breath. "I need you to be a big girl for Mommy, okay? Why don't you play with your toys for a few minutes? I promise I'll be super fast and we'll have breakfast when I get back."

"Okay."

I lock the door, and I'm already halfway to a run when I shove the key in my pocket, Trixie following at my heels.

Mr. James' front door is partly open, propped open with a rock that matches the rocks surrounding the flower beds around his porch. I leave Trixie outside and push the rock out the way so she can't nose her way in.

I find Mr. James in the living room, sitting in a recliner, and for a split-second I think, pretend, he's sleeping. But there's a spray of blood on the wall behind him, bloody paw prints all around, and part of his head is gone. And on the floor beside the chair, a gun.

I sink to my knees, holding both hands over my mouth. *Don't fall apart,* I tell myself. *Not over this. Millie needs you to be strong, so be strong.*

I'm not sure who I should call first, and then I make a sound in my throat, a sound that might be a strange sort of laughter. Call someone? And for what? Mr. James didn't have any family that I know of, only Trixie, and I'm not going to bother anyone in town, not now. But I can't just leave him like this so I grab a blanket from his linen closet and cover him up, careful not to breathe too deep, not to look too close.

When I pull the door shut behind me, Trixie whines and does the strange circle-pace again, but she follows me back. The gun tucked in the back of my jeans feels wrong, feels like a weight of why, but better to put it away somewhere safe rather than leave it lying out in the open.

Millie is waiting in the front hallway; I put on a smile that feels too small and too tight.

"Trixie is going to stay with us for a little while. How does that sound?"

Millie grins, but there's a funny little pause right before she does.

We discover Trixie likes human food just fine and after a bath with the baby shampoo I use for Millie, I let her climb up on the sofa. Millie doesn't ask about Mr. James until I tuck her in for bed.

"He, he went away for a few days, and he knew you'd take good care of Trixie while he's gone."

"But how come he didn't knock on the door? Why did he just leave her outside?"

"I think because he knew we were asleep and Trixie was fine. Remember how she always used to sit on *his* porch?"

Trixie jumps up on Millie's bed and sprawls out beside her, tail going a mile a minute. After I kiss Millie goodnight, she grins.

"You have to kiss Trixie too."

I do. The dog's tail nearly spins in a circle.

"Another kiss for me?"

"Of course."

I kiss her forehead softly, trying not to cry, not to think.

When I'm halfway to the door, Millie says, "Wait."

I spin around and she's holding out her favorite teddy bear. "Here, you keep Teddy tonight. I have Trixie now so I don't need him."

I stand outside her door with the bear clutched to my chest and a knot inside me. This isn't fair.

It isn't fair.

Three days until impact:

"How about you sleep in my room tonight?"

"And Trixie too?"

"Okay, Trixie can sleep there too."

Two days until impact:

"Why don't we make your favorite cake tonight?"

"Pineapple smushside down cake?"

"The very same one."

"Can we have it for dinner?"

"Cake for dinner?"

"Uh-huh. Cake for dinner."

She giggles and Trixie barks.

The three of us have cake for dinner. And for dessert.

One day until impact:

"Mommy, is something bad coming?"

"Why would you think that?"

She shrugs and my heart drops. "It feels that way I guess," she says, her voice little more than a whisper.

My fingernails dig half-moons in my palms. "It's a bad storm, that's all."

She turns back to her coloring book and I'm frozen in place, the lie like ashes in my mouth.

Three hours until impact:

I slip out of bed once Millie is fast asleep and open the top drawer of my bureau. The gun is tucked all the way in the back, underneath a nightgown I haven't worn in years.

Millie is on her side with one hand beneath her cheek; Trixie is a small snoring ball at her feet. I wonder if Mr. James knew she'd come to us or maybe he just didn't care.

My hand shakes as I brush the hair away from Millie's forehead. A kindness, then, to end the waiting? To give our story a definite end and not a maybe? We're at the edge of the impact zone; from everything I've read, the end will be fast. The people left will suffer through the end of everything else.

Unless something changes, unless some of the calculations are wrong, and we're one of the latter.

All I have to do is press the barrel to the side of her head, then to mine, and our stars will wink out. No chance of suffering, of starving, of dying in pain.

Trixie lifts her head, gives a little whine. I cover my mouth, stagger over to the bureau, shove the gun back in the drawer. No. I can't. I won't. Not like that.

Not like that.

My hands are still shaking when I sink down on the sofa. If it were just me, I wouldn't care. It wouldn't hurt. But Millie will never get to start school, never be a teenager, never go on a date or drive a car. She'll never have a chance to grow up. She'll never have a chance to be anything other than a five year old girl.

I double over, my mouth open in a silent O. The concrete in my heart gives way beneath the weight of all the nevers and my dam shatters. The tears come in a rush, hot and angry, and they hurt, God do they hurt. I bury my face in a throw pillow to muffle the sound.

Damn God, damn everyone. It wasn't enough. I want more. I want to see her sixth birthday; I want to see her wave goodbye as she gets on the school bus; I want her to lose her first tooth and wake to find a present from the Tooth Fairy beneath her pillow.

I want so much. I want everything.

Crying over things you can't change is for fools, I tell myself, but I can't listen to the words because once this night is over, I'll never see Millie again and if that isn't worth crying about then nothing is.

"Mommy?"

I scrub the tears from my face and bite back the sobs as I turn around. She's standing in the doorway, holding something at her side, something partially obscured by the dog.

"I'm sorry, I didn't mean to wake you up."

I turn my face and wipe away the rest of the tears. I hear a rustle and a click. She's standing beneath an open umbrella, the white fabric covered in bright pink polka dots. In spite of the lump in my chest, I can't help but smile.

"What's that for?"

"For the storm, remember?"

For a few moments, I can't remember how to breathe. Finally I nod and pat the sofa next to me. "Well, come on then. Let's sit here for a little while."

"Till the storm's over?"

"Yes. Until the storm's over."

I hold the umbrella while she curls up beside me and scoots under my arm. Trixie takes the cushion next to her. I close my eyes and kiss the top of Millie's head, breathe in the smell of her hair and her skin, and hold her tight beneath the umbrella while we wait for the storm to pass.

U is for Umbrella

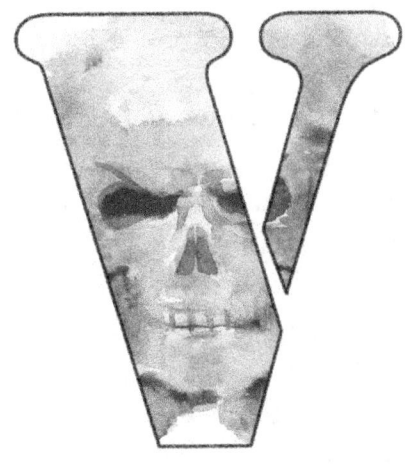

Samantha Kymmell-Harvey

Footsteps awaken me from my nightmare. The cries I hear in my sleep are old now, ancient perhaps. I'm safe for now.

I feel as though I ought to stop holding my breath. But then I remember I have no breath. No heart either. Not anymore. The layers of dust have dulled my senses but not my fear. Do the others here feel the same as I do? Their pages envelop mine like fingers clasped. I am not alone. We are bound together.

A fiery blaze breaks my darkness. It glides silently in the distance like a flickering ghost. Will they torch us for fuel like they did the rest?

Light feet patter across the tile floor below me. Over the shelf's edge, I can barely make out the edge of a small, black outline. It comes closer to us, its warmth emanating through the corners of my brittle skin. That torch I feared is only a candle, and a dying one at that. I now see who has come — a child, her dark hair hanging in ropes around her pale face.

Happiness fills my non-existent heart for the first time since I can remember. Find us. Hold us. Read us.

The city generator sputtered and shrieked, rattling the windows of the abandoned library. The electric lights fizzled out then relit, settling on a dim yellow glow. I jumped and swallowed my vomit back. It burned my dry throat.

"Hurry," I said.

The scriptor nodded as he glanced at his biblo-tablet before turning back to the skin stretched on the easel before him. He steadily applied his stylus to the vellum. Its sound scratched at my ear drums as he wrote. Cringing, I turned my attention to the freckles. The way they dappled the surface made it look like marble, like something that had never been alive. But it had lived. I'd know that pink birthmark anywhere. That skin once belonged to my sister, Johanna.

"Don't you know how to spell?" I said as he leaned into his biblo-tablet again. The battery was already blinking in the upper right hand corner.

The scriptor pressed his lips together. "I doubt you'd do much better with these scientific words. Latin has long since vanished. Now hush, Zoe."

The wooden frames stretched the skin like some sort of torture device. It moaned as the scriptor wrote. I watched him carefully form each loop, ascender, and descender, clearly not understanding the city generator was going to give out at any moment. He was running out of time to finish my sister's pages!

I knew why Johanna wanted to donate her skin to the botany text, but did it not occur to her to ask this scriptor his knowledge of Latin or even of plants? Maybe Mom should have come to tell him stem from stamen.

"So how many books do you have memorized?"

According to Johanna, the scriptors were historians who had started memorizing as many books as possible once we used up our trees.

"In the last 20 years I've donated to the Great Preservation, I have over 100 memorized," he said.

"And have many volunteers picked those books?" I stood and paced by the completed volumes, some thin, some thick.

He shrugged. "Some. It is the choice of the volunteer what he or she wants to preserve."

My hand stopped on a volume with a cover made of wiry hair. It prickled against my hand. This was not human hair. I picked it up and opened it. Even the skin was different, smooth on one side and speckled on the other.

"That's horse skin," said the scriptor. "We bought animal skins until the last animals were bought up and slaughtered for meat."

I closed the volume and placed it back on the shelf. The last of the fresh pork, chicken, and beef was consumed when Johanna was five or so. At least she got a taste of it. I wasn't even born yet. The chicken and beef I ate were grown in petri dishes in agri-labs to ensure maximum nutrition for the lowest production cost possible. It all tasted the same to me. Of course, there would be no more petri-pork after the fuel ran out. "Which is why you needed my sister."

The scriptor dipped his stylus in the porcelain inkwell. "We scriptors were the first volunteers for the Great Preservation. Others followed their hearts here."

The lights flickered again, but the candles on the tables around the scriptorium burned unaffected. I held my breath, prepared for the electricity to finally fail. The electric bulbs buzzed defiantly back to life.

The other scriptors hunched over their desks, faces mere inches away from the vellum they were illustrating. I didn't get how they wasted their time pigmenting human skin when they ought to be considering their own survival. I'd made survival plans for me and Mom, and if it weren't for my stupid promise, I'd be at home preparing. Leave it to Johanna to force yet another sacrifice on me and Mom.

But the scriptors weren't ready at all. They hadn't even built a wall around the Peabody scriptorium. The only thing being constructed around here were books. Tents of human skin were stretched between empty bookshelves, waiting to be sliced into pages. Tables were littered with needles, thread, bindings, glue, and blades. Martyrs, all of them. Like Johanna. But I planned on living. A huff escaped my chest. "Can't you go any faster?"

The scriptor shook his head. "I've met plenty of others like you, Zoe," he said. "Survivalists. I'm surprised you're not out in the city with the rest, fighting for resources, building walls, and such."

"I promised Johanna I'd see her wishes through to the last sentence. So if you hurry up, I can go scout out water sources. I've got our mom to take care of. I'm all she has now."

The scriptor fought back a smile. "You're not much like your sister."

"Never have been."

"Your sister, like so many others, believes in preserving humanity's knowledge in the hopes that we can overcome this ending. Once the fuels are gone, electricity will fail, and all the e-books, e-cyclos, all our stories, history, science, all of it, will be lost. Surely you believe that is a cause worthy of the lives given?"

I kept my promise, Johanna, but does he have to be so preachy?

The heat from the torch warms my spine. I feel her fingers poking and exploring, rattling the other books on my shelf. Swirls of dust hover like clouds. And that's when I feel those thin, bony fingers clasp around me and yank us from our cradle.

Our spine crackles and groans as she peels us open. My instinct is to scream. Our skin has become so brittle now, I fear it will not hold the seeds I had sewn in countless years ago. As she leafs through the pages, the little seeds rub like grit between my skin. They are there for you, child. Be gentle.

The child holds the torch in my face, exposing me. I see nothing but a head with curls outlined in shadow. My reader has come alone. Where are the others? Are there others?

A sensation, like a daddy longlegs scrambling down my pages, makes me want to laugh and shiver. It is her fingers, smoothing my wrinkled vellum down. The granules of dirt tumble into my spine. If only I could laugh when tickled.

Read me. Read us.

The child snaps me shut. My pages sting. Hands lift me and I anticipate the cold metal shelf once more. But when I land, it is not the cold that greets me, but warmth. Fabric envelopes my sore spine like a sling. The child's legs bounce me against her hip as she runs.

"What if these books are never found? Or what if they're burned like all the paper ones were? We haven't solved how to keep people warm without fuel. Will all these volunteers' lives have been wasted?"

He didn't answer. His hand kept at its task. I watched as he leaned closer to my sister. The tip of his tongue lodged in the corner of his mouth, eyes squinting in the dim light. The scriptor paused only to compare his drawing of a root system with the one in his biblo-tablet. He'd detailed bushes of roses like the ones in Mom's garden, roots spanning beneath. Johanna's pink birthmark naturally tinted the buds. Even I had to admit that had been a clever choice of art on his part.

"Too bad they have thorns," I said. I'd snagged myself many a time on those bushes, but Johanna loved them. I think it's because she missed real trees, real nature as she called it.

The only trees I grew up with were the government's engineered kind, arborbots, mandated for city use. Every autumn, the leaves retracted instead of changing color. Johanna hated that, but I thought it was efficient.

The scriptor dipped his stylus in his inkwell. "I have faith that the right humans will find this library," he said. "When they are ready. These lives are not wasted. Every page you see here is the hope that we can still survive. Perhaps future generations will be able to make paper again."

He applied the fresh ink to labeling the parts of the tree and the roots, marking the water table lines.

"Are they all textbooks, like my sister?"

The scriptor shook his head. "Of course not. This is a library after all."

The lights flickered, bulbs sizzling. I gripped the edge of the table, teeth clenched, and started to rock. The sizzling ceased. The lights extinguished.

"That's it, isn't it?" I said, continuing to rock. The scriptors moved their candles closer as if nothing had really changed. I swallowed the bitter taste at the back of my throat.

"Have faith," my sister's scriptor said. "Hold this." He handed me the candelabra.

An electric pulse sizzled and popped as the lights came on once again, only this time they shone duller than the candles.

"What will you do when the generator fails?" the scriptor picked the stylus from the green-colored inkwell. "What do you live for?"

"I don't know." I shrugged. Nobody had ever asked me that before. I'd grown up being told that there was no future for me. In kindergarten, Miss Bell told us there were only four years of fuels remaining. In third grade, my only required class was basic survival. In fifth grade, Mr. Sawyer told us the Earth was on life support and would soon be unplugged, just as the animals already had been.

But what did I live for? Johanna knew what she lived for. I screamed at my sister the day she told our Mom that she was going to commit her skin to the scriptors. She was always such a martyr. Selfish. We were all we had, my sister, Mom, and me. At least Johanna had a choice whether to live or not. Dad never did.

The lights flickered then extinguished. Wrapped in the silence, my heart thumped in my ears. That same bitter taste gathered at the back of my throat. The circuits sizzled, as if to savor its last surge of energy. But it died. All was silent. The End had come.

I jumped when I heard it — a boom so loud it rattled the library windows shattering the weakened panes. I clutched the scriptor's hand, my nails digging into his swollen fingers We clung to one another as colored glass rained on us and pinged off the marble floor.

"What was that?" I whispered. Explosions echoed in the distance.

The scriptor shook his head. "It doesn't matter, it only makes our work here more urgent."

"I have to know." I clambered atop a bookshelf.

"You won't learn anything about out there from within here," he said.

Perched on the bookshelf, I looked out the gaping hole that had been a window minutes earlier. Rows of flames licked the city skyline. What had happened? My eyes stung, my knees weakened, and my calves ached with the jolt of loss.

The scriptor pulled me to my feet. "We cannot mourn yet, not when there is much work to be done." He handed me the candelabrum. "Hold the light close now," he said. "Our future relies on what I commit to skin."

Saliva gathered at the back of my throat. The acrid smell of electrical fire seeped in through the cracks in the glass. I settled in beside Johanna and held the edge of her skin between my trembling fingers. *Johanna, why did you abandon me to face this alone?*

But I wasn't alone. Mom was. I turned to the scriptor. "I'll be right back! I am going to get my Mom. We'll be safer here."

I ran.

They took turns passing me around, leafing through my pages with great hurry. The seeds still rubbed, lodged within me. I could see the curly-headed girl sitting cross-legged by the fire. There is a clumsily-shaped earthenware pot in her lap. Her hand plays in the dirt inside it. Her satchel leans against the stony wall. Are we in a cave? An old cottage?

A new set of hands hold me. They are large, calloused and rough. His fingers pinch one of my corners. And then I feel it. Underneath, something hot licks against my binding. The dry heat sears and curls my corners yet I cannot scream. He's going to burn us. This bearded man does not value the knowledge I contain, he just wants fuel for his fire. He wants warmth.

His cold fingers grip my skin and pull. The sickening sound of tearing echoes within as he rips me. No! Stop it! As he tilts me toward the flame, the seeds slide loosely downward. The flame singes my now dangling page. The End has come for me, for us, again.

And then I feel her dirty hands pluck me from my captor's. Before she closes me, I see him drop one of my pages into the small campfire at his feet. His face is red and bearded, his black eyes are narrow. The girl bends down and swipes her hand in the sand around the river stones encircling the fire. Three white seeds, slightly tanned, glisten in her hand.

If I could shout for joy and kiss that girl upon the cheek, I would, but I settle for an apology. *I lost faith, scriptor. You were right. The right kind of human found me, found us. Our secret lies in her hand.*

She runs again and we emerge from blackness into light. It blinds me. The ground glitters white. Frozen droplets soothe my burn wounds. Snow. I wish catching snowflakes on my pages was the same as catching them on my tongue. My sister and I used to.

Ah, my sister.

The child's grip tightens on me, fingers wet and chilled.

I darted between the crowds of people fleeing their homes. Some screamed, some held their babies to their chests, toddlers gripping their hands. Thieves were already at work, ransacking the abandoned homes. Arborbots and street lamps towered, black giants overseeing the chaos. Thick smoke rolled through the alleys spilling onto the streets. It burned my eyes. I blinked away the tears eyes as I coughed. I had to get Mom out of this chaos.

"Mom?" I pushed open the door of our row house. It moaned as it swung off the hinges, thudding against the wall. "Mom? Where are you?"

The flames outside bathed the hallway in an orange glow, casting long shadows on the walls. The steps creaked uneasily, shards of glass crunching under my feet as I ascended. "Mom?"

Maybe she'd been evacuated already. St. John's was just down on the corner. They'd have her.

"It's me!" My legs felt as if I had been at sea for ages. I forced them down the corridor, toward the heat and flames.

The bedroom door was open. The window gaped, glassless. And there was Mom, on the bed where I'd left her this morning. Her face frozen, marking the moment Baltimore exploded.

Shrapnel.

I didn't even think of shrapnel.

Flecks of crimson dotted her abdomen, scraps of glass and metal glinted in the sticky blood gathered at her neck her and sheet and nightgown were shredded.

I turned away, unable to scream. My stomach emptied itself at the foot of her bed. Tears and heat stung my eyes as I dropped to my knees. There was nothing I could have done. All that training, all that preparation, for nothing. She was gone. Johanna was gone. I buried my face into my sleeves and sobbed.

What did I have to live for now? I couldn't build a wall high enough, store away enough water or collect enough canned foods to shut the End out. And even if I could, what's the use of surviving if you can't even save the ones you love? I didn't want to hunker down behind barbed wire alone for the rest of my life. That's not living.

I teetered down the steps, Mom in my arms. She didn't weigh much. She'd stopped eating long ago, when she learned she'd be losing Johanna. So now they'd both left me. But I didn't have to be alone forever. Survival could mean something else. I stood and grasped the bedpost. I know what I live for.

I kicked the back door down and carried Mom to the place she loved best — her rose garden. And there, as screams echoed around me, smoke blotting out the End, I buried her. I plucked a rose, defiantly in bloom, and placed it on the mound of fresh earth. I knelt down, my scraped knee burned as the dirt mixed with my blood.

"Johanna and I," I said. "we're going to survive. Together." I plucked another fat pink rose. "For you, Mom." I tucked it into my coat pocket.

I wondered if the scriptor had ever seen a real rose before.

She stops running. Her chest frantically rises and falls against me. I can only see parts of the scene from where my pages are exposed.

Dull beige grass pokes through the layer of snow. The arborbots droop heavy with water, their wires poking out from the flaking bark.

The girl sets me down in the cold and begins to claw away at the snow and soil. Her breath is mist on the chilled wind, but she still digs.

Now the soil caked on her fingers is rich and dark. She fills her misshapen jars of clay with it. Then those dirty hands reach for me. My pages flutter as her fingers search through me. Then she stops, poking a finger at a page I know well. She smiles.

Plant the seeds, child. Make them grow.

She wiggles her fingers through the soil to make a small hole. I feel as though my pages could tremble in excitement as I watch her place the seeds in the jar.

Now we wait, child. We wait together.

When I entered the scriptorium, I found Johanna being marked for threading. Another scriptor measured her for binding.

"She's not finished though," I said, pointing the half-sentence in the lower right corner of her skin.

"I did the best I could," said the scriptor, running the pencil down the ruler. "This still fulfills Johanna's wishes."

The dim room began to twist and turn. I sat where I stood, bleeding knees stinging as I bent.

"When was the last time you were out there?" I said.

"Years," the scriptor said.

The skins didn't disgust me much anymore. In here was organization and peace. And love, even.

"I want to show you something." I took the rose from my pocket and laid it on the table beside my sister. The scriptor squeezed my shoulder.

"I'm sorry, Zoe."

"There is no life out there." I thought of Mom. Of Dad. Of the screaming faces, houses on fire. Of the blackness. "I want to finish Johanna's book." I placed a hand on her skin. "Our book."

The scriptor stopped and laid his blade on the table. "Are you sure?"

I nodded. "My mother's roses never died, not even in the dead of winter. I have faith we will be found, and when we are, they will rediscover our library of lost knowledge once again." I handed the rose to the scriptor. "Please dry this and press it into our pages. There are seeds inside."

Did Johanna feel the water in our binding like I did? I wish we could speak, after all, we are bound together by the same needle and thread. Do you see her, Johanna? The child waters her plants like a mother would nurse her child.

The girl cradles us in her arms. The sun warms my spine, the gentle wind ruffles our pages. She brings us back to the jar where she planted our seeds. No more snow holds the jar in its frozen grass, instead the spring muds have taken up the task.

The earth vibrates heavily. Footsteps jolt me. The girl sets her bucket down and scoops me up. She hugs me close and points at her jars.

The tall man with the bearded face emerges from where I cannot see. His arms are folded across his chest. His voice booms.

But my child holds me. Her heart flutters, its beating pulsing through my pages. She points at the jar.

He nears, face flushing red. His giant hands reach to steal us away from her. Her voice pierces the silence. "Look!"

He stops because he finally sees them, the green sprouts pushing up from the dark soil.

And he embraces us, spinning us around in the cold air.

Johanna! Look what we've done!

Soon, they all come to see the sprouts. They all come to hug the girl. They praise her and tousle her curls in their hands. She laughs.

I wish I could too.

We are hope, Johanna. You and I.

V is for Vellum

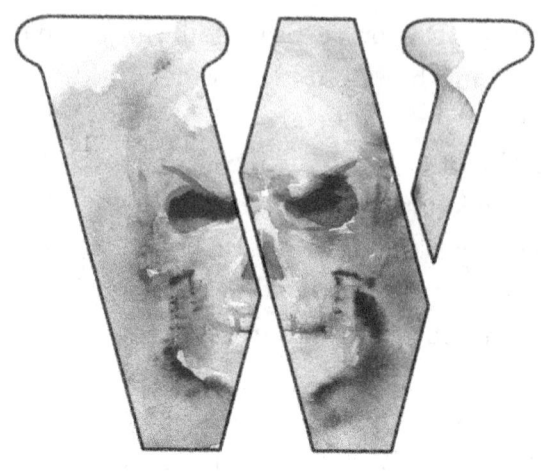

Lilah Wild

The sand between his toes, like flour. Warm and soft. That hadn't changed.

Nicky closed his eyes and hugged his knees to his chest. Willed himself, through filth and exhaustion, not to lose it now. There were no more rollercoaster screams joyfully pealing in the distance, no more appetizing scents of fried clams and funnel cake on the breeze. But there was still the beach, powder-fine and old as time. Nothing but shifting grains to steady himself on, but he'd take what he could get. Right now he had to calm down and focus on what remained. Not all was lost, he hoped. With all his heart.

The salt air was quiet, the town still raw with shock, struggling with the oceanic surge that had bashed its boisterous seashore face into oblivion. Behind him lay an aftermath that defied comprehension but demanded it from him constantly, and he needed a rest. Just a little one, before he fell over. Nicky closed his eyes and hugged his knees to his chest. Willed himself through the filth and the exhaustion not to lose it now. He ran his hands through his buzzed brown hair as he pushed his feet back and forth, back and forth, felt comforting old childhood tics crawl back into his nervous system and take over for just a few precious seconds before the current would twitch up again, push him back to an increasingly desperate search.

"Hey! Nicky!"

His already-clenched stomach turned into a pit of ice.

Sand flew into his lap, and he looked up. Jessabella stood before him in sweats just as dirty as his, curly black hair gathered back in a scrunchie, fingertips bearing remnants of hot-pink polish. All of fifteen, a neighborhood kid learning to shoulder the fresh new steel that had been snapped into her spine, the oldest of four and the one who had to be strong for all of them. Someone else trying not to lose it, even though she'd already lost.

"You haven't found Kristin."

He shook his head.

She dropped to her knees, ran an awkward yet kindly hand over his arm. "The pyre's at South Pier in an hour, they said."

He nodded once. "I'll be there."

"You know I'm praying for her, Nicky. And you too." She kissed his cheek and got up, started walking south towards what was left of her family.

Three days. Three awful, agonizing days. The evacuation was done with the tourists, then the locals, and had now finally reached the mourners. The families of the missing and deceased had been put last in line out of town, and the lighting of the pyre meant his time was up.

He'd be there, even though he didn't know yet if it was time to start grieving. One thing was for sure: it was time to panic.

☠

Even as a teenager, Nicky used to hate the boardwalk. It was obnoxious and gaudy, a hot, crowded tourist trap where people threw their money away on cheap prizes and got into fights. The game barkers smeared the air with free throws and insults to his manhood, oblivious parents rammed their strollers into his legs. Summers meant arguments over parking spots, car stereos booming maximized bass up the boulevard, and splashes of vomit along the sidewalk in the mornings. Grumpily, he'd come to find his place as a disdainful young man in an old-man bar tucked away in the side streets, far from the techno, a dim relic that smelled comfortingly of cigarettes and spilled beer and coastal history.

He did administrative work for the community college, and spent his days sketching, smoking up to marine-life documentaries and going on rambles through the nature walks — the quieter parts of the shore that drew scientists, not weekend warriors.

He'd chanced across an article in the biology lab about the conches and whelks sold in the gift shops — not naturally shed like he'd always thought, but the creatures inside disposed of, their beautiful homes stolen away for souvenirs. Up on the boardwalk, he reached into a bin of small pink murexes to investigate. Each lovely shell had been pierced with the telltale sign of the kill. And no one, not even him, had known this.

The boardwalk was a canker on his hometown, a necessarily evil to be endured. Which he did. The salty winds, the pounding of the surf — lonely as it could be at times, this was home.

Until Kristin.

He'd been wandering the beach half-baked in the sunset, the tourists starting to roll up their towels for the day, and stooped to see if a raggedy curl of black before him was a devil's purse filled with a shark egg, or just a piece of trash bag. Out of nowhere, a body softly crashed into him.

"I didn't know Ed Hardy made Darth Vader t-shirts," teased a female voice, instead of apologizing.

It was actually a knockoff, but he turned around, and — short blonde hair sprayed out into spikes, knowingly arched eyebrows, tattoo-styled silver hoops enclosing the word FOREVER. The glint in her blue eyes reached for the peacock tail that sprouted on every guy who'd ever grown up at the shore. That reflexive swagger came up to the surface to scan her fashion sense and tease her back.

"Italians are still doing it better? Really?" God, she really did look like Madonna, back in the day.

"Come find out."

He grinned at her moxie, but understood. You had to move fast when you were only in town for a summer, or a week, or just one epic night. That was one rare positive about the boardwalk: a refreshing lack of head games.

She linked her arm through his and walked them up on the boards, and soon they were getting smashed in a rooftop bar, staining their mouths red from horrendous slush drinks and laughing their asses off. Her name was Kristin, and he was pleasantly surprised to find out she was a local too — she'd moved here a year ago and looked after a clutch of rental properties on the other side of town.

"Biggest dream right now?" He looked up at the moon, high up in the sky by now, and considered. They were deep into the confessional part of a good drunken evening. "Moving out of clerical stuff to go work in the science department. You?"

"I don't know yet. Not managing property, that's for sure. Getting a pinball machine named after me. Yeah! That would be the ultimate honor, your name up in lights, right? C'mon, let's go play."

No built-in end date to her companionship, Nicky thought hopefully, as she led him down the stairs and into an arcade. The game barkers called at him to win a prize for his lady, but for some reason, it struck him as hilarious instead of aggravating. And the kids in their strollers actually looked kind of cute, with their wide eyes and the way they protectively clutched their stuffed animals. The night was full of glittering delights, the brightest of which was her smile, as she excitedly pulled him towards another game. Attempting skeeball, they were both terrible — matching their steps at Dance Dance Revolution, their budding chemistry attracted a crowd — ending the night at mini-golf, where she drew him beneath the waterfall at the seventh hole, into the darkness of the cave, and consecrated the course with their first kiss.

The boardwalk had been a place he'd never fit in, until she found a place for him within her company. The people making all that noise turned from trashy drunks to cheerful party folk, the COME AT ME BRO shirts somehow fading away behind relaxed smiles, raucous laughter. The bars were packed with people having the time of their lives, whether spinning around in the lightshows of hard trance, or bouncing along on aching knees to classic rock covers. Through a mischievous, ever-present grin, through sparkle-tipped fingers that were always reaching for him, drawing him close — Kristin performed the miracle of transforming him into a giddy tourist himself.

Chocolate-dipped soft serve would always bring him back to those days, cracking the cold sweet shell into his mouth while walking on burning sand, her hand in his and the whole ocean grand and inviting before them. No cheap motel room but the plushy nest of his apartment to chill in, peeling off their wet suits and making love with the salt water drying on their skins. Over time, their dates accumulated bounty. Claw-machine plushies sat next to water-gun mirror art. On top of the entertainment center reigned a pair of dragon wineglasses, scored with all the skeeball tickets they'd saved over the summer. Their pewter tails curled around each other into a heart. High above shells they'd picked up along the nature walks, above his mermaid sketches that had started to look a lot like Kristin, they were the supreme memento, ruling over all the other keepsakes they'd accumulated on their adventures.

On their first anniversary, they climbed up onto his building's roof to watch a fireworks show on the beach. They brought along a bottle of champagne to fill their prizes, and raised a winged, crystal-eyed toast to all the frivolity and fantasy in the world. And, of course, to a long, long life together.

Nicky's sneakers pounded the boards, the boards that were still left. He wanted so badly to keep his head down, block it all out, but time was running out. He swept his eyes across the landscape, relentlessly searching for a glimpse of pink sweats, the twinkle of whatever word would be gleefully rhinestoned across her backside today. He blinked back sudden tears. No. The world could not be that cruel, to take away someone so *alive*.

The phantoms of tram cars rolled by. Beneath his feet, down below in the darkness, the spirits of partying kids passed around bottles of bottom-shelf whiskey, badly rolled joints. Above, the hotel balconies echoed with loud, brazen girls who tossed their hair and aimed lusty hiprolls at the whistling boys below.

Everywhere, hauntings. Kisses on the sky chairs that coasted lazily above the boardwalk, now yanked angrily down to earth. The arcade that boasted a collection of early 80's

treasures, so many nights spent flapping around the boards of
Joust together, ripped off the pier and flung to the beach.
Stuffed animals hung on hooks like soggy, distended carcasses,
and he could feel himself start to lose it again as he looked into
their soft, friendly faces.

He turned a corner and almost ran smack into a pair of
cops.

"Hey. Sorry." Nicky danced back on his sneakers.

"You're packing up, right?" The older cop was scanning the
beach, haggard eyes sharp for stray people.

"Uh, actually, I wanted to ask — if I could stay and
volunteer, help with the search—"

The younger cop let out a dismissive laugh, a foul whiff of
the boardwalk he'd hated before Kristin had made it a
wonderland. Nicky bristled.

The older cop shot a look at his partner — *grow up, son* —
and said basically the same thing, but friendlier. "We
appreciate the help, but manpower's gotta go towards ruptured
gas mains, all these puddles that might have power lines in
them, we gotta start getting them off the street before they kill
somebody."

"Besides," said the younger cop, "it's not likely we'll be
finding anybody alive by now. Just bodies."

The older cop caught the flash in Nicky's eyes and stepped
in front of his partner. "Look, I know you mean well. I know
someone hasn't come home and you want to stay and find
them. But I can't let you. It's much too dangerous here. Right
after the pyre, you gotta go. It's for your own safety."

Nicky kept his face polite, nodded at the older cop who
really was just doing his best to keep order in a place where
there wasn't any, not anymore. Nodded at the younger cop
while inside, his temper lit up like an arcade marquee: *FUCK
YOU FUCK YOU FUCK YOU.*

"Headed home to pack my bag right now, officers."

"Good," said the older cop. "Right after the pyre."

Nicky nodded again and kept walking, tried to keep the stew of dark emotions in check now that anger had been poured into the cauldron.

The boards sloped down to the asphalt, and he walked past the pastel-hued hotels towards the sweet summer cottages. Dead cars lined the streets. Flood water collected in massive pockets and blocked out parts of the road, smelling ominously like gas. The trees and plants had already started to die. The koi pond, a favorite sight on their walks back from the beach...gone, when the salt water came rushing in.

The nature walks. The nests torn out of the trees, the water coursing down into underground burrows, the tiny families below...*keep it together. She needs you now.*

Soon he reached the all-year part of town, where hasty graves had been dug into at least a couple of backyards, families who would not — could not — let the bodies of their loved ones depart the earth by fire. As he ascended the two steps up to his building, and took two more steps towards his ground-floor apartment, he counted his losses, and knew it could have been even worse. Unlike a handful of truly unfortunate inhabitants, at least his home hadn't broken up and floated into the sea.

It had been too late by the time everyone took the news seriously.

Nicky had put in a long day at the college working on a mailing, had caught the oncoming megastorm in glimpses. Severe, the news was saying, but they'd cried wolf many, many times before.

"Alright. So I'll grab some extra food, some booze. I won't forget the ramen, I promise." His phone was crooked against his shoulder as he smoothed labels onto oversized envelopes. The plushy green squid she'd gifted him his last birthday presided imperiously over the chaos on his desk.

"Hah. This does seem more Y2K than Katrina," Kristin snorted from one of the buildings she managed, somewhere down the boulevard.

"We might have the day off tomorrow."

"I don't know — these tenants really fucked the place up before they skipped town. No idea what beef they had with the owner, they dumped a whole bunch of rotten pickles beneath the couch cushions and there's a ton of holes where they punched through the sheetrock. Lots to do."

"I'll be waiting for you with a light gun and a bottle of wine."

It started when the talking head on the TV froze. He'd been on the couch, scrolling through a blog post on emergency preparedness. He was halfway into his first dragon-glass of pinot grigio, her glass empty and ready right beside it, but the way the news had gotten increasingly serious throughout the day, maybe he shouldn't have been laughing it off. He'd already gathered together a slapdash first-aid kit out of the bathroom, and had just slid a fresh pair of batteries into a huge flashlight, when the newscaster went silent.

He looked up, and the anchor's concerned face was caught in a moment of raised eyebrows and moistening pancake, the bright red graphic at the bottom of the screen screaming EXTREME STORM WARNING. All was silent for fifteen seconds, before all the electronics cut out.

He went to the kitchen and grabbed some candles. No big deal, he thought, as he lit them around the apartment. He put three votives down on the coffee table and tried calling Kristin.

No answer. But that wasn't unusual when she was cleaning up after a departed tenant, especially an irate one.

And that was when he heard the trickle coming in by the doorway.

Forty minutes. Forty frantic minutes that started with getting important stuff off the floor. The trickle quickly turned into a foot of water. Soon he was gathering his laptop, wallet, and phone, and he was running up the stairway towards higher shelter. The second-floor neighbors were having a blow-out fight as he passed by, pant legs flapping wetly, up to the vacant third floor. He looked out the window. Below, the entire town had disappeared beneath small gray waves, a deluge of rain and merciless wind.

Up climbed the water, as he ran breakneck trips to salvage whatever he could. It rose up over the stereo speakers, the coffee table — he grabbed a bunch of sketchbooks, a handful of her jewelry. Up it came over the bookcases, the bed — he stuffed a backpack with food and candles and clothes: this could be a long night. It lifted the furniture from the floor and floated it about — he pulled blankets and pillows from the closet shelf, grabbed their sleeping bag. When it rose to his shoulders, he was forced to give up. Nicky glanced back at all the art and remembrances submerged in darkness, all he couldn't save. He sprinted up the steps before the heartbreak could drown him.

A game of musical chairs descended upon the town, trapping inhabitants in place wherever they were until the floodwaters receded. He sheltered in the third-floor hallway and gave her a call.

And Neptune had ruled the land for a night. Something cheesy like that, he could hear her saying, if she'd been with him.

She didn't answer. Wasn't answering, after ten calls in a row.

He knew her well enough to stress about it, but not too much. She had a whole keyring of third-floor places to take shelter, and her phone had probably gotten wet. It was what he told himself, with each frustrating detour towards her voicemail.

Tempting as it was to stay glued to the internet all night, his scan of the news was quick; he had to save battery power in case she called. *Collapse*, and *World*, and *Gone* — the same old tragic words salting the headlines, grabbing for pageviews. He closed his eyes, tried not to think about his home, tried not to think about her. He lit a couple of votives and cracked open an enormous fantasy novel, and began to pass the dark, lonely hours waiting it out.

It hit him when he awoke the next day, when he heard voices outside — people! — when he checked his phone's screen and saw no message, and no internet. He ran downstairs and found himself face to face with a cop about to knock on the building's doors, who informed him that he had five minutes to pack a bag and evacuate.

That was when he began to worry. A lot.

Nicky stepped into his apartment. First thought before anything else: Kristin still hadn't come back.

The place looked ransacked. Everything was overturned and scattered and soaked, as if a gang of cold-blooded henchmen had torn the place apart before tossing the contents of a swimming pool on top as a last kiss goodbye. But, eerily, nothing had been broken. Fragile things of glass and porcelain had been covered in filth, but the water's soft landing brought them all unshattered to the floor. The coffee table lay on its back, angled against a chest of dead comic books. A spill of pewter figurines lay beneath, and he wanted so badly to gather them up, put them somewhere safe. It was a sight that tormented him every time he came back here to check if she'd returned. But there was no time to spare.

That smug prick back on the boards — that heartless asshole scumbag — but, but. Rage was pushing the tremors back. That was useful when he was going to pieces every five minutes.

And, fuck that guy. Nicky had other plans for this evening.

One thing he'd caught from the neighbors: there would be a patrol on the streets. Not that many feet on the ground, but enough he'd have to be careful.

And...

It's much too dangerous here.

He dreaded what the dark would bring.

Back up to his sanctuary on the third floor, the hard linoleum hell on his bones, but he wasn't leaving without her. He dipped a chunk of bread in a jar of peanut butter, and thought about the next cull through his stuff; his whole world reduced to whatever he could fit in his backpack. Everyone would be getting chased out and the patrol would come by here, making sure he'd gone too. He could not come back here again.

He looked at the small scattering of possessions that surrounded his sleeping bag: green glass votive holders they'd picked up at a bed and breakfast, an artisan pillowcase printed with a massive horseshoe crab she'd given him as a semi-joke. ("Think of the dreams you'll have on *that!*") He'd saved his bowl and a bag of smoke, but couldn't touch it. Knew he wouldn't be indulging for a long, long time.

He narrowed it down to the laptop, of course. One sketchbook, only one. Her jewelry could fit in an inner pocket.

The shakes started breaking through again, and he willed himself to stay calm, or he would never see her again.

If Jessabella could keep it together, so could he.

He rooted through the tangle of necklaces and bracelets and dug out her hoops. The tattooed font proclaimed a vow so total it only needed one word, total boardwalk chic and he loved her *so* much. He folded his fingers over them and held his fist to his mouth, felt tears threaten to escape. A megaphone outside issued commands to his block, and he breathed deeply, feeling the mission take back over.

He slipped her earrings into his pocket and hoisted his backpack over his shoulder, and descended the stairs. This time, he didn't look back.

A grim bonfire awaited on the beach.

The unlucky ones who hadn't made it upstairs; recovered, documented, ready for an expedient cremation. They were almost at the water, far away enough that a stray spark wouldn't burn the whole place up. Nicky walked around the gathering crowd as he stared at the bodies, wrapped up neatly on wooden pallets. Was Kristin supposed to be among them? This limbo was torture, not knowing, possibly never knowing. Keeping a light on for her, for the rest of his life…his restless eyes went everywhere, searching for that twinkle. Up on the boardwalk, the benches along the edge — all the times they'd shared a plate of cheese fries and watched the sea — empty.

The mourners had not gone on, not yet. The first ones on that journey had been the families left intact, everyone accounted for, packed up quick and ready to go. But the mourners were slow. They clutched cups of fire-boiled tea and spoke softly about other cities that had been destroyed by the storm, other places in the world that might have washed away as well, as they struggled with varying stages of grief. A couple of them saw him and nodded sympathetically, knowing that this moment had commanded his search to stop.

Jessabella stood near the pallets with her father, her tear-stained sister and brothers nestled beneath her arms like baby birds. No breakdowns for her, though — her face was dry, resolute. The protective maternal branch overhead had come crashing down onto her back, and it forced her up the tree, made her become the woman of the family. He could see the role still settling into her dark eyes, shoving the trauma back behind whatever problems they were all going to face now. She looked up and saw him standing alone, and dipped her chin once. A signal.

A loud voice broke in over the crowd. Not a priest, not a cop, some community figure taking on the burden of ceremony.

"To all assembled here today — we come together to honor our dead..."

Nicky turned away. This was too raw. Too unreal. The voice dissolved into background clamor as he wandered away from the circle.

A life without Kristin — a life without anything familiar anymore — everything would go back to being ugly and empty again. Not even that, because the games of luck and chance, the all-night parties, all the sparkles of the boardwalk — that world was over.

He felt the heat at his back, heard the crackling of the flames. Anguished wails pierced the sky.

He wandered to the edge of the water, and pulled one of her hoops from his pocket. FOREVER, it said, shining up at him. He clenched it tightly to his chest as his neighbors fell to their knees behind him, sobbing, screaming. He drew all his terror up from his heart, all the devastation that surrounded him, and pushed pure agony into the circle of cheap silver metal. He lifted his eyes to the horizon and held out his hand, offering an eternity that smelled like her perfume: a sacrifice to the angry sea gods for an answer. Because that power-drunk masochistic fuckhead was right. The longer this went on, the worse the answer would be.

The air grew thick with the scent of charred flesh.

He cast it into the ocean — hating to lose one of the few keepsakes left, as the horrific smell hurried it from his hand — and knew the gods' only compassion would be the speed of the reply.

Another voice took over. The older cop.

"OK, people. We need to start moving." Almost sounding apologetic as he laid down the law. Nicky had never been comfortable around cops, the way they patrolled the boardwalk for illegal alcohol and seemed almost disappointed when water bottles really did contain water. But he felt a flash of pity for the poor guy, doing his best at one of the world's shittiest jobs right now.

But, as he watched the mourners gather their travel bags and round themselves up, it was going to get a lot harder to be here, from this point on. Getting caught meant getting cuffed and dragged out of town by force. Although…it would be done by cops. Not soldiers. Where was the National Guard? Where was—

Jessabella shattered the air with a scream and wandered towards the flames, slowly. Everyone's attention leapt to the young, half-orphaned girl beset by suicidal urges, the diversionary tactic she'd promised him. Nicky silently thanked her and slipped away before anyone could notice.

Nightfall.

Nicky wasn't the only one who hadn't left yet; there were a few rustlings in surrounding homes, the stray flashlight beam in a window here, the smash of something falling there. He'd hidden out in a parking lot attendant's booth until it got dark, curling on the floor and catching some much-needed sleep.

The search had to continue in darkness, now that the patrol had put the clamp down. Live wires, highly flammable puddles — the moonlight would not reveal everything.

He'd asked the gods for an answer. Here was their ordeal.

He started down the boulevard, which was deathly silent. The town was so strange without music pumping through the air. Which building had Kristin been working in? He'd visited the addresses he knew of while the patrol let him, but this must have been the new property. He'd combed the apartment for jotted-down work notes, but all the paper was wet and totally indecipherable.

Flashlights appeared up ahead. He ducked behind a picnic table as the patrol continued on, not seeing him.

He passed the broken glass of an ice cream parlor where they'd once split a Kitchen Sink, a toppled waterslide where Kristin had fished a rogue bikini top out of a whirlpool. The posters of a nightclub leaked inky tears down the side of a building where they'd once danced to 80's tunes all night long. Hell, he realized, was not some faraway fiery pit of torment. It was a walk down a road as long as your life, where you passed all your happiest memories, and each had been smashed to pieces.

A villa of candy-colored shops was a boom of flame just waiting to happen. A rickety old bar dotted with fake palm trees teetered on the verge of collapse. The cops had been absolutely right, and no wonder they'd been hustling everyone out of town so quick. Everything was screaming at him to leave, leave *now*, before it killed him. And he wanted to. How easy it would be, to turn himself in at the station, catch the transport out, and be gone. But he couldn't. He would die before abandoning Kristin to this wasteland. And that was looking, with each passing moment, like a very real fate.

He implored the sea gods.

Find her — find her —

His eyes fell on the mini-golf course, the halfway point on the boulevard. The cave where she'd led him — the waterfall had dried up and vanished.

That first kiss.

(No, *you* find her.)

A strange, sudden impulse drew him in, guided his feet through the astroturf lanes like a supplicant walking the curves of a divine labyrinth. *Wander in, ye who would seek the truth.* The moon lit up the greens, and he passed a chipped windmill, stepped across tiny gardens of dying flowers. Children's happy screams and disco hits ghosted through the cold air, along with the mouthwatering scent of freshly made pizza from the parlor next door. It was a gentle assault on his senses that should have broken his spirit, but it quieted his anxieties into a weird certainty as he came closer to the center, closer to the answer, to the cave. A holy site, if only to two people.

The smack of a putter had sent her bright orange ball like a tiny sun into the darkness. She'd run after it, and called his name. Her laughter invited him beneath the water, brought him closer, ignited the best years of his life with a soft sugary kiss...

Something inside the cave caught the light. Rhinestones, spelled out across a pair of sweatpants.

IMMORTAL.

His heart pounding, he ran inside and found her fast asleep on the ground. He dropped to his knees and drew her into his arms.

She opened her eyes. Bright with delirium as she reached for him, tried to speak but her words came out garbled. Her skin was freezing. He held her tight, relief sending shudders through his body as he willed heat into her cold flesh, her voice chiming beautiful nonsense into his ear. He could stop now. He could stop. He'd gotten his answer, and it was unexpectedly merciful.

Two deep, sweet, grateful breaths before he threw his head back and screamed for help.

Side by side, slumped together, sipping burnt coffee from a pair of folding chairs. All around them, people bustled through the communal area of an unfinished senior citizens' complex, pressed into service as a shelter. They were dressed in dry, clean secondhand clothes, and paper plates of pasta were being passed around. Making do with the resources at hand.

Warmth, pumped into her body intravenously. A cleanse, antiseptic to rid her skin of whatever was in that floodwater. Kristin was still a little weak, but most of the spark had come back into her eyes.

"So yeah, they trashed the furniture, drew all over the walls. The power was already shut off inside the unit so I didn't get everything blowing out like you did. I got so wrapped up in cleaning the kids' room - they made their kids sleep in the storage room, can you believe it - I didn't notice until my sneakers started squeaking. And that was when I found out they'd fucked up the locks."

Most of that spark. There was still a little bit missing.

From a nearby corner came a burst of hard trance. Someone had plugged a pair of desktop speakers into a laptop, tried to make it a little happier in here. A young hippie-esque mom got up and started to dance with her scraggly-haired toddler. A few more people joined her, their kids too.

The images Kristin painted for him...Nicky went into a room of horror that would always be there now. A windowless room painted pale pink, sheets and tiny clothes and plastic dolls cluttering the floor. A wooden door that wouldn't open, not even when hit with a bunkbed ladder, a cheap old door that wasn't cheap enough. A dead wet brick of a phone in her back pocket. A slice of oxygen that was getting smaller and smaller. Clambering up the bunkbeds to get away, the water calmly following her.

It covered her hands as she lay on the mattress, played with her hair. Shaking from the cold, and the fear, staring at the stained ceiling, she waited on a little girl's bed for the coffin lid to close over her face. The shell had been pierced, and the water poured in.

But the creature inside hadn't been killed.

"The water emptied out, but it was slow. I felt like shit. Just, really dizzy, and weak, and oh my god, the smell. I was so itchy, I'd never felt so dirty in my life. It took me a really long time just to get up off that bed, I kept falling asleep and waking up and falling asleep again, and just wanting to barf the whole time. Finally I felt OK enough to get down. The door was soaked through and easier to smash now, even though I could barely lift my hands."

When the internet came back on, he would track down Jessabella and help her and her family in whatever way they needed, for the rest of his life. Then he would find those tenants at their new home, break down their door, and tear them apart with his bare hands. It sounded like their kids deserved better parents, anyway.

"I found some water in the fridge – God, it tasted so good – and I went outside, and it was dark, and the streets were empty. Everything looked deserted. I thought, had everyone died? Or had I lost my mind? I could barely stay upright, my clothes were still damp and I was freezing, but I had to keep walking. I had to get back to you. But after a while...I saw the mini-golf, our cave, and I thought...nothing bad could happen *there*, right?"

(*Terminal burrowing, hide-and-die behavior*, the medics had said as they got their hands on her. Nicky had glared at that asshole cop, who turned tail and walked away from the rescue team fast.)

Immortal. Immortal enough. The proud strut of a mouthy boardwalk chick, pulling herself together to keep going. But the shock of coming so close to the end, two inches from death — that pink bedroom would be hiding inside her dreams, waiting to wake her screaming for the rest of her life.

"It's all gone," said Nicky, finishing his cup, the sugared warmth over all too quickly. "It's just us now, and that's all."

A small tremble had crept into his skin as it became okay to feel now, now that the search was done. A smiling ice cream cone smashed from its rooftop perch — an inviting arrow of arcade lights that would never flash again — a gingerbread porch torn from a yellow Victorian — all those glimpses of the wreckage were free to surge forward and knock him over. The roller coaster really had fallen into the ocean, holy shit. His blood burned with the need to go back, now. To rescue the tiny fragile things scattered all over the living room floor, to find the pieces of the ferris wheel and start putting it back together.

But.

The murmurs of reconstruction were coming to a halt.

"Us is enough." Kristin's look sent a jolt through him, blue eyes lucid and loving, feet still unsteady but getting to walk the earth another day. He reached for her hand and squeezed, gratitude silent and immense that she was here with him, that he was not going through this alone. It had been devastating, the thought of losing her. It was absolutely unthinkable, now that a whole new unease had started to descend.

For there had been no word from the outside world. The town's distress calls had cast desperately about for help, but had gone unanswered. Within the waiting-room limbo of folding chairs and bad coffee and wary patience, the evacuees came to learn that a lot more had been lost than just one seaside town.

There was no next destination, no incoming aid. No further directions.

"Us has to be enough," he said, putting his cup down and winding his body around hers, wanting to keep her warm always, this last bright neon light coming with him into an ominous silence. She clasped him tight in her arms, and their embrace was quiet amid the dancing children and the dire rumors and the mass confusion, nothing certain at all now but each other.

Back in town, inside the apartment, a pair of wineglasses lay on the floor. Filthy but whole, as if set down by gentle hands. Their jewel eyes sparkled in the coastal sun, and their pewter tails waited to curl together again.

W is for Water

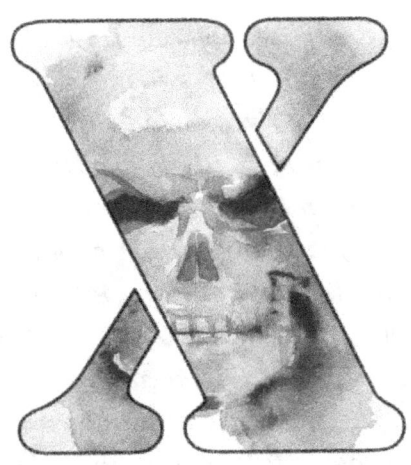

Jonathan C. Parrish

"We write our histories on the pages of others."

I'm terrified of the rats. They've been stealing tiny pieces of me, shredding me to line their nests and to smear their filth on. Every day there's less of me that I can remember. I didn't mind that they took the first few pieces, childhood is not so hard to put down again and they all come off so goddamn similar. It's when they started pinching my formative years, the ones Cyrus hadn't tainted with his lies, that I started feeling afraid. Afraid I wouldn't be able to remember or, worse still, I'd stop trying to. Of course, they started with the pages I kept close, stained and soft. I can't remember how many there were, damn them, can't remember any of it.

Cyrus is here again, his eyes burning yellow red, his lips breathing the name I hate, the name he calls me that isn't my name, the name he decided to call me after; after dad left, after mom went squirrely, after all the shit happened, Xerxes. Fuck him, fuck everyone. He's probably here to regurgitate a new story, he keeps moving my past around every time he comes up with something new, says we've done that. We haven't done shit, we've just been sitting here getting more thin and more squirrely and more alone. Cyrus is getting louder and his eyes more yellow. Little scabs around his eyes and his nose and always that dirty snot on his lip. I close my eyes because it makes them hurt to look at him, think about how I wish I was in the woods with bears, feeling flesh yield to my fangs and the blood and—holy shit am I hungry. And still I can feel his breath and I can't open my eyes because then I'll see him and fuck that. I want to get away, away from the next past and the fucked up now and the no future and find a hole and live in it with maybe an animal pal and we'd be a super awesome team at being awesome. The hole would smell like leaves and earth and paper.

I breathed in through my nose imagining it. Something bounced off the back of my throat so I started coughing. I peered into the recesses surrounding me, trying to identify the clicks and faint whispers. There's nothing there, I hope more than I believe, the faint sound of tearing was something I was imagining, all my imaginings fleeting and tenuous. I coughed again.

Mom and Cyrus are looking at me, scared as shit I've been too loud, that someone might come and find our staked out kingdom in this dump. I spit on the ground, one more memory lost to the soil. Mom's silent but her sneer shows me how nice she thinks that was; Cyrus just rumbles 'less than human good for nothing doesn't even deserve my stories' while I try to remember how good my hole should have smelled.

The smell, mom, Cyrus, the rats, they are all fucked in the head and the crazy's going to take me too if I don't do something soon.

The rats have taken Cyrus. They took the last copy of mom, they took my stink and replaced it with the smell of wet fur and rat piss. They're taking pieces of me and covering the pages with piss and shit. I can't remember my name, all I can remember is Xerxes and it makes no sense, no sense at all. I can't even remember why I am terrified of the rats, I think I am not. I think they remember me, I think the rats and I are in league together, down here in this hole. I am the ink and they are the pens, and it seems right that they can write the story because I am too tired to do it any more.

X is for Xerxes

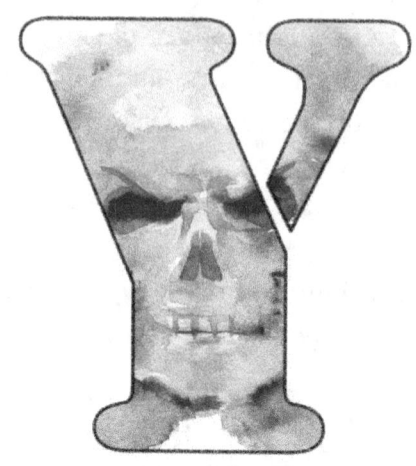

Alexis A. Hunter

Animam Poetae 7.4 Launching...

...

...

System error. Scan required.

...

Aural/visual stimulants present. Record to file?

...

Y.

Recording Started. Scan resuming.

A hand holds either side of my face. The grip is tight, cool... Desperate? I struggle to determine this without visual aid. System errors and corrupt files pop off inside me as I attempt to assess the damage.

My last memories are...

Playback
Three hundred and nine gathered in the Orios Court; six hundred and eighteen eyes, lit like fireflies winking back at

me. Encouraging. Eager. They hunger for illumination, and I swell with the thought of providing it for them. I look down at the thin scrap of paper clutched in my metallic fingers. It is so fragile in my hands. So outdated, but it provides its own stimulus.

I wish to be as the poets of old. The Human poets.

So I wrote my words on this paper and I stand to recite them.

There are no voices as they wait, but their bodies make a gentle susurrus that breathes around me. Fans expelling heat, eye lenses dilating to watch me closer, the subtle hum of their processors, their minds working.

I look to the paper and open my mouth to begin—

...

...

File corrupt. Attempt diagnostic?

I am jarred by the notification, timed with the return of my visual feed. My eyes zoom in and out, attempting to focus on the face pressed close to my own. The metallic bump of his nose almost brushes mine. His mouth flashes, I can't hear anything, but a steady blue light on the right corner of my heads-up display tells me I'm still recording.

My fans sputter, seeking more power.

I check and find that my power-cell is low. Lower than I've ever seen it. These cells are supposed to last for decades and longer. How—

The entity shakes my head. His face is an old model: sleek titanium shaped to mimic human features; lips and mouth replaced with a curved box, emanating light alongside words. His eyes burn copper, never leaving my own. But he lacks the sophistication which a digital overlay can provide — his face does not move, does not reveal his emotion. Still, by his grip on my head, I determine he is desperate or angry or... broken?

I try to shake him off. My limbs move with fractal delay, caused by insufficient power. I feel a tug at my gut and look down.

A tether. A cord stretched between us.

The light in his eyes is fading, his grip lessening.

My powercell levels are rising and it is then that I realize.

He's passing all of his energy to me.

"What are you doing?" I vocalize, unable to even hear my own voice. "Stop, what—"

He does not listen. He slumps against me, his forehead clanking against my shoulder. His hands slide off my face.

My aural facilities return just in time to hear the soft whine of his systems shutting down. The sound pierces me. Now at full power, I move to shift him off of me. I ease him up against the wall of the Orios Court — for I am where I last remembered being, in the court and on the podium with the glistening marble wall behind me. It is engraved with the names of our ancestors, the ones who created us.

I do not unplug myself from the entity, do not move from his side as I crane my neck to survey the court.

Three hundred and nine androids. No, three hundred and eleven counting myself and this entity — I glance back to him and scan the tag on his chest. He is called Ghrus. A host of other data filters in, overlaying the right side of my vision — Ghrus, a commercial pilot currently grounded for taking a ship off course. He had tried to return to Earth.

I am struck by the silence.

No fans, no humming processors, no dilating lenses.

My people are slumped where they stand. Crumpled metal heaps on the pavement like...like crushed soda cans, abandoned on the street.

I call out. "Is anyone there?" My voice is a symphony of plaintive, metallic cords; my words echo back to me, unanswered.

Tension rises in me. This silence is oppressive. I cannot make sense of what passed between my blacking out and this reawakening.

Looking back to Ghrus, I access the recording my systems began before even waking fully...

Playback.

Entity Ghrus shakes me. His voice is not high and desperate, it is low. It is broken and resigned.

"You only have one life to live. This my mother said to me and this I say to you." He stops. Seems to choke as he looks down at the cord stretched between us. "This is our new cycle. This is our new life. Spend upon Lumirius all the time which you will. But take care — for you will not find another body. No more Reawakenings."

His grip relaxes, brushes gentle across the metal face under my digital overlay. "This is the one life I give to you, as it was given to me."

For the rest of the video, he merely shakes me and cries out. Broken phrases and fragments I cannot make sense of. His grip tightens until it lessens, until the light fades again—

I snap out of the file, shuddering at the thought of reliving the moment he shut down.

It is evident something has occurred. The bodies around me tell me this as much as Entity Ghrus' rote words.

I delve again into my last memories, before everything went black.

Playback.

I look to the paper and open my mouth to begin—

...

(The file skips. I attempt to discover the damage and repair.)

...

Before I can recite my "magnum opus" to my people, something distracts them. They look to the sky — my peripheral cameras tell me this — but I do not. I have spotted a word awry in my great masterpiece. Pulling up the poem's file in my harddrive, I open it and move to change the word.

I am saving the change...

...

And all goes black.

I ease the tether out of Ghrus' gut. Out of mine. I kneel beside him. Grab his hands in my own and the clicking of our fingers echoes, through the whole of Lumirius.

I squeeze his hands, wishing he would return to me a least for a moment. But he is silent and slumped. I do not know what has happened to my world, but I know that he has given me something. Something I am not sure I want.

"Thank you, Mother," I say.

He is not my mother in the strictest sense, of course. He did not birth me from between his metal thighs, not as the humans come into life. If anything, humanity is my mother and science my father. But they have abandoned me. They have abandoned all of us.

So Ghrus I take as my mother. I kiss his hands because it feels right to do so. I thank him because I sense he gave his life for me. Does it matter if he no longer wished to live it? Does it mean anything that he no longer found value in his life?

I am born of his suicide.

I ponder it. Wish to write about it, even as I hold his cold hands.

New File.
I am born of my mother's suicide.
She passed to me the life
She no longer desired
Should I desire it?
Should I want that
which is unwanted?

To whom will I turn
Will I ask
All the questions
That suffuse my programming
How can I learn
If no one will teach
How can I live
If no one will—

Error: Vocabular Library Banks Corrupt.
...

...
How can I live
If no one will—

Error: Vocabular Libr—

I curse. Shut down the file and save it as it is, incomplete. Run yet more diagnostics in the background as I stand. Something is broken. Whatever knocked me offline — whatever took us all out — it did so while I was saving a change.

I am broken.

I yell this, to the gray clouds marbling the sky.
I am broken and I am alone.

I wander out of Orios Court, cringing as I step between the slouching entities. The curved walls of the court give way to the city outside it. The view has not changed: sleek white buildings, sharp and angular against the gray sky; the sun remains, though its placement has changed, casting a pale light across the city, across the green mountains beyond.

All looks as it did before. Except there are no vehicles buzzing around the buildings, homes, and places of employment. There is no smoke. No damage. No crumpled buildings. No ash and waste like I have seen of human apocalypses.

But devastation remains. A devastation felt by one.

One at a time. No more will live until I give them the life, the energy that is in me.

Again, I feel the urge to write a poem. It is who I am — that impulse. Yet, I do not wish to fight my corrupt files. Do not wish to heap more despair upon myself.

I step forward. Once and twice. And on.

All around, the bodies lie where they fell. The lights in their eyes are gone, but still I scan each one as I pass. Their shining forms are unscarred, unscathed. No bullets, no missiles, no violent catastrophe.

For hours, I continue thus, weaving aimlessly through our city. I go to Jhalis, my teacher. She lies over her desk, the pale white of her arms nearly blending with the pale white of the desk. I shake her, but she does not wake.

I should have brought Ghrus' cord.

For how am I to continue alone?

I find the circle on the northern outskirts of the city. It is a garden, formed of blockish hedges, once neatly clipped. Now stray fingers of greenery stretch up toward the sun, waving under the breath of a cool breeze. And here is the change. Here is the difference, only here in the wild where life continues without power.

The hedges live on. The garden continues to bloom, spreading in viny trails like a green sun expanding upon the earth. And the wind passing through its leaves, that faint rustle, is enough to ease, for a moment, my pain.

Then I see them.

In the ring of pavement just inside the garden, there are twelve benches circling a fountain. A still fountain that no longer sprays water. In this ring, more entities lie. Spaced evenly so each lies against a bench. Their hands are joined, all but the two on either end — their hands are outstretched as if reaching for...the next.

I squat beside the one closest to me, touch her arm which trails out like the vinery around her. Scan her chip: Vaurosa. An ambassador to humanity. One of the few allowed entrance into Earth space. She had risen through the ranks of our political system quickly and spent the past years off-shore, amongst the humans.

She had registered no return flight-plan.

She was not supposed to be here.

Faint mounds of dirt and crumpled leaves abound in this garden. The vines have begun to overtake the bodies, and it is by their reaching that I tell the time. The time of these eight predecessors. Vaurosa appears to have been first — the most dirt and leaves and entangling vines lie upon her.

I touch her face. "What calamity ended us?"

To hear my own voice is a mild comfort. A disruption to the heavy wake of silence.

It is then that I notice the numbers burned into the bench, just above her head.

01001110 01001111.

Shifting about the circle, I discover the same message burned or scored into the surface of the benches above each entity. *No.*

"What does it mean?" I ask Vaurosa, the first.

She does not answer.

Night. Darkness.

I have never known it.

I sit in the garden circle. I am still like the bodies around me, resting against a bench with no message burned in it. As desperate, as lonely, as broken as I am, I am not ready to take their hands. I am not ready to burn 01001110 01001111 into my tombstone.

Maybe I must understand that message before I will be ready.

I cast light from my eyes, illuminating only the narrow circle around me. Their faces are even more haunting in the solo white light of my making. Perhaps the yellow light of the sun gave them more warmth. Perhaps it glinted more kindly against their sleek features.

But my own light glares off of them, until I cannot bear to look. I turn toward the city, but I am not strong enough to pierce the darkness. It is a heavy black wall around me. It crushes in on every side and I cannot spin my light fast enough to keep it at bay. Always, the darkness touches me.

I shut down my lenses, making a darkness of my own choosing.

I seek the poem, the masterpiece I was ready to recite on the last day of my last life. The parts of it are jumbled. I can make no sense of their words. But I remember the meaning. I laugh at the meaning. I intended to lament that we as synthetic life forms are given endless life, that we cannot enjoy, that we cannot experience fully the pains and joys of life if we know it will never end.

My laugh is coarse. It barks against the hedges and back at me. And I fall silent, no longer wishing to hear my own voice, my own sins trumpeted through our silent world.

When the sun brings warmth back to the world, I rise. I return to the Orios Court, to Ghrus. I wonder why he strayed so far to find me. Did he know me?

"Thank you, Mother," I say again, but I mean it less this time.

I take up the cord that passed his life to me. I pocket it in the compartment in my left thigh. Then I lift Ghrus into my arms. He is heavier than I had imagined. An older model. Still, I have no trouble carrying him through the city. I step over the synthetic bodies.

I try to summon a song. A dirge, like the humans would offer, to serenade my fallen mother, my fallen people.

But I know no such songs.

So I let the hum of my fans and the *whirring* of my joints sing their own song. I hope it will be enough.

I lower him against a bench in the circle garden. I entwine his fingers with the newest entity lying there, assuming she is his mother as he is mine. I wonder if he would like 01001110 01001111 burned above his head. Would he say no to the question I do not understand?

I recall the recording of his last moments.

The low, resigned note in his voice.

He would say *No.*

I have no laser tool in my swivel arm. My tools are all designed toward the poetic lifestyle. It is how I designed this body in my last Reawakening, after my last body broke down fifty-three years ago. So I return to the city. I search the empty stores, murmuring apologies to their owners.

I return with a human tool from a musuem. A handheld, old fashioned screw driver.

And I begin to scratch an answer for my mother into the bench.

01001110 01001111

No.

My system continues to fight me. Error notifications pop up at every turn.

I ache to write poetry. To express the desperation and the loneliness.

I could write it in my own files. I could save it there as I always did before. But it means nothing squirreled away inside me. What use is a poet if no one lives to hear her words? What use are words if no one reads them? There is no network to upload my files to. I cannot reach the humans in their far away space.

And so I scrawl my words into the smooth sides of the city. In bits and pieces. Broken, fragmented bits of poetry. I scrape with the screwdriver, gouging my words into marble and stone and metal.

They will remember me this way, I begin to think. Then I remember we will never be as we were. Only one will remember me. One by one.

Until the energy that is in me fades. For energy can only be passed about for so long.

I discovered early in my first days that there truly is no energy here, no power. I flipped switches in the buildings. I attempted to power up vehicles powered by cells like my own. The smallest machines and the largest — none of them work. I passed from one city to the next, and always return here to our capitol. But the whole of Lumirius has been sucked clean of energy.

Why and how I do not know.

And does it matter?

Often I replay the file of Ghrus, the rote words he recited.

"This is the one life I give to you, as it was given to me."

I will call this recording My Rebirth Sequence (*"My Rebirth Sequence.vid"* saved to file). Though, of course, I was not technically *reborn*, but rather *reawakened*. As all the times before, yet different. Still, I prefer to think of it in terms of human birth. The world into which I have been so violently expelled is utterly different, almost unrecognizable. Does that not match the definition of birth? Surely humans passing from the dark warmth of their mothers' bodies to the bright, noisy world experience just what I have — only, my birth worked in opposition: I passed from a bright, noisy world to the dark warmth of this dead world.

I feel as a child, bewildered. Humans are spared this aching confusion. They are spared the burden of remembering passing from one life to the next.

So it will be the Rebirth Sequence. The last new beginning. A concept unknown to us — no, to me.

Me.

I am surrounded by my people, by their bodies. I can look into their eyes, I can entwine my fingers with theirs, I can embrace them.

Yet, they are not here. They are lost in the black space of nothing.

No light greets me from their eyes; their fingers do not squeeze my own; they are stiff and lifeless in my embrace—

They are corpses.

Corpses.

The word has never applied.

Now it applies to all... save me.

Save me.

☠

I had never realized the beauty of a sunrise. In a faint way, I knew. In such a way that I knew it was good to live and bad to die — because that knowledge was written into me.

But as I sit in the garden on its faint rise, I watch the sun crest over the mountains far. It is a burning orb. It is life and power. A sharp gust of wind buffets my face. The cities are shielded from these winds by their towering buildings scraping the sky.

But here it is a relief.

It is like the breath gusting from an entity's fans. Warm sometimes, cool sometimes, always touching my face.

It is constant.

The breath of the world.

The...

Constant?

I hurry away from the garden, into the oppressive shadows of the city. When did I cease to take comfort from my home? How now is the garden my succor? It matters not. An idea has occurred, a memory arisen from the days of my studying at Lumirius University for the Arts. I return to that place, the familiar buildings where I plugged in and absorbed knowledge at incredible rates.

But there is not always room in the head for all of it. So much was saved to the cloud. Now that too is gone and I cannot find what I need in my own head.

I pass through the halls, step over gleaming limbs untainted by dust or detritus. I skim through rooms of entities plugged into the walls, struck down in the middle of learning, of enlightenment. Deeper into the university, into the darkness where fewer windows cast paler shreds of light. I turn on my beams, light bursting from my eyes to guide my path.

Until at last I reach the abandoned place. A backup of sorts. Files and books that were long ago scanned into the cloud and should have been destroyed or sent to the Human Museum. Thank Science, they were not.

I spend many days there. I long for the kiss of the wind. My fingers itch to write more poems on the walls of this place. But I keep myself there, skimming through the books. The rustle of pages makes its own kind of music. In my haste, I tear more than a few.

Until at last I find it.

An answer to our problem.

Days fade into months and years. Or maybe I only think they do. Regardless, I toil on. It takes three attempts, for I am not as skilled in engineering as I should be. Still, I am a synthetic entity. I may learn all.

So it is that I construct a windmill in the center of our circle garden. I empty the water out of the fountain, knock down its ornamental angels, and arise, arise ye windmill! It is cobbled together with bits of metal, stripped from homes and cars and, Science forgive me, even a few entities.

Now I must choose.

Choose who to revive first.

I stare at the messages above their heads. And maybe now I begin to understand, even as desperation and hope war inside me.

01001110 01001111

No.

Do not resuscitate?

But I need answers. I whisper an apology to Ghrus, my mother, and turn instead to Vaurosa. I take the cord from my thigh and plug it into the windmill, plug it into Vaurosa, The First. And the wind blows as I cheer for it. The blades spin, slow at first. Then quicker as the gray clouds gust up from the south.

It will take so long.

But time I have.

And I will wait.

She is waking.

I press my hands to either side of her head. I shake her as my mother shook me. I speak to her, but not the rote words I was taught by the ReBirth Sequence. I call to her.

"Wake! Wake, Grandmother!"

Her charge is so weak, so low. Minimal systems running, my scans tell me. Still, the windmill spins on. The hedges are grown wild around us. They have overtaken the garden, they have begun to storm the walls of the city. I am not sure I can pry Vaurosa loose from the vines that have entombed her body.

This is how much time has passed.

My poetry is scrawled over every wall. At least one line, at least one word.

They will think me mad. Am I?

At last, her eyes dilate. Violet light. A digital face overlay flickers to life over her bland titanium features. It whispers her confusion, forming human expressions of grief and anger.

"What have you done?" she cries.

I smile. "I return your life to you. Yet I keep my own."

"No," she says as her body begins to stir. Blue, digital tears streak down her projected face. "No. It means no. It means—"

"I'm sorry," I say. But I'm not. Her voice is the human's heaven to my ears. I touch her face. I touch her hands and she tries to push me away, but I delight in even that touch.

Still, she is weak. She cannot move. She begins to weep and still I am not sorry.

"You must rest," I tell her. "You must charge. And we will charge them all one-by-one, or until we have enough to make a new life. To find new power. And you will tell me what fell upon us that ended us so."

She shakes her head and there is guilt on her face. In her voice as she whispers apologies. "I didn't mean to...I didn't... They made me watch. Sucked every bit of power out and then... Dumped me. I didn't mean—"

I hush her. No matter what she did, I forgive her. No matter what happened on Earth, so far away, that led to this calamity, I will forgive her because her voice is all I have. Her eyes glow with a light that is not of me and is not of the sun. It is of the wind. It is a sweet thing to me.

I touch her again and she does not pull away.

I pull her to me and she weeps against me.

"Shh," I whisper. "Would you like to hear a poem?"

Y is for Yolo

Steve Bornstein

David walked into the bedroom with his backpack. From the den down the hall Annie could hear CNN breathlessly recapping the event, as if anyone within earshot of a media device hadn't already heard the thing.

"...We'll play it again, for those of you just joining us..." Annie rolled her eyes. *"...Citizens of Earth. Greetings and apologies. We come to rescue you from the disaster..."*

"Goddamnit Brad, I don't care if it really is aliens," Annie snarled into her phone. "I warned you I wasn't going to be available and I meant it! Let that jackass Sam take it." She could hear the newsroom chaos in the background behind her editor's wheedling. It's not every day someone managed to hack every satellite feed on Earth for some kind of treehugging manifesto.

"Annie, you've got connections at NASA and MIT, we need you!"

She could practically see his sweaty brow and bugging eyes. "Goodbye Brad. I'll see you in a week." She stabbed the phone's screen with her thumb and tossed it on her bed.

"They want you to come in," David muttered as he fished around in his pack.

"Of course they do." She sighed and returned to packing her camping gear. She needed to show him she hadn't even considered it, even though – no, because – she had. "Brad acts like I have Neil deGrasse Tyson's personal cell or something."

The bed creaked a little as David set his pack down and started securing his blanket roll to it. He wasn't talking, which meant he was sulking. She let the silence stretch while they packed their bags.

"*...out of our control. We apologize. We come with all speed...*"

David yanked on a strap, finally breaking his silence. "Do you think it's real?" Small talk was better than no talk, Annie thought. He hefted his pack again and set it on the floor.

Annie shrugged and shook her head as she stuffed her toiletry bag into a side pouch, thinking about what she'd learned as one of the network's top science journalists. "It's the perfect cover story. A runaway black hole coming to destroy the planet? Sure, it's possible I guess, but so is a meteorite coming through the roof and hitting you in the nuts. Everything's got a statistical probability. You couldn't see a black hole coming until its gravity actually started affecting things, but it's a lot more likely for an anonymous splinter group of environmentalists to hack the feeds and make their point with some end-of-the-world story that couldn't immediately be disproven. It's Occam's Razor."

"*...regret we cannot save all of you. We apologize...*"

She turned to finally look at him and was surprised by the worry she saw creasing his brow. "Oh honey..." She crossed the room to him and hugged him, burying her nose in the shoulder of his flannel. She forgot for a moment what she was going to say and let herself relax in the strong grip of his arms. "It'll be okay, seriously. Look, we're already going out to the cabin. We'll just go there and let all the doomsday preppers jerk off and by the time we get back this will all have blown over."

"...take this time to prepare. End." "And there you are, either actual contact from an alien race or a more mundane but still amazing mass simultaneous hacking of every major media feed. Either way, this is unprecedented. With us now is Dr. Silverman from..."

He grinned down at her with the little curl to his eyebrow that meant he wasn't faking. "Well we better get going then before the streets get clogged with zombies." He hefted his pack onto a shoulder and grabbed hers, heading out to the den. She turned off the TV just as some rent-a-geek started bemoaning the lack of network security at satellite uplink sites.

The drive took twice as long as it should have thanks to all the people already freaking out. Annie had no idea where they thought they were going. Maybe "destruction of the Earth" was too big of a concept for them. Cooler heads seemed to be prevailing, but there's always someone willing to believe the sky is falling. Literally.

The cabin had that musty smell of disuse that went right to the part of the brain that made you feel guilty for leaving it like that for so long. David set down the battery lantern, casting the room in harsh white LED light and razor sharp shadows. Annie felt like the cabin was glaring at her.

This trip was going to be just the two of them spending some much-needed time together away from all the distractions that kept pulling them apart. Annie liked the odd symmetry of the rest of the world panicking about some end-of-the-world hoax at the same time they were putting their relationship back together.

The next day they settled in, unpacked their food, and tidied up the last couple years' worth of dust and cobwebs. They listened to satellite radio while David chopped wood and Annie stacked it next to the stump. Without flying saucers landing on the White House lawn or Jupiter spinning out of orbit, everyone was lining up behind the "hackers did it" explanation for the previous day's event.

It wasn't until the next day that everything started going to hell.

They stared at the radio, their dinner going cold, as they listened.

"*Reports are coming in from dozens of amateur astronomers across the world, images posted online all showing the same thing: Neptune being pulled apart by what is now assumed to be the black hole referenced in Thursday's mysterious broadcast.*" The voice shifted from newscaster to an obvious interpreter, talking over someone who sounded Slavic. "*The message gave us a direction to look and I knew it would cross close to Neptune, so I started looking and there it is. What are we going to do? I'm sorry, I need to go.*"

Annie looked up from the radio to find David staring at her. The guy on the radio went on talking but the only thing she could hear was her pulse pounding in her ears. She could hardly breathe, feeling the tragedy on his face mirrored on hers. "It could still be a hacker hoax thing, right?" he whispered.

She swallowed, willing her voice into being. "I don't know," she lied. It had to be real. Something of this magnitude was impossible to fake. Now that the word was out, everything stronger than a set of birdwatching glasses was turning to look

267

at Neptune, or what was left of it. She was glad they didn't have a TV.

Suddenly she had to see it. She had to see for herself. Annie bolted from her chair and ran out the door. She didn't know what direction to look and knew she wouldn't have been able to see anything even if she did, but she had to go outside and look. If she couldn't see it then it couldn't be real, right? She stared up into the clear night sky, her breath puffing in little white clouds while the stars twinkled down at her. She didn't know how long she'd been out there before she felt David's arms wrap her up, his damp cheek against hers.

The numbers had been crunched by morning. There was a lot of guesswork simply because it's hard to measure what you can't see, but the consensus was that a small black hole was on a glancing path through the solar system and that, worst case, its trajectory wouldn't take it closer to the Sun than the orbit of Mars. Not that it mattered, because by the time it crossed the orbit of Jupiter in two days the tidal forces would have kneaded the Earth like a stressball, causing global earthquakes in the double-digits on the Richter scale and eventually reducing the surface of the planet to magma before turning its stately orbit around the Sun into something a lot more elliptical. There was nowhere to run to and nowhere to hide. Nothing would survive.

The sheer enormity of the whole thing left David and Annie shellshocked. They took their morning coffee on the porch, huddled together under a blanket as they listened to the satellite radio. Annie watched a plane fly overhead, a needle-thin white contrail heading west, and tried to imagine the plane, the contrail, and the air around it all simply gone three days from now. She just couldn't. Her brain recoiled from the very idea. She hugged herself closer to David.

Then his phone rang. They both jumped as Trent Reznor's tinny voice started screaming from inside the cabin. David raced inside to grab it and came back with it on speakerphone. "Annie's here with me, we're up at the cabin." 'It's my mom,' he mouthed to her. He looked white as a sheet, wide-eyed and scared. Annie opened an arm and hugged him as he sat down again, the phone cradled in his palm like a kitten.

"I'm here, Rose," Annie said, bracing for the worst.

"Annie? How are you, honey?" Annie blinked at the question and looked at David, mouth agape. He was rubbing his forehead, eyes closed. Before she could manage more than an uhm, his mother continued. "Do you think this is for real?"

God, was she about to squash Rose's last bit of hope? Was this going to be Rose's last memory of her, as the person who confirmed that the world really was ending? She tightened her hand on David's leg and took a deep breath. "I think it might be, Rose, yeah." Her heart pounded in her chest. She suddenly felt very, very small.

Rose tsked, as if annoyed the looming apocalypse was going to get in the way of her Tuesday bridge game. "I don't know, you can hardly trust anything they say anymore. I think they're just trying to finally lay down martial law." Annie looked at David again, horrified speechless.

"...Mom..." David began, grasping for words.

"It can't be true!" Rose insisted, her voice starting to waver. "I can't lose you too, not after your father. Annie, what's going to happen?"

It had always irritated her that Rose could never grasp the fact that she was just a science reporter and not an actual genius polymath, but all Annie could feel now was heartbreaking sympathy for the woman pleading on the other end of the call. "Rose..." she said through dry lips, at a loss.

"Mom, I love you." David took a breath and wiped at his eyes. "Don't worry about us, o-"

A tremendous noise started from the other end of the call, like a dozen gravel trucks all dumping their loads onto steel plating. Rose shouted into the phone over the din. "Goodness, what is that? Dav-"

The line went dead.

Annie stared at the phone's patient "Call Ended" message, unable to breathe. David scrambled to call her back, pleading for her to pick up, but the only answer was the network's prerecorded apology for being overloaded. After a while his pleading gave way to sobbing and they clung to each other on the porch's bench, the phone clattering forgotten to the deck.

There was no way to get back to the city in time to see anyone or say goodbye. Traffic had been bad enough on the drive to the cabin, and now that word was out phone networks had overloaded and social order was rapidly giving way to chaos. It seemed like half the world was trying to scare off the approaching singularity with screams of rage while the other half huddled together and tried to deflect it with prayers.

For dinner they broke into the wine, picnicking on cheese and crackers on the porch as they listened to the world closing up shop, toasting memories of old places and things that would never, ever be the same again. Taking their cues from the latest reports, Annie would tell a story about somewhere the network had sent her or David would talk about a co-worker from overseas. There were other reports of buildings and whole areas of countryside being swallowed up, but as the chaos spread there was no way to sort fact from rumor and hearsay.

That's when they felt the first tremor. David dropped his wineglass as the ground suddenly lurched. Annie shouted and grabbed a post. Both of them waited, holding their breath for more that didn't come. That was the moment the idea came home for her, that what was happening a world away was happening here too, and the distance afforded them by radio and phone wasn't going to spare them.

Annie looked at David and for the first time knew, really knew, that she was going to lose him. Until that moment she'd secretly wished that this had just been a big misunderstanding. Someone didn't carry the three and they'd go back and check their numbers and find out, whew, it was just a big mistake. She slowly crumpled to the floor, her heart swelling and throat closing up as hot tears welled up and raced down her cheeks. She was dimly aware of her voice screaming and David's familiar scent being close, and somehow that just added fuel to the tragic fire. She tried to smell as much of it as she could, burying her face in his chest and grabbing at him, trying to sear his memory into her brain for the afterlife.

Annie clung to him as David scooped her up and carried her to bed. Mental and emotional exhaustion won and they stayed like that until morning, with Annie sobbing herself to sleep and David, despite his efforts to keep watch over her, quickly following her.

The radio didn't work when they woke up for the last day of Earth. The ground had rumbled several more times during the night but had finally settled down again. They spent the morning nude under the blanket on the porch, trying to experience as much as they could, while they could. Annie watched another jet contrail fly west and nudged David, pointing it out to him. "I wonder who that is," she said. Her words felt funny in her mouth.

David shook his head, watching it until it disappeared behind the trees. "I wonder where they're going. How could it even matter?" He looked back to her.

"Maybe..." Her voice trailed off as her throat threatened to close up again. She took a breath. "I'm sorry. I'm sorry David, for all the canceled dinners and postponed plans. God, now it seems just so fucking pointless. I worked away my best years, our best years–"

He stopped her with his lips. She tasted him, felt that scar on his lip with her tongue, and swore to remember it. "We don't have time for regret," he said with a sad smile. "I forgive you because I love you. I'll always love you, and I want to spend this day loving you."

His image wavered through her tears and she kissed him again. "I love you, too," she managed to say. "I don't want the... end to be without you."

David tightened his arm around her and kissed her forehead. "Where else am I going to go?" She gave a little laugh and dropped her head on his shoulder.

The rest of the day was mercifully free of quakes, or anything else untoward. Even the knowledge of their impending doom had mostly numbed over, as if being constantly punched in the brain had left their emotions deadened. If it wasn't for the death sentence that had been broadcast for the last few days, it'd almost seem like any other day. Maybe being this far out in the mountains was shielding them from the worst of it. But the math was reliable and cold: tonight the tension in the Earth's crust would reach a critical level and, literally, all Hell would break loose. They were cleaning up from dinner when David stopped, plates in hand, then set them down on the table.

Annie looked at him, confused. "What the hell are we doing?" he asked with a lame little laugh. "Of all the things to be doing right now, dishes isn't one of them."

Annie grinned crookedly. "Force of habit?" He grinned back at her and took her hand in his, pulling her towards the bed. "Oh, this is a much better idea."

In the afterglow, with just the brightness of the full moon lighting the cabin, they listened to each other breathe until they fell asleep.

☠

It was 7:26am when Annie opened her eyes, and she watched the alarm clock's second hand tick three times before she bolted out of the bed screaming. "David!"

He jumped and sat up, looking around in a tangle of sheets. "What?!" Recognition dawned on his face when he saw her backed up against the wall, staring at the morning outside. "What the fuck...?"

She swallowed, trying to calm the hope swelling in her chest. "I really don't want to sound cliché, but is this the afterlife?"

David slowly got out of bed. "I dunno, I slept through that part of Sunday School." He carefully set his foot down on the floor, watching it as if he expected it to pass right through. When it didn't, he grinned at her like a kid at Christmas.

She leaped into his arms with a whoop and they kissed until they ran out of air. "How is this possible?" she asked, panting. "Did they screw up the numbers?"

"How the hell should I know?" he replied. He looked past her, out the front windows to the trees waving in the morning breeze and the radio still sitting on the porch railing. "The radio." He grabbed her hand and ran outside, their flesh goosepimpling in the freezing air. It had never felt so good.

The radio remained silent, but it had lost the satellite signal the previous day. It was probably too much to hope that it was back already. "I guess we should have cleaned up after dinner last night," David said with a smirk. Annie punched him in the arm. "That wasn't a complaint!" he laughed.

They enjoyed the rest of the morning nursing their coffees from under the blanket on the porch. Annie spotted another jet contrail heading west in the bright warm sun. "Hey, look!" David grinned up at the sky with a chuckle. "I guess at least some of the world didn't totally go to shit."

As if on cue, the radio suddenly sprang back to life. Without so much as a burst of static, a voice said, "You and your local surroundings have been transported aboard a ship. We are exiting your local space and returning to [Hoothoooonk]." Annie and David looked at each other simultaneously, then stared at the radio, silently daring it to say it again. After a moment, it did.

"More hoaxes?" David said.

"The first one wasn't a hoax," Annie replied, the bottom falling out of her belly.

"...Shit," David said, as logic's implications caught up with him. They sprang from the porch bench, running inside to get dressed.

"Where are we going?" Annie asked him as they ran to the car. David slipped into the driver's seat and started it up. "To find out what the hell's going on." Annie turned on the radio as the car headed off down the dirt road, only to be greeted by the same message regardless of what station she tuned. She was making another slow pass up the AM band when she felt the car coast to a stop. She looked up at David. "What's up?"

He was staring straight ahead. "I think we found our radio announcer."

She looked down the road, and saw it. At first glance it looked like a small tree had grown in the middle of the packed dirt path, but then her eyes started latching on to details. They weren't roots, they were four squat legs. That wasn't a smooth trunk, it was some kind of brown jumpsuit. And those weren't four branches waving in the breeze, they were four arms waving at them. "Holy shit," she breathed. "Is... that...?"

David grunted, trying to avoid hyperventilating.

She opened and closed her mouth, at a loss. "What... I mean, should we..." It kept waving at the car. "I think it's trying to get our attention."

David put the car in park and turned it off, stared at it for another moment, then turned to her. "It probably could have killed and eaten us already if it wanted to, so we might as well see if we can get some answers."

They stepped out into the crisp air and started crossing the hundred feet to the not-tree. Now that they were walking towards it, it had stopped waving at them. Annie could see more details as they got closer. What looked like smaller branches resolved to stalks of some kind sprouting from between what she assumed were the alien's arms, and some kind of device hung between two of its arms. Whatever it was, it definitely wasn't from Earth.

They stopped about ten feet from it, close enough that they could hear the hollow sound of its breathing. It let out a hoot and the device spoke. "I greet you."

Annie immediately thought it sounded like Siri. She glanced at David. He widened his eyes and shrugged at her, shaking his head. She widened her eyes back at him and shrugged in return, turning back to the not-tree. "Uh, hello. Uhm..." She looked around at the familiar woods surrounding them. "This still looks like Earth..."

Siri The Tree hooted. "You have been saved."

"Shit," David muttered. "We're dead after all."

"That is an incorrect statement," SiriTree said. Annie snorked back a laugh in spite of herself. It continued, "I stopped you here because this area's barrier is a short distance away and we did not want you injuring yourselves in a vehicular collision."

The brain-numb feeling fell over Annie again like a wet towel. "Earth really is gone," Annie mumbled. "But… I saw a jet contrail in the sky this morning. How much did you take?"

"That is a correct statement," SiriTree said. "The line in the sky was determined to be part of your global environment and was introduced into the simulation to better replicate it. We have rescued 5.8% of Earth's biosphere from our escaped singularity. We believe this to be a representative sample with adequate diversity for introduction into a suitable environment after a period of rehabilitation and acclimation. You will be safe here, but for your safety you cannot intermingle with [Honkhoonk]."

The ground fell out from under Annie's feet. "What did you say?"

SiriTree dutifully repeated itself but Annie was hearing a researcher at the San Diego Zoo, from a piece she did last year on efforts to save the black-footed ferret: *You need a broad enough sample of the population to ensure genetic diversity, he'd said. Then once you provide the right kind of environment you put on some Barry White ferret music and let nature take its course!*

"We're breeding stock," Annie said, staring numbly at SiriTree. David looked at her. SiriTree swayed gently, the gesture indecipherable.

"That is a correct statement."

Z is for Zoo

Contributors

Brenda Stokes Barron is a writer from southern California where she lives with her husband, daughter, and two cats. This story is dedicated to her father, who wore a turquoise ring for years, and instilled in her a love of the written word after giving her a copy of Stephen King's The Regulators. She wouldn't be a writer without him. You can find out more about her at www.thedigitalinkwell.com.

Marge Simon's works appear in publications such as Strange Horizons, Niteblade, DailySF Magazine, Pedestal, Dreams & Nightmares. She edits a column for the HWA Newsletter, "Blood & Spades: Poets of the Dark Side," and serves as Chair of the Board of Trustees. She won the Strange Horizons Readers Choice Award, 2010, and the SFPA's Dwarf Stars Award, 2012. In addition to her poetry, she has published two prose collections: Christina's World, Sam's Dot Publications, 2008 and Like Birds in the Rain, Sam's Dot, 2007. She won the Bram Stoker Award ® for Superior Work in Poetry with Charlie Jacob, Vectors: A Week in the Death of a Planet, Dark Regions Press, 2008 and again in 2013 for Vampires, Zombies & Wanton Souls, Elektrik Milk Bath Press.

Michael R. Fosburg, a recent Pushcart Prize nominee, is a senior Literature major at the University of South Florida Sarasota-Manatee. His work has appeared in Star*Line, Niteblade, MindFlights, Illumen, and elsewhere. He can be harangued through email, fosburg@gmail.com, or through his perpetually-neglected blog, http://m-roderick.livejournal.com/

Milo James Fowler is a teacher by day and a speculative fictioneer by night. When he's not grading papers, he's imagining what the world might be like in a few dozen alternate realities. He is an active SFWA member, and his work has appeared in more than 70 publications, including AE SciFi, Cosmos, Daily Science Fiction, Nature, and Shimmer. His novel Captain Bartholomew Quasar and the Space-Time Displacement Conundrum is forthcoming from Every Day Publishing. www.milojamesfowler.com

Beth Cato's debut steampunk novel THE CLOCKWORK DAGGER will be released by HarperCollins Voyager in September 2014. She's originally from Hanford, California, but now resides in Arizona with her husband and son. Her short fiction, poetry, and tasty cookie recipes can be found at http://www.bethcato.com.

Simon writes fantasy and SF from deep in the English countryside. He lives with his wife, two daughters and black cat. His fantasy novel Hedge Witch has just been published. Find him at simonkewin.co.uk.

Suzanne is a tattooed storyteller from South Africa. She currently lives in Finland and finds the cold, dark forests nothing if not inspiring. Although she has a Master's degree in music, Suzanne prefers conjuring strange worlds and creating quirky characters. Her published works include the novels Dragon's Teeth, Obscura Burning and The Other Me. You can also find a bunch of her short stories scattered throughout the Internet. When not writing, Suzanne teaches dance and music to middle schoolers and eats far too much peanut butter. She is represented by Jordy Albert.

Alexandra Seidel is a writer, poet, and editor. She does not believe in fortune telling, and that tarot deck on her desk is really just there for research purposes. Alexa's writing can be found in Mythic Delirium, The Red Penny Papers, Jabberwocky, and elsewhere. She edits poetry for Niteblade and loves nothing more than finding just the right poem in her slush pile. If you are so inclined you can follow Alexa on Twitter (@Alexa_Seidel) or read her blog: www.tigerinthematchstickbox.blogspot.com.

Sara Cleto is a PhD student at the Ohio State University where she studies folklore, literature, and the places where they intersect. She specializes in fairy tales, vampires, the 19th century, and disability theory, an unlikely brew that spices her creative writing and academic endeavors. Her creative work can be found in Ideomancer, Cabinet des Fees: Scheherazade's Bequest, Niteblade, the anthology Metastasis, and others.

Despite all the hearts that break in his stories, **Kenneth Schneyer** is usually pretty happy. He sold his first story in 2008, attended the Clarion Writers Workshop in 2009, joined the Cambridge Science Fiction Workshop in 2010, and received a Nebula nomination in 2014. His work appears in Analog, Strange Horizons, Beneath Ceaseless Skies, Clockwork Phoenix 3 & 4, Escape Pod, Podcastle, and elsewhere. Born in Detroit, he now lives in Rhode Island with three talented people and an opinionated cat. He thinks the world ends every day.

KV Taylor is an avid reader and writer of urban fantasy and dark speculative fiction, even though the only degree she holds is in the history of art. (Or, possibly, because the only degree she holds is in the history of art.) In her spare time she enjoys comic books, Himalayan Buddhist art, loud music, her Epiphone, and Black Bush. Her fiction can be found at kvtaylor.com.

Gary B. Phillips is a writer and software developer. He blogs irregularly for Apex Publications. He is currently working on writing a YA Horror novel and growing a wizard-length beard. He lives in Arizona with his wife, three children, three cats, and two chickens. He has no plans to shave his beard until the novel is done or wizard mode is activated, whichever comes first.

His work has appeared in Stories in the Ether, Interstellar Fiction, Lacuna: A Journal of Historical Fiction, Daily Science Fiction, Kazka Press, Flash Fiction Online, and the Another 100 Horrors anthology.

BD Wilson is a writer from Edmonton, Alberta, Canada whose work has appeared in the anthology Dark Pages from Blade Red press, Liquid Imagination Online, and Niteblade Fantasy and Horror Magazine among others. A firm believer in a virtual existence, BD's home on the Web is located at http://www.bdwilson.ca

Ennis Drake is the author of a dozen critically-acclaimed works of fiction and non-fiction; his novella, Twenty-Eight Teeth of Rage, was shortlisted for the Shirley Jackson Award, and has been called "a masterpiece of modern horror". He currently lives in Central Florida.

C.S. MacCath is a writer of fiction, non-fiction and poetry whose work has appeared in Strange Horizons, Clockwork

Phoenix: Tales of Beauty and Strangeness, Murky Depths, Witches & Pagans and other publications. Her poetry has been nominated twice for the Rhysling Award, and her fiction has received honourable mention in The Year's Best Science Fiction: Twenty-Sixth Annual Collection.

Ceallaigh's first collection of fiction and poetry entitled The Ruin of Beltany Ring has been called 'wonderful, thoroughly engaging, always amazing', a book of 'tiny marvels' and 'well-worth reading'. At present, she's working on a science fiction series entitled Petals of the Twenty Thousand Blossom and a second collection of fiction and poetry.

Michael Kellar is a writer, poet, and occasional online bookseller living in Myrtle Beach, SC. He has had fiction appear in "Side Show 2: Tales of the Big Top and the Bizarre", "Metastasis: An Anthology to Support Cancer Research", and the recently released "Bones II". He has also had fiction appear on the "Flashes in the Dark" website, and had poetry published in "Gothic Blue Book III: The Graveyard Edition" and at "The Cynic Online".

Upcoming pieces will include stories appearing in "The Ghoul Saloon" and on the "Dark Futures Fiction" website.

Cindy James lives in Edmonton, Alberta with her husband and two children. After twenty years working as a court reporter and listening to other people's stories, she decided to engage the right side of her brain and tell a few of her own. She is pursuing a degree in English and History, and is committed to one day write something truly great. She now works as a broadcast closed-captioner, volunteers at the local art gallery, and agonizes in what remains of her free time over whether she should be writing or painting.

Brittany Warman is a PhD student in English and Folklore at The Ohio State University, where she concentrates on the intersection of folklore and literature. Her creative work has been published in Mythic Delirium, Stone Telling, Ideomancer, Cabinet des Fees, Niteblade, and others.

K.L. Young is an award-winning screenwriter of such films as "H.P. Lovecraft's Strange Aeons: The Thing on the Doorstep", "The Shunned House", and "The Small Stuff". He is also an Executive Editor and publisher of the quarterly print anthology Strange Aeons Magazine, now in its fourth year of publication.

Pete Aldin has been writing stories since he was a kid. In his 40s, he finally decided to start finishing the damn things and get some published.

His day job involves assisting longterm jobseekers with disabilities in reclaiming their lives and careers. Pete lives in Melbourne, Australia, with his family and their small yappy dog. The family are good for his sanity. The yappy dog, not so much.

Pete's addictions include alcoholic ciders, movie soundtracks and the FIFA franchise on Xbox. He don't like pina colada, nor taking walks in the rain.

He can be found lurking in the shadows at http://www.petealdin.com

Cory Cone lives, works and writes in Baltimore, MD. He studied painting at the Maryland Institute College of Art, where he met and married his wife. His work has appeared in a

handful of fine journals, including Niteblade, Grim Corps, The Colored Lens, and Every Day Fiction.

Writing as **Damien Walters Grintalis**, Damien's short fiction has appeared in Lightspeed, Strange Horizons, Beneath Ceaseless Skies, Interzone, Fireside, Daily Science Fiction, and others, and her debut novel, Ink, was released in December 2012 by Samhain Horror. As Damien Angelica Walters, her work has appeared or is forthcoming in Year's Best Weird Fiction Volume One, Apex, Shimmer, Shock Totem, Strange Horizons, Lightspeed, Daily Science Fiction, Nightmare, Drabblecast, Pseudopod, PodCastle, the anthologies Glitter & Mayhem and What Fates Impose, and others. Sing Me Your Scars, and Other Stories, a collection of her short fiction, will be released in Fall 2014 from Apex Publications.

She's also a freelance editor, a staff writer with BooklifeNow, the online companion to Jeff VanderMeer's Booklife: Strategies and Survival Tips for the 21st Century Writer, and until the magazine's closing in 2013, she was an Associate Editor of the Hugo Award-winning Electric Velocipede.

You can find her online at http://damienangelicawalters.com.

Samantha Kymmell-Harvey's work can be found in Waylines Magazine and Spark: A Creative Anthology just to name a few. She is a 2012 graduate of the Odyssey Writing Workshop. You can follow her adventures by checking out her blog: http://samanthakymmell-harvey.blogspot.com/

Lilah Wild's scrawlings have appeared in Pseudopod, Not One of Us, and Morbid Curiosity. Her debut novel, Goddess of Thunder: A Death Metal Fairytale, is available on Amazon and other online bookstores. Besides writing dark urban fantasy and horror, she can be found dabbling in tribal fusion bellydancing, conducting experiments with vegetarian cuisine, and unlocking the deco puzzlebox of Manhattan. She lives in Queens amid a clamor of doom metal noodling and four cats. Her online home can be found at leopardmoon.com.

Jonathan C. Parrish is known by many other names. He goes by Jo because of a poem by A. A. Milne and by Jopa because of an email address he received in 1990 (and a blissful ignorance, at the time, of the Russian language). He spent most of his life in Canada, particularly in Alberta and Nova Scotia and he once made the mistake of taking the train from Halifax to Edmonton and back again.

Alexis A. Hunter revels in the endless possibilities of speculative fiction. Short stories are her true passion, despite a few curious forays into the world of novels. Over forty of her short stories have been published, appearing recently in Kasma SF, Spark: A Creative Anthology, Read Short Fiction, and more. To learn more about Alexis visit www.idreamagain.wordpress.com.

Steve Bornstein has been in the military, travelled to distant lands, and held the sorts of jobs you watch shows about on the Discovery Channel. His stories have been published alongside the likes of Ed Greenwood and Mercedes Lackey. He lives in Central Texas with his wife and five insane pets, and is totally not building a Mars rocket to use to escape the coming zombie apocalypse.

Thank you for reading

A is for Apocalypse

We would appreciate it a great deal if, in addition to sharing your thoughts with us directly, you would leave an honest review for it.

A few words and some stars can go a very long way toward determining a book's success or failure!

Always Be The First To Know!

Whether it's a new release, a call for submissions, cover reveal, super sale or I just want to share a new story I've written, you will always be among the first to know if you sign up for my newsletter.

I promise to respect your privacy and your inbox. I will only email you when I have something exciting to share, probably about twice a month.

Subscribe now and you'll receive a free download of my award-winning post-apocalyptic short story, "Starry Night" as a welcome-to-the-newsletter present!

Subscribe to Rhonda's Mailing List!

http://bit.ly/StarryStory